REBEL

Also by Amy Tintera

Reboot

REBEL

AMY TINTERA

HARPER TEEN

An Imprint of HarperCollinsPublishers

HarperTeen is an imprint of HarperCollins Publishers.

Library of Congress Cataloging-in-Publication Data
Tintera, Amy.
    Rebel / Amy Tintera. — First edition.
      pages cm
    Summary: Having broken free of HARC, seventeen-year-old Wren and
Callum escaped north but the Reboot Reservation is preparing to wage
all-out war on the humans and the two are torn about their loyalties until
Micah commits the ultimate betrayal and their choice is made.
    ISBN 978-0-06-221711-0
    [1. Adventure and adventurers—Fiction. 2. Soldiers—Fiction. 3. Dead—
Fiction. 4. Science fiction.] I. Title.
PZ7.T4930Rd 2014   2013047726
[Fic]—dc23   CIP
                                                                  AC

Typography by Torborg Davern
15 16 17 18 19 CG/RRDH   10 9 8 7 6 5 4 3 2 1
❖
First paperback edition, 2015

For Mom

ONE

CALLUM

WREN WAS SILENT.

She stood completely still next to me, staring straight ahead with that look she got sometimes, like she was either happy or plotting to kill someone. Either way, I loved that look.

The other Reboots around us started jumping up and down and yelling in celebration, but Wren just stared. I followed her gaze.

The wooden sign must have been hammered deep into the orange earth, because it didn't move even though the wind was brutal. The sign was at least a few years old, the words slightly faded. But still, I could make out every one:

REBOOT TERRITORY
ALL HUMANS TURN BACK

But "Reboot Territory" appeared to be nothing but flat, dry land and powerful, gusting wind. I was sort of bummed, to be honest. The Texas I knew was lush and hilly and green. This Texas was flat and orange. Who'd ever heard of orange dirt?

"It should be a couple miles that way!"

I turned at the sound of Addie's voice. She brushed her long, dark hair out of her face as she studied the map to the reservation that the rebels had given us. She glanced back at the two crashed shuttles behind her, then turned and pointed straight ahead to empty space. The flat land gave way to a small hill in the distance, so perhaps there was something over there we couldn't see yet. I certainly hoped so, otherwise Reboot territory was looking pretty pathetic.

Wren held out her hand and I laced my fingers through hers. I caught her eye and smiled and she attempted one in return, the way she did when her thoughts were elsewhere. A strand of blond hair escaped from her ponytail and she pushed it back, as usual not appearing to care where it landed or how messy her hair looked.

We started walking and the Reboots around us stole occasional glances at Wren. They all slowed until they were slightly behind us, letting her lead, but I didn't think she noticed. I was pretty sure Wren was proud of her One-seventy-eight—her impressive number of minutes dead before the KDH virus caused her to Reboot—but she often seemed oblivious to the way people treated her because of it. Or maybe she was just so used to it that it didn't faze her anymore.

Personally I would have been freaked out if everyone stared at me like that.

We walked in silence for almost half an hour as the Reboots behind us chattered, but now didn't seem like the time for conversation. My stomach was in knots, my mind buzzing with what we were supposed to do if the reservation wasn't here. How much fuel was left in those shuttles we just abandoned? Would Wren's even work after that crash landing? It had only been hours since we escaped HARC. What if they were on their way to find us right now?

I held Wren's hand tighter as we approached the hill. It wasn't terribly steep, and we climbed to the top quickly.

I stopped, my breath catching in my throat.

If that was the reservation, then someone hadn't explained it right. Someone should have piped up and said: *"Oh, it's not really a reservation. It's more like a huge compound in the middle of some ugly orange dirt."*

They'd built a fence all the way around the compound, not unlike the HARC fences that surrounded the cities of Texas. Except this fence was made of wood and stretched at least fifteen feet high, hiding the interior from our view. Towers even taller than the fence were at either end, and there was a person standing at the top of both of them. The towers were simple wooden buildings that seemed to only function as lookouts. On each one, long blocks of wood crisscrossed in between the four beams of the tower, and a ladder ran up one side. At the top was a bare slab of wood with a roof, but it was open on all four sides.

Beyond the reservation was a lake and large patches of trees, and past that more flat, orange dirt. I couldn't get over how big it was. *That* was a Reboot city? It had to be almost the size of Rosa.

Wren took in a sharp breath and quickly pulled her hand from mine. "They have guns," she said, pointing. "Look at them. They all have guns." She glanced around at the other Reboots. "Put your helmets on if you took them off. Raise your hands!"

I squinted at where she was pointing and took in a sharp breath. In front of the compound, lining the gate, was an army. There were maybe seventy-five or a hundred people, and it was impossible to tell if they were Reboot or human from this distance.

I tightened my helmet strap and raised my hands. "They could be humans, couldn't they?" We had a hundred near-invincible Reboots, but if those were armed humans we could be in a lot of trouble. Only a shot to the head could kill a Reboot, but a few of us didn't have helmets, and we hardly had any weapons at all. I swallowed as I looked at them again.

"They could." She squinted as she raised her hands. "We're too far to tell."

If it turned out we escaped from HARC—the Human Advancement and Repopulation Corporation, which enslaved Reboots and made us do their dirty work—only to get killed by a bunch of humans living in the middle of nowhere, I was going to be pissed. If they killed me, I was coming back from the dead (again) to hunt down the human rebels who told us about this reservation.

"If they're humans, let's pick a state now," I said in an attempt to stay calm.

Wren's expression twisted into confusion. "A state?"

"Yeah, you know. Those things they used to have in the rest of the country. I vote for California. I'd like to see the ocean."

She blinked at me, that *"Are you being serious right now, Callum, we're in the middle of a very tense situation"* blink. But a corner of her mouth turned up. "I vote for North Carolina. We can go to Kill Devil Hills and see where the virus started."

"That's great, Wren. I pick the ocean and you pick the death state."

"Doesn't North Carolina have a beach? Wasn't it on the water?"

I laughed. "Fine. Death state it is."

She grinned at me, her bright blue eyes searching mine for a brief moment. I knew what she was looking for. I'd been cured of the drugs HARC gave us to make us better, more compliant

Reboots, but instead just made us insane, flesh-craving monsters. It had only been a few hours since she'd given me the antidote, and she was watching to see if it didn't work, if she'd have to stop me from killing and trying to eat someone again.

She hadn't been fast enough in Austin.

I quickly dropped my gaze to the ground.

One of the men pulled away from the group and strode across the dirt, his black hair shiny in the morning sunlight. A gun swung from one of his hands and he had another tucked into the waist of his pants.

"Reboot," Wren said quietly.

I looked from her to the man. How could she tell from this distance? I couldn't even see his eyes yet.

"The way he walks," she clarified, off my confused expression.

I turned to the man. He walked quickly, but evenly, like he knew where he was going but he wasn't going to panic about it. I didn't see how any of that said "Reboot," but I wasn't a badass five-year veteran Reboot who could take down nine men by myself. So what did I know?

The Reboots around us slowed as the man got closer, and many of them were watching Wren. I lowered my hands, nudging her back, and she looked at me as I tilted my head toward the man.

"What?" She took a quick glance around at the other Reboots, then turned back to me with a slightly exasperated expression.

"Am I elected to talk to him or something?"

I tried not to grin, but I failed. Wren was so oblivious some-times to how other people saw her, interacted with her, looked up to her. She'd been elected to talk to him miles back, before we ever saw anyone.

"Go," I said, giving her another gentle nudge on the back.

She sighed that "What do you people want from me?" sigh and I bit back a chuckle.

Wren stepped forward and the man stopped, lowering the gun slightly. He was in his mid to late twenties, but his eyes were calm and steady. He didn't have any of the insanity of the adult Reboot I'd seen on an assignment in Rosa, meaning he must have Rebooted as a child or teenager.

Adults who Rebooted couldn't handle the change, but if you were younger when you Rebooted, you could age normally without going crazy. Not that I'd ever had that theory confirmed until now, since I'd never encountered a Reboot who'd turned twenty. They all "mysteriously" disappeared from the HARC facilities before they reached that age. I suspected HARC either killed them or experimented on them. Wren and I were seven-teen, so we would have had less than three years left if we hadn't escaped.

"Hello," the stranger said. He crossed his arms over his chest and cocked his head to one side. He scanned the crowd briefly and settled on Wren.

"Hi." Wren glanced back at me for a moment before turning

to the man. "Um . . . I'm Wren. One-seventy-eight."

He had the same reaction as everyone else. His eyes widened. He stood up straighter. Wren's number earned her extra respect, even here. The reaction bugged me every time. Like she didn't matter without that number.

Wren lifted her wrist, and the man stepped closer to examine the number and bar code printed there. I closed my fingers over my own 22 and wished I could scrub both numbers off our arms. A higher number supposedly meant a Reboot was faster, stronger, less emotional, but I thought that was just a line HARC fed us that the Reboots bought into. We all used to be humans, before we died and came back to life as Reboots. I didn't see why the number of minutes dead mattered so much.

"Micah," the man said. "One-sixty-three."

One-sixty-three seemed very high to me. Wren had been the highest number in the Rosa facility, but I didn't think any of the other Reboots had been that close to her. A guy named Hugo was the closest and he was, what, One-fifty?

Micah held up his arm. His ink was more faded than Wren's, and I couldn't make out the numbers from this distance. But Wren tilted her head and stared at him blankly. She gave people that look when she didn't want them to know what she was thinking. It worked.

"I see you brought a few friends," Micah said, a smile spreading across his face.

"We . . ." She turned and found Addie in the crowd and pointed. "Me and Addie broke into the Austin facility and released all the Reboots."

Addie unhooked her helmet, her dark hair blowing in the wind. She ducked her head behind the taller Reboot in front of her, like she didn't want to be recognized for this feat. I couldn't really blame her. She hadn't really asked for any of this. Wren came to rescue her as part of a deal made with Addie's father, Leb—one of the HARC officers at Rosa—in exchange for help-ing Wren and me escape. Addie had just gotten caught up in the whirlwind.

Micah's smile disappeared. His face was expressionless, his mouth open a tiny bit. His eyes flicked over the crowd again.

"That"—he pointed—"is the entire Austin facility?"

"Yes."

"You released all of them?"

"Yes."

He stared a moment longer before taking a step closer to Wren. He put his hands on her face and I saw her body jolt. I resisted the urge to tell him only a dumbass would touch Wren without her permission. He'd discover that one for himself if she decided she didn't like it.

His hands covered most of her cheeks as he gazed down at her. "You. Are my new favorite person."

Yeah, get in line, dude.

Wren laughed and stepped away from his grasp. She tossed

a look back in my direction like, *"Really? You made me deal with this guy?"* I grinned, stepping forward and offering her my hand. She slid her fingers between mine.

Micah stepped back to address the group. "Well, come on then. Welcome."

A few cheers erupted, and people began talking excitedly all around us.

"We already took their trackers out," Wren said to Micah. "Way back near Austin."

"Oh, that doesn't matter," he said with a chortle.

It doesn't? I frowned in confusion and saw a matching expression on Wren's face, but Micah had already turned away to talk to a cluster of eager young Reboots. He began leading the way to the reservation and I started to follow, but I felt a tug on my hand as Wren stood her ground, watching the Reboots stream after Micah.

She was nervous, although it had taken me a while to learn what that particular expression looked like. She took in a small breath, her eyes darting over the scene in front of us.

"Everything okay?" I asked. I was nervous, too. When Wren was nervous, I was nervous.

"Yeah," she said softly like it wasn't. I knew she wasn't as excited to go to the reservation as I was. She'd told me she would have stayed at HARC if it weren't for me. I couldn't begin to understand that, and it occurred to me for the first time that maybe she hadn't just convinced herself she was happy as a HARC slave. Maybe she really was.

I wanted to think that she'd adjust and be happy here, too, but it was hard to say. I wasn't even entirely sure what made Wren happy, besides beating people up. Of course, if I were as good at that as she was, it might make me pretty happy, too.

She barely nodded, as if convincing herself of something, and began walking in the direction of the reservation. The Reboots lining the gate were still as we approached, their guns all pointed at us.

Micah stepped away from the group, holding one hand up to his troops. "Weapons down! Hold your positions!"

As soon as he shouted the command, every Reboot lowered their gun. Their bright eyes were glued to us, and I took in a breath as I glanced down the line. There were so many. Most of them were about my age, but I spotted a few who seemed closer to thirty or forty.

The reservation Reboots were dressed in loose, light-colored cotton clothes, nothing like the black uniforms HARC made us wear, with the exception of the helmets on their heads. They were strong and well fed, and even though they were positioned for what they thought was an attack, no one seemed scared. If anything they were . . . excited?

Micah lifted a black box to his mouth that looked like one of the coms HARC used. He spoke into it, glancing up at the tower to our right. He listened for a moment, nodded, and said a few more words into it before sliding it into his pocket.

He took a step backward and beckoned in our direction with two fingers. "Wren."

She stood still next to me, her shoulders tense. Micah gestured with his head for her to come, and she let out a tiny sigh as she slipped her fingers from mine. People moved aside as she walked toward him, and I felt uncomfortable on her behalf. They were all staring.

Micah beamed as she stopped next to him. He reached down and grabbed her hand, making her jump. He had an expression of such pure adoration on his face that I would have been jealous if she weren't looking at him like he was an alien.

Okay, maybe I was slightly jealous. She'd looked at me like I was an alien at first, too, but now I was pretty sure she liked me.

Well, more than pretty sure. Mostly sure. As close as you can get to sure without being totally sure. She had left her "home" (prison) for me, and then risked her life and took down an entire HARC facility to save me. I thought that was like Wren's version of "I'm totally into you." I'd take it.

Wren yanked her hand from his, but Micah seemed oblivious, beaming as he faced the reservation Reboots.

"Guys, this is Wren One-seventy-eight."

A few of them gasped and I sighed inwardly. Any hopes I'd had of our numbers not mattering here were being further dashed by the second. Some of the Reboots were gazing at her with such awe and excitement that I wanted to slap them and tell them to stop being weird.

"She brings with her the entire Austin facility," Micah continued.

More gasps. At least they were excited to see us.

"I didn't do it by myself." Wren scanned the crowd, but didn't seem to find Addie. "Addie Thirty-nine and I did it together."

Micah sort of nodded in that way people did when they weren't really listening. He was grinning at the crowd of reservation Reboots. They were whispering, their faces cautiously optimistic.

Wren cast a confused look at me as Micah raised his hand. The crowd went silent.

"All right then," he said. "I have good news."

Thank goodness. I needed good news. I hoped it was something along the lines of "I have food and beds for all of you right now."

Micah gestured to the tower. "I just got word that there are more HARC shuttles coming. They're on their way right now."

Wait. What?

"About a hundred miles out," Micah continued. "At least seven confirmed."

Which part was the good news?

"So." Micah grinned as he lifted one fist in the air. "Ready?"

Every reservation Reboot responded together in one loud yell.

"ATTACK!"

TWO

WREN

I FROZE AS CALLUM CAST A HORRIFIED LOOK IN MY DIRECTION. *Attack?*

"Wren." Micah put his hand on my shoulder. I shrugged it off. "You came in HARC shuttles, didn't you? Where are they?"

I blinked. How did he know that? How did he know there were more HARC shuttles on the way?

"We left them a couple miles back," I said. "We didn't want to alarm you by getting too close in them."

"We were alarmed, obviously," Micah said with a laugh, gesturing to the army of Reboots behind him. He stuck his fingers in his mouth and whistled. "Jules!"

A girl a few years older than me joined us. Her red hair was in a braid, and she had a HARC bar code stamped on her wrist, but I couldn't make out the number.

"Go fetch those shuttles." Micah lifted his hand, made a sort of circular motion with his finger, and the massive wooden gate immediately began to creak open. The Reboots in front of it scrambled away.

I felt a hand on my back and turned to see Callum behind me. He stared at the opening gate. "What's going on?" he asked quietly.

"I don't know."

The gate swung open the rest of the way to reveal about ten Reboots sitting on contraptions I'd never seen before. They had two big wheels—one in back and one in front—and looked sort of like one of those motorcycle things I'd seen pictures of, but bigger. Three people could probably fit on the wide, black seat stretched between the two tires, and they were obviously not made to be discreet, because a loud rumbling noise came from each one.

"Kyle!" Micah said, waving. A tall, beefy Reboot inched his bike away from the others. "Take Jules and—" He stopped and turned to me. "Who flew those here?"

"Me and Addie."

"The Thirty-nine?"

"Yes."

He nodded and turned back to Kyle. "Take Jules and

Thirty-nine to the shuttles. Quick. No more than twenty minutes round-trip."

Kyle twisted his hand around one of the handlebars and the bike roared forward, coming to a screeching stop next to Jules. She hopped on and eyed the crowd of Austin Reboots expectantly.

"Thirty-nine!" Micah yelled.

Addie stepped out from the crowd, arms crossed over her chest. She ignored Micah completely and stared at me like she was waiting for something. I wasn't sure what it was. Did she want me to tell her it was okay to go?

I avoided Micah's gaze as I strode across the dirt and stopped in front of her.

"They want you to take them to the shuttles," I said. "And probably fly one over here."

Her eyes darted behind me. "And you think we should trust them?"

I paused. Of course I didn't think we should trust them. I'd just met them, and so far, they seemed weird. But we'd strolled up to their home and asked to be let in, so maybe it was too late to think about trust.

"No," I said quietly.

She looked taken aback by my answer. "No?"

"No."

She blinked as if waiting for more, and a smile began to appear on her face. "Okay then. I feel better." She took a deep breath. "Right. Ride off with the strangers. Hope for the best. Got it."

She nodded her head as she finished, and I blinked, suddenly realizing what I was asking.

"I can go instead—"

She laughed as she stepped back. "That's all right. Can't fault you for being honest." She jogged across the dirt and hopped on the back of the bike, pointing in the direction we'd come from. Kyle peeled out, the bike spitting dirt as they disappeared.

"One-twenties and over with me!" Micah called to the Austin Reboots. "Let's do this!" He was practically jumping up and down, he was so excited.

I didn't understand.

I took a glance behind me at the Austin Reboots to see similar confused expressions on their faces. Beth One-forty-two, a couple girls, and two guys who I assumed were Over-one-twenties broke off from the group and slowly headed in Micah's direction, but they kept turning puzzled faces my way. There were less Over-one-twenties in Austin than there had been in Rosa, but I'd been stationed in the toughest city in Texas. More assignments meant they needed more skilled Reboots. They were all close to my age except for one of the guys, who was probably only twelve or thirteen years old.

"Micah!" I called, following him as he darted for the gate. "What's going on? How do you know HARC is coming? How did you know we were coming?"

He stopped. "We have people stationed in strategic places outside the cities, and equipment that monitors air traffic in the area."

I raised my eyebrows, surprised. I hadn't expected them to be so advanced.

Micah spread his arms wide, beaming at the Austin Reboots. "Guys! Let's see some excitement!"

We just stared.

He raised his fist. "Whoop!"

"Whoop whoop!" a hundred reservation Reboots yelled at once, and I jumped. What the hell?

"Oh, come on," he said with a chuckle. "Who wants to kick some HARC ass?"

That produced a few laughs. Someone at the back of the crowd of Austin Reboots raised his hand. "I'm in!"

I'd actually kicked enough HARC ass this past week to last me a very long time. I glanced at Callum. He'd never wanted to fight anyone, human or Reboot.

Micah chuckled as he caught my expression. "I know you're probably tired. And you're going to have to tell me the story soon about how you got out of Rosa, ended up in Austin, and stole two shuttles filled with every Reboot in that facility." He stepped closer to me. "But right now, we've got a bunch of HARC officers on their way here to attack us. So we don't have much choice."

I looked at Callum and he lifted his shoulders, like he wasn't sure what to do.

I knew what I wanted to do. I wanted to hightail it out of here before HARC arrived. I didn't know where we'd go or how we'd get there, but we certainly didn't have to stay and fight.

Or maybe we did. I regarded the group of Reboots I'd brought here and saw several faces turned in my direction, watching to see how I'd react. I'd busted into the Austin facility and ushered them all into shuttles and dumped them into this situation. If I asked Callum to make a run for it, he would tell me they needed my help. And he would be right, unfortunately.

But this was the last time. If it seemed like there were going to be more attacks from HARC, I'd grab Callum and go. I didn't want to spend the rest of my life fighting off the humans. I'd be perfectly content never to see them again, actually.

I sighed and barely nodded at Micah. He clapped his hand on my back like he approved.

"Under-sixties with me!" a thin guy yelled, stepping from the line.

I shook my head at Callum and held out my hand. We weren't doing that. A corner of his mouth turned up as he walked toward me.

Micah glanced down at Callum's wrist. "One-twenty-two?" he asked, squinting.

"Twenty-two," Callum corrected.

Micah pointed to the crowd gathering around the thin man. "Under-sixties with Jeff."

"Callum's with me." I held his hand tighter.

Micah opened his mouth, but closed it with a hint of a smile. "Fine." He turned to the reservation entrance, gesturing for us to follow him.

We walked toward the line of bikes guarding the entrance and I glanced back to see the remaining Austin Reboots divided into two groups: Under-sixties on one side, everyone over sixty but under one twenty on the other.

I faced front as we passed the bikes and heard Callum suck in a breath of air as the reservation within the fence came into view.

There were more Reboots inside. This must have been the second wave, and it was maybe half the size of the first. About fifty or so stood in neat lines in front of a giant fire pit, guns in their hands but barrels lowered so they were facing the ground. A Reboot ran past us and started talking excitedly to one of the guys in front.

The reservation was laid out in a circle, with thin dirt paths snaking in between brown-and-tan tents. There were very few permanent structures in the compound, but sturdy tepee-style tents lined each side of the paths. There were tons of them, at least a hundred, as far as I could see.

To my right were several much larger rectangular tents. The material they'd used was dirty and worn in some places. How

long had they been here? Why didn't they build more permanent structures?

To the left, near the fence, were two long, wooden buildings
that looked like they might be a shower area. Pipes ran up the
side of the building and the ground around it was wet. At least
we didn't have to bathe in the lake.

I scanned the lines of Reboots. When I discovered rebels
were helping Reboots get away from HARC, Leb told me that
my trainer, Riley One-fifty-seven, had escaped to the reservation and wasn't dead like I'd previously been told. But I didn't
see One-fifty-seven in the crowd.

I stopped behind Micah as we approached a tent and he
pulled back the flap, gesturing for us to enter. I ducked my
head and stepped inside, followed by Callum and the five One-
twenties from Austin.

Weapons. Everywhere.

I'd never seen so many weapons in my life. Guns of all
sizes lined every wall, were stacked on the dozens of shelves
around the tent. There were grenades and axes and knives and
swords and things I didn't even recognize. They had enough
weapons to arm the entirety of Texas. There were a bunch of
empty shelves, but I assumed those weapons had gone to the
Reboots outside. Still, they had enough to give everyone a second weapon. Or a third.

"Impressive, right?" Micah said with a grin.

There was a bit of nervous laughter and I took another quick glance around. It was certainly impressive. And maybe a little comforting. A long wooden table ran down the middle of the tent, its legs disappearing into the dirt. A large bed stood in the back right corner, and I wondered if this was where Micah lived. There were two fire pits surrounded by rocks on either side of the tent, with smoke holes cut out of the fabric above them.

"We don't have time to do much of an introduction here," Micah said. "HARC will be here soon, and they will likely bring the big guns this time."

"Whoop whoop!"

I jumped at the sudden outburst and turned to see several reservation Reboots standing behind us. Their penchant for yelling random noises was going to take some getting used to.

"I'm going to get you all weapons, do a very fast tour, and assign you a location." He turned and started pulling guns off the shelf.

"This time," Callum said quietly.

I looked up at him. "What?"

"He said 'this time.' Like HARC has come here before."

"They've been here several times," Micah said, holding a handgun out to me. "We always win."

I took the gun, eyebrows raised. "Always?"

"Every time." Micah offered a gun to Callum.

Callum glanced from the weapon to me and for a moment I thought he wasn't going to take it. Guns were not Callum's thing. I'd had to escape HARC with him because he refused to use one to kill an adult Reboot. HARC saw no point in keeping Reboots who didn't follow orders.

But he took the gun from Micah without a word. I doubted he'd use it.

"Why would they come back if you always win?" I asked as he distributed the guns and extra ammo.

"They regroup, figure out what they learned, and try again. They've gotten smarter. It's been almost a year since the last attack." Micah strode out of the tent and we followed him. "That's one of the reasons we don't build many permanent structures." He gestured at the tents. "The bombs will bring a lot of stuff down today."

"The bombs?" Callum repeated.

"Yes. We'll stop some of the shuttles in the air but expect some bombing." Micah stopped near the fire pit and faced us. "All right. Shuttles coming in from the south. You'll stay here with the second wave. Protect the reservation, don't die. That's all you gotta do. If you lose a body part in a bombing, don't panic. We've got a bunch of kits to sew parts back on. Don't take other people's body parts. Unless you know the person is already dead—then have at it."

Callum's face twisted. "Seriously? We can just put our body parts back on?"

"Yes," I said. "If you sew it on fast enough. It's like when you have a broken bone. Get it back where it belongs and it'll reconnect."

"That's disgusting." He looked at me in horror. "Has that ever happened to you?"

"Yeah, I lost a few fingers on an assignment once. It's not that big of a deal. Feels funny going back on, though."

Callum winced, examining his own fingers.

Micah chuckled as he stopped in front of me. "Newbie?"

"Yes," I replied. Sometimes I forgot that Callum had only been at HARC a few weeks before I figured out an escape to save his life. This last month or so felt more like a year.

"Does newbie want to stay here with the second wave? Because I'm going to put all the Austin Reboots in a third wave at the back of the reservation, except you guys. I don't want to throw them into the fire and scare them their first day here."

I hesitated, glancing at Callum. He'd be safer in the third wave. *I'd* be safer in the third wave, but I didn't think anyone would appreciate that. The strong Reboots needed to be on the front lines. I met his eyes and he nodded at me like he understood.

"That's fine," he said to Micah. "I'll go with the other Under-sixties."

Callum started to walk away and I grabbed his hand, turning aside from Micah. "Use it if you have to, okay?" I said quietly, glancing down at his gun.

He nodded, but our definitions of "have to" were likely very different. He probably wouldn't even take the safety off.

He squeezed my hand, his dark eyes soft when he looked down at me. "Be careful."

I watched as he walked away, wishing I'd mentioned the whole fleeing idea. Maybe he would have gone for it.

"Wren, do you want to come with me?" Micah asked. He glanced at the other One-twenties. "You guys stay here."

I took a quick look back at Beth. She was the highest number in the Austin facility, but had told me on the way here that she'd only Rebooted five months ago. She seemed comfortable stepping up as the voice of the Austin Reboots, but I wasn't so sure how she felt about preparing them for battle. Her face was neutral, but she was frantically twisting a strand of hair around one finger.

"Okay with you to stay here in the second wave?" I asked quietly.

She swallowed, her expression unsure. "Yeah."

A guy with dark hair stepped forward, his expression calm and reassuring. "We'll catch them up on what's going on."

Beth nodded, gesturing for me to go, and I ran to catch up with Micah. I followed him out the reservation gate, glancing around at the first wave of Reboots. They were relaxed now, leaning against the wooden gate and chatting. The atmosphere was calm, yet still filled with anticipation. I'd always enjoyed the thrill of chasing and fighting, so I could almost understand how some of them seemed eager for the fight. Summoning up some excitement helped to take away the fear.

"How'd you do driving that shuttle?" Micah asked, stopping and squinting into the distance.

"Okay, except for the landing. Mine took a pretty good beating."

"We'll have someone else drive, then. You and I are going to go up in a shuttle, and we'll pick off as many in the air as we can before they get here." He gave me an approving look. "Awesome idea, stealing some HARC shuttles to escape. How'd you do it?"

"We had help from the rebels. Tony and Desmond and some others. You know them, right?"

Micah laughed, although I wasn't entirely sure why. "Yeah, I've known them awhile. Helpful bunch."

Truthfully "helpful bunch" might have been an understatement. I wouldn't have made it into the Austin facility to get the antidote for Callum if it weren't for them. I certainly wouldn't have been able to free all the Reboots and escape without them. I probably owed them something now. That was unfortunate.

Micah paced as we waited for the shuttles, occasionally speaking to one of the towers on his com. I almost wanted to pace back and forth with him. I wanted this to be over. I wanted to crawl into Callum's arms and sleep until spring.

The shuttles we'd stolen appeared in the distance a short time later and landed softly on the ground not far from us. The one I'd piloted was dented on both sides and there was a long crack across the front window, but it seemed to fly fine.

The door to the other shuttle opened and Addie jumped out, cocking her head in confusion at something behind me. I turned to see two guys jogging in our direction, holding something that looked like a giant gun in each hand. Two more Reboots were close behind them, carrying the same things.

"What are those?" I asked as they stopped next to Micah.

"Grenade launchers." He pointed to the Reboots at the gate. "They've got some launchers over there, too. It's our best anti-aircraft defense."

Where did they get all this?

"Nice job," Micah said to Addie. "Go on inside and they'll get you a weapon. Under-sixties are with the third wave at the back."

She walked past us, barely nodding at me. She looked about as thrilled as I was to be thrust into this fight.

Micah ordered everyone onto shuttles and I piled into the one Addie had piloted. Two of the guys holding grenade launchers followed me inside.

"I've never shot these from the air before, but I'm pumped to try," Micah said, handing me one of the launchers. It was heavier than a gun, maybe ten pounds or so, but not unmanageable. It was like a really giant revolver with a much longer barrel.

"It goes on your shoulder," Micah said. "One hand at the back, one in the front."

I grabbed a spot under the barrel and another behind the

revolver. I leaned forward to look through the black tube thing mounted on top and saw a smaller circle inside a bigger circle, to help aim.

"That's your sight," Micah said. "I know you've never used one before, but just aim best you can and pull the trigger. You have six rounds, then hand it off to one of these guys and they'll give you a new one and reload for you. I have a feeling you'll be awesome at it." He punched me lightly on the shoulder with a grin.

He had a lot of faith in me based solely on my number. Riley must have told him about me, and I guess he approved of me freeing the Austin Reboots, but still, he seemed just as obsessed with my One-seventy-eight as HARC was. I didn't know whether to be relieved or disappointed.

"Take her up!" Micah yelled to the man sitting in the pilot's seat. He pointed at me. "Scoot back. We're leaving the door open so we can shoot."

I edged back until I hit the corner of one of the seats. The shuttle lifted into the air with a jerk and I tucked my chin into my chest as a strong wind swept over me. I watched the Reboot shuttle pilot, who seemed calm and comfortable steering us into the air, even in this weather.

"Has he done this before?" I called over the wind.

Micah nodded, taking a quick glance back at him. "We have a couple old HARC shuttles we repaired after shooting them down. Only one still works, though. And we're out of fuel."

"We have visual on four shuttles." The voice came from Micah's com and I gripped my launcher tighter.

Micah pointed, getting on one knee as he rested the launcher on his shoulder. "There they are!"

I took my place beside him as four black HARC shuttles dotted the clear blue sky and soared straight for us.

"Wait until they get closer," Micah ordered. "Wait . . . wait . . . now!"

One of the shuttles roared past us, and another hung back. The two remaining raced in our direction, and I aimed the launcher at the wide pilot's window of the nearest shuttle.

I squeezed the trigger. I missed.

A loud bang ripped through the air as Micah's shot made contact with the side of one shuttle, and the two boys beside us promptly let out a "whoop!"

"Faster!" Micah yelled at me. "Aim for the pilot window!"

I had been, but it wasn't exactly easy with the wind and new equipment. I decided now wasn't the time to mention that.

The shuttle I'd missed shot past me and I jumped as an explosion rocked the ground. One of the towers burst into flames and I took in a slow breath.

Focus.

Our pilot whipped us around and I tightened my fingers around the launcher as I peered at the shuttles that had just taken out the tower. I aimed for the window. I took a breath. I fired.

The shuttle lurched as the windshield exploded, and I ignored the "whoop whoop!" as I took aim again. The second grenade soared through the open window and what was left of the shuttle hit the ground so hard I'd swear I felt it.

Micah took out the straggler shuttle but three more roared in, one making it past me as it headed for the Reboot shuttle hovering over the reservation. Smoke rose from inside the walls and the gunfire was constant. I felt a twinge of fear for Callum as I discharged my last rounds at a shuttle. Maybe I should have brought him with me.

A blast rocked our shuttle and I was suddenly glad he was on the ground. A large piece of the back end of our shuttle was missing, the metal above a row of seats breaking off and tumbling through the air.

I turned my attention back outside to see even more shuttles. At least ten whizzed around me.

Ten HARC shuttles. And we had two.

I glanced at Micah to see his brow furrowed in concentration, his finger pressing down on the trigger. Another shuttle fell from the sky.

"You gonna watch me, or are you going to do something?" he asked as he handed off his launcher and took a loaded one. Some of his excitement was gone, replaced by intense concentration and maybe even a hint of fear.

I tightened my grip on my launcher as I aimed. I wasn't going to escape from HARC only to be killed by them a few hours later.

I fired. Again and again, until two more shuttles fell from the sky. I handed off my launcher as our shuttle took another hit and the pilot swung us around so hard I had to grip the doorframe to keep from falling out.

"Having a hard time holding them off, guys!" the pilot called.

"Keep trying!" Micah yelled.

We were losing altitude with that second hit, and I shot as fast as I could at the remaining shuttles. There were only four now and, as I watched, someone on the ground destroyed another one.

Micah managed to obliterate one more, but we were headed down so fast I abandoned my launcher and threw my arms over my helmet. We slammed into the ground and I flew through the door, rolling to a stop several yards away.

I coughed as I got to my hands and knees, wiping the dirt off my face with the back of my hand. There was some blood, too. My left arm was broken in several places, and it felt like most of my ribs were either cracked or bruised.

I scrambled to my feet just in time to be knocked down by another explosion. I curled up into a ball as pieces of metal crashed all around me.

When the smoke cleared I got to my feet again, shaking off the pain tickling me all over. There was only one HARC shuttle left in the air.

My eyes widened in surprise and I looked back at the

reservation, half expecting it to be entirely gone. But the walls still stood (minus one tower). Smoke billowed from a few spots inside, but it wasn't like total destruction.

These Reboots were good. Scary good, actually.

"Who's got the last one?"

I turned at the sound of Micah's shout to see the last shuttle hovering in the air not far away. Someone on the ground fired, hitting the very edge of it. It lurched and spun and Micah made a sound of approval as it crashed into the dirt.

"Whoop whoop!" Micah's yell was followed by more cheers and whoops from a few Reboots in the area.

He turned to me, grenade launcher resting against his shoulder, a wide smile spreading across his face. "Not bad, huh?"

A trail of shuttle pieces littered the ground between us, and the Reboots around us were laughing, talking excitedly. They hadn't just beaten HARC, they'd crushed them.

I met Micah's eyes, returning his smile.

Not bad at all.

THREE

CALLUM

"SO, YEP, THAT'S THE GROSSEST THING I'VE EVER DONE."

The boy in front of me snorted as he patted the arm I'd helped him sew back on. The skin was already starting to re-attach, the blood and bone disappearing from sight. "You must not get out much." He ran a hand over his dark hair as he hopped to his feet. "Thanks."

"No problem. Be more careful with it next time."

He chuckled, since we both knew there wasn't much he could have done about a bomb exploding a few feet away from him. After I'd left Wren, I'd been lucky enough to stay away from most of the action, but the first and second waves had been hit pretty hard. Not all the Reboots made it.

I'd felt the beginnings of panic until Wren walked through the gates with Micah about an hour ago. He'd ushered her into one of the big tents with a few other One-twenties and I hadn't seen them since.

"Isaac, by the way," the boy said, sticking out his hand. There was no bar code on either wrist. He was about fifteen or perhaps a bit older. He was several inches shorter than me and had a slight build, which I thought probably made him look younger than he was.

"Callum," I said, shaking it. I pointed at the dark skin of his arms, where he was missing a bar code. "Never at HARC?"

"Nope."

"How'd you get here?"

"Just lucky, I guess." He stared past me, like he didn't want to discuss that further, and shoved his hands in his pockets, his shoulders slumping forward. "What's your number?"

"Twenty-two."

He let out a short laugh. "Well, I'm sure you have other qualities."

"Thanks," I said dryly.

"I'm just messing with you," he said with a grin. "I'm an Eighty-two. Not that impressive, either."

"How do you know your number if you were never at HARC?" I asked.

"They have death timers here."

"I don't know what that is."

"It takes your body temperature and determines how long you were dead. A Reboot's temperature always stays the same, so we can use it even if it's been a while since the Reboot happened." Isaac gestured behind him, where Reboots were gathered around the fire pit, holding bowls. "Want to go eat?"

I nodded, brushing the dirt off my pants as I got to my feet. I squinted in the late afternoon sun at the big tent, but the flap was still closed. No sign of Wren.

"That's Micah's command tent," Isaac said, following my gaze. "You can't go in unless invited."

"What do they do in there?"

"I dunno. Pat each other on the back for staying dead so long and being awesome?"

"I can't really see Wren doing that," I said.

"One-seventy-eight? They're probably all fawning over her in there."

I sighed, tempted to go in and save her. But Wren never needed saving. She'd come find me when she was ready.

I followed Isaac to the fire pit and grabbed a bowl of something that looked like oatmeal, glancing at the Reboots around the fire. The mood was mostly relief, with more than a few somber faces scattered through the crowd. They'd been excited and celebrating earlier, but now that it was over they looked exhausted and sad about the friends they'd lost.

I walked past unfamiliar faces and found a spot next to Addie. Isaac plopped down next to us.

"Addie, Isaac," I said. "Addie helped Wren rescue all the Austin Reboots."

Addie nodded at him. "Hey." She passed off her empty bowl to a Reboot coming around to collect them. She turned and gave me a quick once-over. "I appreciate you not dying. I would have been pissed if we went to all that trouble to get you the antidote and then you just up and died a few hours later." A smile twitched at the edges of her mouth.

"I tried my best," I said with a laugh. "Did I say thank you? For helping Wren?"

She waved her hand. "Don't thank me. I know what it's like to be on those drugs." Her eyes met mine briefly and I nodded, quickly dropping my gaze to my bowl. Addie was the only other person beside Wren who knew I'd killed an innocent man while on the HARC drugs, and I could see the sympathy in her eyes. I didn't want any sympathy. I wasn't sure what I wanted, but sympathy felt wrong, considering what I'd done.

"So do you guys usually rebuild after this?" Addie asked Isaac.

I glanced around to where she was gesturing. The tents lining the paths to my right were destroyed, fabric flapping in the strong winds. Plenty of the smaller tents had made it, especially those toward the back of the compound, but I'd estimate that fifty or so were in pieces on the ground.

The shower and restroom area had taken a hit as well. I'd visited them earlier and found a large hole blown out of the men's side. At least their plumbing system still worked.

The tower on the right side of the compound was completely gone, as well as a small part of the fence in that area. But overall, we'd sustained way less damage than HARC. I'd only glimpsed it for a moment, but there were fragments of their shuttles littering the dirt in front of the compound for as far as I could see.

"Yeah, we'll probably start tomorrow," Isaac said. "Patch together as many tents as we can first."

"It's not really that bad," Addie said. "You guys are impressive."

"We'd been preparing for a year," Isaac said with a shrug. "And our monitoring systems are new. They had no idea we knew exactly when they'd be coming."

I opened my mouth to ask where they got their equipment, but I heard a shuffle and turned to see Wren plunk down next to me. She had dark circles under her eyes, but when she looped her arm through mine and smiled, she looked genuinely happy. I introduced her to Isaac and she quickly shook his hand before leaning against my shoulder again.

"Everything all right?" I asked, taking a quick glance at Micah's tent.

"Yeah. Micah just wanted to hear the whole story. How we escaped from Rosa, got to Austin, met the rebels." She gave me a look between amusement and annoyance. "He had a million questions."

I leaned forward, brushing a piece of hair away from her face. I pressed my lips to her cool forehead, trailing my other hand down her neck. The sun was just starting to set, but I wanted to pull her close and ask if we could find a tent and stay there the rest of the evening.

"Isaac, take her for me for a few minutes, will ya?"

I looked up to see a girl passing Isaac a chubby baby. He was less than thrilled, but he took her, arranging her in his lap and sliding an arm around her tummy as the woman walked away.

"What the . . . ?" Wren pulled away from me and stared at the baby, her lips parted. "Is that baby . . . ?"

I glanced down at it and took in a sharp breath as I realized. The baby had bright blue Reboot eyes.

"Did it die and Reboot?" Wren asked.

"Nope, she was born like this," Isaac said. He grabbed the baby's arm and made her wave. "Creepy, right?"

"So creepy," Wren said, poking the baby's arm quickly, like it was going to bite her. "So when Reboots have kids, they come out like this?"

"Yep."

"Do they heal?" Addie asked.

"They sure do," Isaac said. "They're total Reboot."

"But . . . without a number, I guess?" Wren asked.

"Yeah, no number, obviously. We think they might take after the higher parent, but eventually the numbers won't even matter."

"Is she yours?" I asked, trying to keep the horror from my voice. I mean, babies were cute and all, but Isaac seemed a little young.

"God, no." He made a face. "I'm just holding her." He glanced around, thrusting her in Wren's direction. "Here, take her for a minute. I've got to go to the bathroom."

"What? No." She quickly leaned away.

"Only for a minute. I'll be right back." He plopped the baby in her lap and hopped to his feet. Wren held her at arm's length and frowned. She did not appreciate that, because she immediately began wailing.

"Here," Wren said, thrusting her in my direction. "Take the mutant baby."

I laughed as I took her. I'd never held a baby before, or not that I remembered, anyway. I was four when my brother, David, was born, but I doubted my parents let me hold him. Apparently I was doing it wrong, because the baby was still screaming. I glanced at Wren. "You've angered it."

"Oh my God," Addie said in exasperation, plucking the baby from my grasp. She bounced her in her arms and the cries began to quiet.

Wren blinked at the baby a few times, turning to give me a "weird" expression. I pressed my lips together to keep from laughing.

"You're not a mutant," Addie said, grabbing the girl's hand and giving it a gentle shake. She turned to Wren, her expression changing to worry. She ducked her head, lowering her voice. "Is there anything we should know?"

"About what?" Wren asked, covering her mouth as she yawned.

"About Micah? And everyone here?"

"You know as much as I do." She shrugged as she took a quick glance around. "They sure can fight, though."

Addie kept her gaze on the baby, biting her bottom lip as she nodded slightly. I got the feeling she wanted Wren to reassure her, to tell her we were safe and she could relax. But Wren just stared straight ahead, watching as a group of Reboots laughed on the other side of the fire pit.

I considered pointing out that people would be looking to her for answers, but she rubbed a hand across her eyes and yawned again and I felt a burst of sympathy for her. Maybe now wasn't the right time to mention that.

"Hey," I said, running my hand down her back. "How long has it been since you slept?"

She frowned and cocked her head. "A couple days ago? When we were at your house."

"I'm going to see if I can find us a tent or something," I said, getting to my feet. "Are you hungry? I can grab you some food."

She shook her head. "No, Micah gave me some."

"Okay. I'll be right back."

She smiled at me over her shoulder as I headed in the direction of the big tent. Micah appeared to be the only one in charge here, and I had a feeling he'd be more than happy to accommodate a request on Wren's behalf.

The flap to the big tent was closed, and I scanned the area, unsure of what to do. They needed a knocker or something on these things.

"Micah?" I called.

He poked his head out a moment later, his eyebrows lowered. "What?"

Apparently his friendliness didn't extend much beyond Wren. I crossed my arms over my chest. "Wren hasn't slept in, like, two days and she's exhausted. Do you have somewhere she can rest for a while?"

His frown disappeared. "Oh, of course. I should have told her. I had a tent cleared out right over there."

I turned to where he was pointing at a small tepee-style tent that had been untouched by the blast. I wondered who he had "cleared out" to make room for her.

"Hey, Jules!" he yelled. "Did you get pillows and blankets and everything in that tent?"

"Yeah, it's all set!" she called from behind him.

"Thanks," I said, turning to walk away.

"Let me know if you need anything else!" he called.

I sort of waved in reply, torn between being annoyed at her special treatment and grateful that had been so easy.

I found Wren in the same spot. Firelight flickered off her blond hair and, even exhausted, she was striking, the most

interesting girl I'd ever seen, in several ways. Her small, deli-
cate features contrasted with the tough, almost terrifying
expression she often wore. It was one of the first things I
noticed about her. I remember lying on the ground, looking
up at her, being sort of scared and sort of turned on at the
same time.

Addie was trying to make conversation but not getting very
far, and I extended my hand down to Wren. "Come with me?"

She took my hand and let me pull her up. As we walked,
she slid an arm around my waist and leaned against my chest,
which made a few Reboots turn to look at us. The numbers
seemed just as important here as they were at HARC, and I
wondered if they were staring at just her, or because a Twenty-
two and One-seventy-eight were together.

I led her to the tent and pulled back the flap. There was a
small fire pit in the middle, but it wasn't lit. Next to that were
two blankets and two pillows on top of a thin, homemade mattress. Given the amount of clothes and linens they had, they
must have been growing cotton somewhere. Successfully, it
seemed.

Wren plopped down on the mattress as I climbed in after
her. "Is this just for us?"

"Yeah, Micah said he had it cleared out for you." I stayed
crouched near the tent flap, suddenly aware of the fact that we
didn't have to sleep in the same tent if we didn't want to. When
we escaped from Rosa, we had to stay close, huddled together

behind trash bins or against tree trunks. We'd had the night in my old bedroom, but I didn't want to assume we were going to sleep in the same bed every night.

She looked nervous, playing with a loose string on her pants and not meeting my eyes. I wanted to crawl onto the mattress and hold her without the threat of HARC hanging over our heads, but maybe that wasn't what she wanted.

"I don't mind staying with the other Reboots, if you'd like to be alone," I said, shifting closer to the edge of the tent to prove I was serious.

She gave me a confused look. "Why would I want to be alone?"

I laughed softly. "I meant if you'd be more comfortable sleeping in here without me. I didn't want to assume. . . ."

She shook her head, holding her hand out to me. I slipped my fingers in between hers and scooted toward the bed, until I was close enough for her to lean down and brush her lips against mine.

"I'm always more comfortable with you," she whispered.

I smiled, kissing her again as I slid onto the mattress. She kicked her shoes off and I did the same, slipping beneath the blanket she held out for me. She was still wearing the shirt I'd given her when we visited my parents' house, and it smelled a little like home when I pulled her close.

I didn't want to remember home, or my parents, or how they rejected me. How I'd killed a man minutes after I'd told them I was the same person they remembered. I knew it was the HARC drugs that had made me an insane, flesh-craving monster, but I couldn't help but feel I'd lied to them. After everything I'd seen and done on our escape, I wasn't nearly the same person who'd left them a few weeks ago. It was ridiculous to think I was.

But I often didn't feel like a Reboot, either. I wondered if Wren really didn't feel anything about the people she'd killed, or if she just hid it well. If being less emotional was truly a Reboot trait, then I hadn't acquired it in my twenty-two minutes.

Being able to brush off terrible things the way Wren did might have been useful, actually. I could see how numbness would be preferable to the weight sitting on my chest.

I winced. The human version of me never would have considered that. He would have been horrified by the prospect of shutting off guilt.

Wren looked up at me and I ran my hand into her hair and kissed her more intensely than I had intended. She wrapped an arm around my waist and kissed me back, tilting her head up as she pulled back slightly. Her eyes searched mine and I suspected some of my emotions were showing, because she seemed to be trying to find the right words.

"I think we're okay now," she said softly. "I think we're safe here."

I pressed my hand into her back, touching my forehead

against hers as I smiled. I got the feeling she was lying, or at least stretching the truth, because there was no way Wren felt safe yet. But I appreciated that she wanted to make me feel better.

"Thank you," I said quietly as I kissed her again.

FOUR

WREN

I WOKE TO BIRDS CHIRPING AND I JERKED, MY HAND INSTINCTIVELY reaching for the gun at my hip. I found nothing but my old HARC pants. The heavy material at the front of the tent flapped in the wind, and I let out a slow breath.

I was safe.

Well, sort of. Safer than a few days ago, at least.

My second instinct was to find Ever in the bed next to me, and my head turned to the left before I could stop myself. There was nothing there but the fabric of the tent. I took in a shaky breath as I looked away. At least I didn't have to stare at her empty bed in my old HARC room.

Callum was on my other side, hands behind his head, his

gaze fixed at the small opening at the top of the tent. He was so still that for a moment I panicked, thinking he'd slipped back into insanity, but his eyes shifted to me and he managed a small smile. I could tell what he was thinking without him having to say it. The horror of what he'd done, the memory of the man he'd killed, was written all over his face. There was nothing I could say. My only hope was he found a way to forget, or move on, or do whatever normal people did when they had guilt about taking a life.

Someday I'd ask him how he could torture himself over one human life when I'd taken too many to count. I'd ask him why he liked me when he despised killing so much. Someday I'd point out the weirdness of that.

But not now.

I sat up and ran my hands through my hair, avoiding Callum's gaze. I needed a shower. And new clothes. I was still wearing his old three-sizes-too-big T-shirt. They couldn't possibly have enough clothes for everyone, though. I might just have to wash the ones I had.

"Wren?"

I sighed at the sound of Micah's voice from outside the tent and crawled across the dirt to pull back the flap of the tent, squinting in the early morning sunshine. I must have slept, like, fifteen hours. "Yeah?"

Micah looked down at me, hands on his hips. "We're splitting people into groups to start cleaning and rebuilding today.

You want to be with me? I can take you on a tour around the compound, show you everything."

I got to my feet, trying to think of a legitimate excuse to stay in my tent with Callum all day instead. I had nothing.

"Sure," I said, suppressing a sigh. Callum climbed out of the tent, and Micah didn't extend the offer to him.

"Can I shower first?" I gestured down to my dirty clothes. "And any chance of getting something to wear?"

"Yeah, sure." He turned, beckoning for me to follow. "This way."

"You want to come?" I asked Callum.

He shook his head, regarding Micah with amusement. "I'm good. I'll meet up with you later."

I rolled my eyes behind Micah's back, and Callum grinned at me as I turned around to follow him.

I jogged to Micah's side. It was still early, the sun just starting to rise, but there were already quite a few Reboots milling around. I scanned their faces. "Is One-fifty-seven here?" I asked. "Riley?"

"Yeah. He's on the hunt with a few others. They should be back soon, actually." He smiled at me. "He'll be thrilled to see you. He talks about you all the time."

The Riley I knew hadn't talked all that much, but maybe Micah was exaggerating. Still, I was relieved. Riley and I weren't exactly friends the way Ever and I had been, but I'd still felt sad when I thought he was dead.

Micah took me to a midsized tent at the back of the reservation that had been used as a makeshift sleeping area. Blankets and pillows were scattered everywhere, and a few Reboots were still sleeping in corners. There were stacks of clothes on a table in the back.

"Pick something that looks like it will fit," Micah said, pointing. "I had everyone turn over their extra clothes so the new Reboots could have something."

I took a quick glance around, wondering if the reservation Reboots secretly hated us. I would.

I grabbed a pair of pants and a long-sleeved shirt about my size and walked back outside with Micah.

"I'll meet you over by the fire pit for breakfast when you're done," he said.

I nodded at him and headed across the reservation to the shower area. A Reboot told me yesterday that the plumbing system had been in place for several years, and it appeared to work impressively well. The bathroom stalls were small, closed-off wooden compartments, but the showers had nothing but a wall to separate one shower from the next, the front totally open. No curtain to hide behind.

I grabbed a tiny scrap of fabric (it looked like they'd cut all their towels in half) and scurried to the last one in the row, careful to keep the scars on my chest hidden as I showered quickly in the icy water. I was already enough of a freak here. I didn't need people whispering about my ugly scars, too.

I shivered as I toweled off and reached for my clothes.

"Hey, Wren, you in here?"

I paused at the sound of Addie's voice. "Yeah?"

Her footsteps came closer and her face appeared around the side of the wall.

"Hey!" I snapped, pressing the towel against my chest. I motioned for her to go away. "Can you give me a minute?"

"Jeez, sorry." Her voice was annoyed as she took a step back and disappeared from view. "Didn't realize you were weird about that."

I quickly jerked a shirt over my head. "I'm almost dressed."

"Good, because we have a problem."

I sighed as I tugged on my pants and toweled off my hair. Wonderful. That was just what I needed. More problems.

I stepped out of the stall and found her standing a few feet away, arms crossed. I dumped my dirty clothes in a bin labeled *Laundry* and she followed me from the showers and into the sunlight. "What's the problem?"

"The nut jobs who run this place are the problem." Addie said it loudly, so that several of the Reboots around us turned and frowned.

I stopped and faced her. "I'm not sure that pissing them off right away is the smartest idea," I said quietly.

"I don't care." She pointed at something, although when I followed her finger I couldn't tell exactly what. "That crazy girl is rounding up all the girls and telling them to take their birth-control chips out."

I raised my eyebrows. "Which crazy girl?"

"The redhead. Um, Jules. Micah's sidekick."

"Did you tell her no?"

"Yeah, I told her no. Apparently it's my *duty* to have children. Apparently procreation is *encouraged*. And since I'm an Under-sixty, I'm *especially* encouraged." She threw her hands in the air. "Some of the Austin Reboots are buying this crap!"

I shifted uncomfortably as I glanced at Jules, who was standing outside a tent not far away. Her red hair blew in the breeze, her eyes narrowed as she watched us.

That was weird. And not exactly something I wanted to deal with.

"You don't have to do that," I said.

"Damn right I don't have to do that!"

"Is there a problem here?"

I turned around to see Micah standing behind me, one eyebrow cocked. He peered at me, then Addie.

"Your sidekick wants to take my birth-control chip out," Addie said.

His eyebrow lifted higher. "My sidekick?"

"Jules," I said quickly, giving Addie a "calm down" look. I barely knew her, and her loudmouth tendencies were already getting on my nerves.

"Yeah." She ignored my look. "She says it's my duty."

"Well, I don't know about duty, but we're a big fan of

Reboot children here," Micah said evenly.

"I'm not doing it."

"HARC forcibly sterilized you," Micah said.

"I'm cool with it."

Micah's jaw moved, like he was trying to control his temper.

"It should be her decision," I said quietly. "You're not going to force her, are you?" I tried to keep the question light, but I was actually worried.

"Yes, it's her decision." He sighed, like he was disappointed.

"What a relief," Addie said dryly. "Me and my baby maker are going to go over there and tell the others."

I didn't know whether to give her an exasperated look or laugh at that comment, and the edges of her mouth turned up in a smile when she caught both expressions on my face. I quickly wiped away my amusement as I turned to Micah.

"I'm surprised she survived at HARC," Micah said, watching her walk away. "Doesn't seem like she takes orders well."

I shrugged. Addie had been at HARC for six years, so she must have done something right. And I couldn't help thinking that maybe she was simply tired of taking orders. I certainly was.

Two Reboot kids ran around the fire pit, and Micah followed my gaze. He grinned. "Cool, isn't it?"

"Weird," I murmured. The girl Reboot was maybe four years old, and she shrieked as a shorter girl chased her dangerously close to the fire. No one seemed concerned by this, and

I guessed it wouldn't matter if both of them fell in and rolled around in the flames.

If Reboot babies were encouraged, it didn't look like that many people were feeling inclined. I'd only seen the one baby last night and I'd only noticed one little boy, other than the two girls at the fire pit.

"Are there a lot of kids here?" I asked.

Micah headed in the direction of the food table, motioning for me to follow him. "No," he said, eyes downcast as he handed me a bowl. "There were more, but they're gone now."

"Gone where?" I asked. A girl about my age shoveled oats into my bowl. Everyone was close to my age, actually. The makeup of the reservation was similar to HARC, with most Reboots falling between twelve and twenty. Where was everyone else? Shouldn't there have been more people around Micah's age? Or older?

He was silent until we sat down in the dirt. "We had more people about a year ago." His voice was low.

"Where'd they go?" I gripped my spoon tighter.

"A group of fifty or so took off by themselves."

I lifted my eyebrows. "Why?"

"You've noticed there aren't a lot of older Reboots on the reservation?"

I nodded.

"We had a falling-out," he replied. "The older generation wasn't happy here, didn't like the way I was running things, so they left. Most of the people with children decided to go with them. Thought they'd be safer away from here."

"Do you know where they went?" The idea of a second safe community for Reboots was comforting, especially if this one didn't work out.

"They all died," Micah said, a pained expression crossing his face. "I tried to tell them it wasn't safe, that our biggest advantage was our numbers and our weapons, but they went anyway. I found them a week later, on a hunt. It looked like HARC got to them."

"Did they go south?" I asked, surprised.

"More like west," Micah said, shielding his eyes with his hand as he gazed in the direction of the sun. "But HARC has ways of tracking and hunting people everywhere."

I swallowed a bite of oats, a blip of fear running through me. If that was true, my backup plan of running off with Callum wasn't looking so good.

"How did HARC get them?" I asked. "Weren't they armed?"

"Barely. Our weapons are reservation weapons. I wasn't handing them off to a group of people deserting us. They took what they had, but it wasn't enough. From the looks of it, HARC sent in a lot of officers. More than they could fight off."

It seemed like Micah had more than enough weapons to spare. I wondered if everyone at the reservation was okay with him sending Reboots away who were barely armed to defend themselves. "How many people are here now?" I asked.

"A little over a hundred. Maybe a hundred and fifteen. We were a hundred and twenty-seven yesterday before you guys got here, but I'm still waiting for an accurate count of how many we lost." He jumped to his feet, clearing his throat. "You done? I'll take you on that tour."

I wanted to ask why exactly all those Reboots had left, but the way Micah had said they didn't like the way he was running things made me doubt I would get a full answer. Maybe that was a better question for Riley, or one of the other Reboots here.

We dropped our bowls off to be washed and I followed him through the reservation. He pointed out areas where they made clothes and other necessities, like soap and furniture. They used one tent for school, and he said some of the younger Austin Reboots should start attending again. He was probably right. I'd managed to hold on to a lot of my education, but I'd received nothing after the age of twelve. Maybe a trip to that tent would be a good idea for me, too.

He led me outside and we walked to the edge of their expansive crops. They grew oats and wheat and beans, among other things. A large barn was one of the only permanent structures on the compound, and it was full of livestock.

I had to hand it to Micah. This place was organized and thriving under his command. I had the feeling that if HARC let him into the cities he would clean them up in less than a month and have everyone fed, clothed, and organized.

"Is there going to be enough food to feed everyone with a hundred extra people?" I asked as we started walking back toward the reservation. "I don't know a lot about growing, but you already harvested everything from last season, right?"

He nodded. "It might be tight, but we'll be okay. We've got some gardens on the reservation, too. I'm working on a plan to make sure everyone is taken care of. Plus we were still producing enough for the Reboots who left."

He looked sad every time he talked about them, and I felt a spark of pity for him. It must have been a huge amount of pressure, taking care of so many Reboots while HARC was constantly trying to kill them.

"The hunting team should have been back by now," Micah murmured as he stared at the sky. "They were scheduled to return this morning."

"Are they usually back on time?"

"Yes, when Riley goes. You know him. He doesn't deviate from the plan."

That was true. He'd been an even stricter trainer than I was. He probably would have let Officer Mayer kill Callum without protest.

"Where are they?" I asked. "Can you go look for them?"

"Let's go see if they got one of the shuttles running," he said. "They went pretty far, about a hundred and thirty miles north, but it won't take us long in a shuttle."

I raised my eyebrows in surprise. They went that far to

hunt? They must have stripped the land clean in this area. Or did people always have to cover that much ground to hunt? I'd never hunted, so maybe that was normal.

We walked into the reservation and down the dirt roads toward the front gate. Reboots around us were busy erecting tents and cleaning away debris. They'd made huge progress in just the couple of hours I'd been with Micah. It was starting to look like nothing had happened at all.

Two shuttles were outside the front of the reservation. Reboots surrounded both of them, and a few others walked around picking up trash. One of the shuttles was in bad shape, its side completely smashed in, but the other one could have been worse. It was dented and dirty, and missing a small corner on the back pilot's side, but otherwise wasn't bad.

We walked closer to the good shuttle and I spotted Callum in the pilot's seat, his brow furrowed as he fiddled with something on the dash. He had grease on his hands and arms, like he'd been working on other parts as well.

"Does this one work?" Micah asked.

Callum lifted his head, smiling when he caught sight of me. "Yeah. We replaced a couple parts with stuff from the more destroyed shuttles. And I just finished fixing the navigation system."

Micah gave him a surprised look and leaned over him to examine the dash. "Thank you. Good work. Not that I know how to use the navigation system." He chuckled.

Callum hopped out of the shuttle. "No problem. I can teach you sometime if you want." He wiped his hands on his pants. "You going somewhere?"

"Our hunting party didn't come back. I'm getting a little worried." He turned to me. "Would you want to come? If there's trouble I could use your help."

I hesitated, taking a glance at Callum. I wasn't exactly pumped at the idea of hopping onto a shuttle to charge into trouble again.

"We shouldn't be long. Back tonight at the latest. And hey, if they're all right maybe we can do some hunting ourselves." Micah punched me lightly on the shoulder. "The hunt is pretty awesome. I think you'd enjoy it."

He might have been right about that. It was probably sort of like hunting down the assignments in Rosa, except deer and rabbits could run faster. More challenging, with no humans barking orders in my ear.

"Yeah, all right," I said.

"You can come, too, if you want," Micah said to Callum.

He made a face at me like he'd rather not and I almost laughed. I couldn't imagine Callum enjoying shooting animals. He didn't even enjoy eating them.

"I think I'll pass," he said. He pointed at the other shuttle. "We were going to work on that one next."

Micah nodded. "I'm going to grab Jules and Kyle, then." He touched my arm. "You want to wait here for a minute?

I'll get you some weapons."

I nodded and he jogged back through the gates and disappeared around the corner.

"Everything all right?" Callum asked, taking a step closer to me.

I nodded, a smile spreading across my face as I glanced down at his grease-covered arms. He looked happy and relaxed. I wasn't sure I'd ever seen that particular expression on his face before. "Good," I said. I decided not to tell him about Addie and the birth-control chips. It was an awkward conversation, and not one that was relevant to us at the moment anyway.

I closed my hand over my upper arm, where my own chip was. I was going to leave it in, though. Just in case.

"You don't mind if I don't come with you, do you?" He grinned. "I think we both know I'd suck at hunting."

I stepped forward, rising to my tiptoes to brush my lips against his. "I wasn't going to say that. But yeah, probably best if you don't come."

He chuckled, leaning forward to kiss me again, keeping his arms at his sides. I rested my hands on his chest and melted into the kiss, not caring about the Reboots all around us.

"Tonight, when you get back, let's do this," he said, pulling away slightly and kissing my cheek. "No more attacking or socializing or hunting. Just this."

"Agreed." I ran my hands up to his neck and sighed. "Now I wish I didn't have to go."

"I think it's nice you agreed. If we stay, hunting will probably be your thing here. Hunting and saving people. Your two favorite things."

I let out a soft laugh. I didn't know about the latter—he was the only person I'd ever saved—but hunting probably was "my thing." It was nice to think I might have something I'd be good at here. I'd never been good at anything but hunting down humans for HARC, and that wasn't something I ever planned to do again.

"Wren! You ready?"

I glanced back to see Micah standing by the shuttle with Jules and Kyle. A young Reboot sat in the pilot's seat, and the shuttle roared to life. I stepped away from Callum with a sigh. "I'll see you."

"Bye. Don't get shot."

FIVE

CALLUM

I FROWNED AT THE CRUSHED FLIGHT CONTROLS IN FRONT OF ME, touching the spot where a button used to be. This shuttle was in worse shape than the one Wren and Micah had just taken off in, but it was possibly still salvageable.

"Need any of these?"

Isaac stood next to the shuttle door, a bag of assorted shuttle parts in his hands.

"Maybe," I said, taking the bag and plopping it down on the seat next to me. "Thank you."

"No problem." He slid his hands into his pockets and leaned against the shuttle door. His tendency to slouch made him look even shorter than he was. "You know, shuttle cleanup was the job most people were avoiding."

I smiled as I sifted through the bag. "Probably because we had to haul out some body parts first." I shrugged. "But I'm pretty good with tech stuff. I thought I might be useful."

"Very," he said. "Most Reboots come in without knowing much besides how to punch people."

I rolled my eyes. HARC and their dumb priorities. "I'm sure."

"Where did you say you were from?" he asked.

"Austin."

"Never been. Never been to any of the cities, actually. Is it nice?"

I gave him a confused look. "You've never been to the cities? Were you born out here?"

"Yep."

"Oh, were you born a Reboot?" I asked, surprised. Hadn't they said the Reboot babies didn't get numbers?

"Nope."

"Oh." I waited for more of an explanation, but he didn't give one. He was holding something back and, given the way he was avoiding my eyes and frowning, it wasn't good.

I took a quick look at the scene behind him. About ten Reboots milled around, picking up shuttle parts or working on the fence. Some of the somberness of yesterday was gone, but the reservation Reboots didn't seem to be making much of an effort to talk to the new arrivals. In fact, no one except Isaac had approached me.

I returned my attention to the mess in front of me. I hadn't approached any of them, either, so maybe we were all still adjusting. I picked out a button and tried to fit it in the hole on the dash. No luck.

"So, Austin," Isaac said, crossing his arms over his chest. "It's nice?"

I shrugged. "It's okay." When I thought of Austin all I could see were my parents slamming the door in my face. All I could hear was the gasp of that man I killed as I wrapped my fingers around his throat.

I closed my eyes, swallowing. Part of me was relieved the memories were returning from the time I'd lost. They'd started slipping back, little by little, last night. Jumping on top of that woman in the restaurant, the smell of her flesh overwhelming me. Waiting for Wren to grab Addie and getting distracted by movement in the next house over. Breaking the door in and pouncing on the man.

I opened my eyes with a sigh. Isaac was staring at me, his face scrunched in sympathy.

"You HARC people are seriously messed up, huh?"

"Probably," I said with a hint of amusement.

"What's it like there?"

"Being in the facility isn't so bad. I got beat up a lot the first couple of days, but then that stopped and it was just Wren kicking the crap out of me and that was sort of fun."

He gave me a baffled look. "Seriously messed up. All of you."

"She was my trainer," I said with a laugh. "She was nice about it."

"Oh, well, if she was nice about it."

"The assignments, where we had to go out and capture humans, were kind of awful. I'd probably have died in less than a year if I'd stayed." I sighed. "The humans really hate us."

Isaac nodded as he took a step back. "Well, they sort of have a point sometimes, you know?"

I looked at him in surprise. "What do you mean?"

"I'd be scared of us, if I were them. We're tougher and stronger and most of you can kick their asses, thanks to HARC."

He did have a point. As a human I'd been more curious about Reboots, but I was definitely still scared of them. I never encountered a Reboot until I became one myself, but I might have run away, too.

Although I could say for sure that I never would have grabbed a baseball bat and tried to bash their heads in. I shivered at the memory of being attacked by humans in Rosa. I had understood Wren's dislike of them, for a moment.

"Do you like it here?" I asked.

"Yeah." He shrugged. "I mean, it could be worse, right? I could be at HARC."

"True."

"It's not so bad. By the time I got here, most of the kinks were ironed out. They've got stable crops and everyone is fed and clothed."

"I used to work the fields in Austin, before I Rebooted," I said. "I could help with that here."

"Nice," Isaac said, like he was genuinely impressed. "More useful skills. Micah might start liking you as much as he likes your girlfriend."

I gave him an annoyed look and he snorted in amusement. It faded as he caught sight of something in the distance, and I leaned out the shuttle door to see Beth and Addie headed in my direction, their faces grim. I turned to Isaac again but he was already walking away.

I jumped from the shuttle, wiping my hands on my pants as they approached. Addie was pale and Beth was nervously tugging on her hair.

"Have you seen Wren?" Addie asked.

"She left with Micah." I lowered my voice, stepping closer to her. "She'll be back tonight. Is everything okay?"

Beth and Addie exchanged a horrified expression and a sick feeling started to build in my stomach.

"On the hunt?" Addie said, her voice barely above a whisper.

"Technically she went to find the Reboots who didn't come back, but I think they were going to hunt if they could." I swallowed. "Why? What's wrong?"

"Did they tell her what the hunt was?" Addie's eyes were big, worry mixing with fear.

"I . . . I don't know." I glanced from her to Beth. "What's the hunt?"

SIX

WREN

I SETTLED INTO A SHUTTLE SEAT AS WE LIFTED OFF THE GROUND.
Micah claimed the big seat usually occupied by a HARC officer, and a big pile of guns sat on the floor at our feet. Kyle
One-forty-nine sat next to me, his wide shoulders taking up
part of my seat. Jules sat on my other side and I avoided her
gaze, worried she would start lecturing me about taking out my
birth-control chip, too.

"Do we have enough fuel?" I asked. Last thing I wanted was
to get stuck a hundred miles away from Callum.

"We do," Micah replied, leaning back in his seat. "Although
we may take a trip down to Austin soon to get more fuel from
those helpful rebels. Seems like the kind of thing they'd be good

for." He smirked in a way I didn't quite understand, like he was being sarcastic, and I shifted uncomfortably in my chair. I hated feeling indebted to those humans. I almost felt like I needed to stick up for them.

The shuttle flew through the air smoothly, like there was a HARC officer in the pilot's chair. "How'd you guys learn to fly the shuttles?" I asked.

"We fixed the ones we shot down and taught ourselves," he said, stretching his long legs in front of him. "It's not hard; I teach all the younger Reboots how to do it. They're made so HARC monkeys can drive them without any trouble."

The Reboots laughed but an image of Addie's father, Leb, popped into my head. Not all the HARC officers were bad.

I took a quick glance around. That wasn't the sort of thing I could say here. I sat back in my seat and everyone quieted down. It was like being with the One-twenties at the HARC facility. The silence was comforting.

"You look better today," Jules finally said, smiling at me as she pushed her long, red hair over her shoulder. "You seemed overwhelmed yesterday."

"You did," Micah said, his voice sympathetic. "I'm sorry. You must have had a hell of a few days, huh?"

"Yeah," I said with a short laugh. I'd told them the story last night, an abbreviated version of our escape from Rosa and break into Austin to rescue Addie and get Callum the antidote.

It felt like a million years ago, even though it was just early yesterday morning that I'd been running down the halls of the Austin HARC facility.

"You were at the Rosa facility how long?" Jules asked.

"Five years. Since I was twelve."

"You were shot, weren't you?" Micah asked. "Riley told me that's how you died."

"Yes."

"Who did it?"

I shrugged. "I don't know." It was a common question, but not one I could bring myself to care about. It was some drug dealer or shady friend of my parents', and it didn't matter now. Chances were good HARC had caught the human who killed me and my parents and executed him anyway.

"Humans," Kyle said with a roll of his eyes. "Go around killing each other all the time."

Micah shook his head, running his hand along the stubble on his chin. "It's like they want to be extinct."

Everyone was amused by this, but once again, I wasn't sure I got the joke. I shifted in my chair uncomfortably.

I cleared my throat and pointed to the stack of guns in the corner. "Where'd you guys get all the weapons?"

"We took some from the HARC shuttles that attacked us," Micah said. "We made some. But we scavenged most of them. Well, I shouldn't say 'we.' They. The very smart Reboots who evaded HARC years ago immediately started scavenging weapons left over from the war. Even though they'd lost, they were still in battle mode."

That made sense. HARC had rounded up all the Reboots and killed them after the war, before they figured out they could use the young ones to help clean up the cities. The Reboots who managed to escape would have needed to be well protected.

"HARC was busy with the new cities in Texas and building their facilities and by the time they sent crews out to the old military bases north of Texas, they were stripped bare."

"Hank used to tell this story about driving a tank right past a HARC officer one day," Kyle said with a laugh. "He just rolled right on by and the HARC guy never looked twice. They had no idea they'd missed so many Reboots, and they were out there, stealing stuff."

"And back then, HARC still thought we had limited brain-power," Micah said. "I actually think the Reboots' organized plan to strip every military base from coast to coast is what prompted all the experiments HARC does on us now. They realized they didn't know crap about us. Or what we were capable of."

"But the Reboots didn't attack back then, did they?" I asked. I'd never heard of a Reboot attack after the war.

"No, the numbers were too small. They just stockpiled the weapons for protection. When I moved everyone here out to the open, we brought them all with us."

I opened my mouth to ask why he would move everyone into the open, leaving them vulnerable to HARC attacks, but the shuttle started to descend and Micah walked over to the pilot. He sat down in the passenger's seat, pointing at something to the east as he murmured to the driver.

"They're right in front of us," he said with a smile, turning to us. "Looks like everyone is okay."

I slid forward in my seat to see a few figures below us. The flat earth that surrounded the reservation was gone, replaced by huge stone structures, almost mountains. It was like someone had carved a random huge hole in the middle of Texas.

"You should see the one farther north," Kyle said, catching my expression. "Makes this canyon look tiny."

There was a river not far away, and the land was dotted with trees. This area seemed much nicer than the location Micah had picked for the reservation.

The shuttle landed softly on the ground. Kyle handed me two guns—a shotgun and a handgun—and extra ammo. These Reboots really didn't take any chances. I had to admire them for that.

The door to the shuttle slid open and a burst of anticipation zipped through my chest. I didn't know how to act around Riley outside of HARC. I might have counted him as a friend, but one who barely spoke to me.

I stepped out from behind Jules, scrunching my face up against the powerful wind that slammed against me. Less than

a day, and I was already entirely annoyed by the wind here. I'd
never felt anything like it.

Micah climbed out the door behind the short Reboot pilot
and raised his hand at something in the distance. I squinted,
lifting my hand to block the sunlight.

Four—no, five—Reboots were walking toward us. Two
bikes were behind them, one of them toppled over in the dirt
with a busted tire.

A guy at the front of the group was walking a bit faster than
the rest: the leader. His hair was longer than last time I'd seen
him, almost a year ago. The thick, dark blond strands tickled
at his neck. His eyes were a light, piercing blue. It was Riley
One-fifty-seven.

"Hey, Micah," he called as he got closer. "Sorry, we—"

He stopped short, his eyes widening as they met mine.
"Wren?"

Micah chuckled, turning to glance at me. "Surprise."

"Wren?" Riley said again, with a hint of laughter. I lifted
my hand to wave but he was running toward me and I froze,
unsure what he intended to do. He scooped me up in his arms,
my feet almost leaving the ground. I stiffened. How odd. Riley
never touched me. His blank, emotionless demeanor had been
my favorite thing about him. We'd been the same that way.

He released me, his face more excited than I'd ever seen.
He was almost as tall as Callum but wider, although he was
slightly less muscular than last time I'd seen him. Working out

had been the only thing Riley enjoyed at HARC.

"How are you here? What happened? Did Leb help you?" His words came in a rush, and by the time he got to the last question I wasn't sure he wanted me to answer the first anymore.

"Yes," I said slowly. "Leb helped me. I . . . uh, escaped."

Riley laughed like that was the funniest thing he'd ever heard and pulled me into another hug. What was happening? Since when did Riley hug? Since when did Riley *laugh*?

"She forgot the part where she rescued every Reboot in the Austin facility and brought them with her!" Micah called over his shoulder as he headed toward the other Reboots.

Riley frowned in confusion. "Austin? What were you doing in Austin?"

"It's a long story," Jules interjected, giving me a sympathetic look. She gestured to the bikes. "What's going on there?"

"Tire busted on one of them," Riley said. "We were trying to patch it up well enough so we could all ride back. It's not working out." He peered behind me. "Is that a new shuttle?"

"Wren rides in style," Jules said with a grin.

Micah knelt down next to the busted bike. "We can put this one in the shuttle. Two of you can ride the other one back." He straightened, scanning the area. "Hunt didn't produce anything this time?"

"Sorry, man, we couldn't find them," Riley said.

Micah pointed to the east with his shotgun. "I just saw them right over there. You're losing your touch, friend." He nodded

his head at me. "Wren, with me. Jules and Kyle, follow on the
south side." He looked at Riley. "You guys stay here and watch
the shuttle. Get that bike loaded."

I took a step toward Micah and stopped as Riley wrapped
his cool fingers around my wrist. Most of the happiness drained
from his face, the blank look I knew so well plastered there
instead.

"Maybe Wren could stay here?" Riley asked.

Micah rolled his eyes. "You'll have plenty of time to catch
up, I promise. I told her she could hunt."

Riley's gaze flicked to mine as he released my wrist, and I
frowned, confused. I couldn't read the expression on his face.
Was he . . . worried? I hadn't seen him worried about me since
he was my trainer.

"Let's go!" Micah said. He winked at me. "It'll be fun."

I cast one more glance back at Riley as I followed Micah,
but he just stared at me blankly. Weird. I was going to have to
ask him what that was about when we got a moment alone.

We walked through crunchy dead grass, the trees sparse
around us, and Micah adjusted the shotgun strapped to his
back and clicked the safety off the handgun. A handgun seemed
like a weird choice for hunting, but he knew more about it than
I did.

"You ever think about revenge?" he asked after we'd been
walking several minutes, his voice low. "On that human who
killed you and your parents?"

"No. I'm sure HARC already caught him anyway. I don't think he was subtle about killing us."

"But if they didn't? Would you go back and kill him?"

I shook my head. "I really don't care. I don't feel anything when I think about my death. Or even my parents' deaths." I looked at him quickly. Maybe I shouldn't have said that last part. That would have horrified Callum.

But Micah nodded like he understood. "Yeah, your parents would have rejected you once you Rebooted anyway."

I thought of the look on Callum's mother's face as she stared at her son. Micah was right about that. My parents could barely stand me as a human.

"I admire your ability to separate out your emotions like that," he said, carefully stepping over a rock and offering me his hand to help me. I ignored it. "I'm not always good at that."

I raised my eyebrows in surprise, but he didn't elaborate. I thought about what Callum had said to me once, about the numbers not mattering. Was I less emotional because I was a One-seventy-eight, or because I was just me?

The prospect of it being just me was worse.

We walked into a thick patch of trees, Micah leading the way. I could see a hint of the river in front of us, and Micah took in a breath as he stopped behind a tree trunk. He reached for his com.

"In position?" he whispered into it.

"*In position,*" Jules replied.

He tucked the com into his pocket. "Ready?" He nodded in approval at my handgun. "Adults get one in the head. Anyone who looks young enough to Reboot gets a few in the chest. Got it?"

I froze.

Micah turned away, stepping out from behind the tree with the gun pointed straight ahead. My fingers crept to where my shirt covered my scars.

"Anyone who looks young enough to Reboot gets a few in the chest."

We weren't hunting animals.

The screams pierced the quiet and I jumped, almost accidentally firing a bullet into the air.

I stumbled out of the trees to see Micah taking wide strides toward a small band of humans, squeezing off shot after shot. They were running in every direction, splashing through the dirty water of the river as they tried to escape.

Jules and Kyle emerged from the trees opposite us, picking off the ones Micah missed.

There was no return fire. They weren't armed.

My eyes flicked over the scene. Tents. A fire. Abandoned food. No sign of HARC gear. They were simply regular humans, living here.

"Wren!" Micah turned to me, a happy-crazed expression on his face. Was this the emotion he was talking about? Delight in killing people?

"Go for it!" he yelled.

I lowered my gun with a slight shake of my head. I wasn't killing these unarmed humans.

I wasn't that much of a monster.

Micah rolled his eyes in exasperation as he turned back toward the humans. There were only two left.

Maybe I should have saved them. Maybe I should have stepped in and attempted to take on these three Over-one-twenties by myself.

I didn't. I stood there, frozen, as Micah shot the last two humans in the chest. The boy was so young I had to turn away. The other one, a girl, was probably about my age.

"Is there a problem?" Micah asked as he lowered his gun. He cocked an eyebrow at me. It was a challenge.

"They were unarmed," I said, choking back the urge to yell it at him.

He walked to me. He didn't seem mad. In fact, he looked sympathetic. He placed a hand on my arm and I shrugged it off.

"I know it's weird at first," he said softly. "But just because they weren't armed right now doesn't mean they wouldn't kill us the first chance they got. Just because we made the first move doesn't make it wrong."

I wasn't sure that logic made any sense. I'd have to run it by Callum later, because I could almost see Micah's point.

He shoved his gun in his pocket and looked at me expectantly, but I didn't know what he wanted me to say. I wasn't going to agree with him. I wasn't going to argue. Silence seemed the best course of action at this point.

"Let's pack it up," Micah said, turning away from me and heading toward the camp.

"They don't have much," Jules said with a sigh, yanking one of the sticks of a tent out of the ground.

My gaze turned to the two kids. Were we waiting for them to Reboot? Then what? They were going to join us after what we'd done to them?

I cleared my throat. "Are there a lot of humans out here?" I asked.

Micah smirked. "There used to be."

"I thought HARC got all the humans together and took them to Texas. Do they escape?"

"Rarely. HARC couldn't possibly get them all after the war. Especially those people from that country way up north." He glanced back at Jules and Kyle. "What was that one called?"

"Canada," Jules said.

"Right. Canada. The humans left in Canada mostly evaded HARC and started migrating south for better weather when they thought it was safe." Micah grinned. "It wasn't."

"And the ones who Reboot just come with you willingly?" I asked. "After you killed them and their families?"

"Where else are they going to go?" Micah said, shoving an animal hide under his arm. "They can either stay out here alone, go to the cities and become a slave, or join us. Not exactly a difficult decision."

I would have picked staying out here alone, actually. Hands down.

"But, yes, there's a transition period." He gestured to the dead teenagers. "Grab one. It's best we get them on the shuttle before they Reboot."

Apparently they did not come willingly.

Kyle reached for the boy, yanking him to a standing position by one of his arms. The blood had soaked through the boy's T-shirt and I sighed.

"Did they have a medical kit?" I asked, rubbing my fingers across my forehead.

"Yeah," Jules said, holding out the bag she'd packed. "Why?"

"Give it to me. You should stitch them up now."

"Why?" Micah asked with a frown. "There's no guarantee they'll Reboot."

"But they might," I said, walking closer to Jules. "If you stitch it now the wound will heal better. Especially if they're over One-twenty."

"Oh yeah, that's true," Kyle said. "The skin doesn't always grow back together right if it's left open too long."

Micah's gaze briefly moved down to my chest, a flash of sympathy crossing his face. My wounds were worse than these kids; I'd been younger and the bullet holes had been much bigger, but still, I knew what I was talking about.

"Quickly," he said, a hint of softness in his voice. "Jules, do one of them."

Jules handed me a needle and a length of thread. "Give me whatever you have left over. There isn't much in here."

I nodded as I took it and walked to the girl. Her long, dark hair covered part of her face and I left it there, glad I wasn't able to see her eyes. I took a swift glance behind me as I grabbed the bottom of her shirt, but no one was watching us. Micah was deep in conversation with Kyle and Jules was hovering over the other dead human.

I yanked up the shirt and stitched the two bullet holes back together as best I could. I used the bottom of my own shirt to wipe away some of the blood, but there was too much to get it all. I pulled her top down and handed the thread off to Jules. When I turned around, Micah had the dead girl swung over his shoulder.

"Take those," he said, pointing to a pile of animal hides and clothes at his feet.

I grabbed them and trailed behind Micah as we headed back toward the shuttle. The girl's dark hair bobbed as we walked, and I didn't know what to hope for. Was it better to die permanently, or wake up to find that you've become a Reboot and everyone you knew is dead?

I didn't know what I would have picked, if someone had given me a choice.

Micah slowed, letting Jules and Kyle pull ahead of us, and I was forced to walk beside him.

"I know this isn't ideal," he said quietly. "But we need as many Reboots as possible."

"Why?"

"Because right now, the humans outnumber us. If we're going to go after HARC, we need an army."

I looked at him quickly. "Go after HARC?"

"Sure. Don't you want to take revenge on them?"

I paused. Sometimes I still fantasized about snapping Officer Mayer's neck. It would make such a satisfying sound. But I mostly just wanted to get away from them.

Maybe if they'd killed Callum I'd feel differently, but they didn't. I won, and I was fine with enjoying my victory from a distance.

"No," I said.

"What about all those Reboots left in there?" he asked. "Do you want to save them?"

My chest tightened as I realized where this was going. Did I want to jump back into the cities of Texas and fight off HARC *four* times? Four facilities, four break-ins, four battles. Or five, if HARC transferred Reboots back to the Austin facility soon.

But the intensity of Micah's stare made me hesitant to admit how little I cared what happened to the rest of the Reboots. Now wasn't the time for outright argument. I needed to get back to the reservation first. Find Callum. Figure out what to do.

"I think it would be very hard," I said slowly.

A grin spread across his face. "But it wouldn't. I already have it all planned out."

I cleared my throat, beating down the rising sense of dread. "What do you mean?"

"We've been preparing for battle for years. I managed to get schematics to all the HARC facilities. Those rebels." He laughed, gently punching my shoulder. "They're such trusting souls, aren't they?"

That sounded bad. That sounded really, really bad.

"Now that we have increased our numbers so unexpectedly, we're going to fast-track the next phase. We're going to release the rest of the Reboots in the facilities into the cities, starting with Rosa. Then we'll eliminate the human population."

I sucked in a breath. *Eliminate* the human population? All of them?

"You'd be a big help in Rosa," he continued. "Riley is the only other Reboot from that facility." He adjusted the girl on his shoulder. "I get the feeling you'd be an asset on the front lines of anything, though."

I swallowed before I spoke, steadying myself. "Why eliminate the human population?"

"Because they enslaved us and killed us and evolution has spoken. Our turn."

"Evolution has spoken?" I repeated.

"They treat us like we're some sort of evil virus gone wrong, when in reality we're the evolved ones. The human race was dying out, and the strong found a way to survive. We should be celebrated, not enslaved."

"Why not free the remaining Reboots and leave?" I asked. "You'll lose more Reboots fighting a war against the humans. Not to mention we lost last time."

"Reboot numbers were smaller last time, and they didn't have the weapons we have. Once we get all the Reboots from the four remaining facilities we'll be three times the size we are now. And if we leave, humans will continue to Reboot and we'll have to keep coming back to save them. It's easier just to get rid of them all."

The humans were screwed. Utterly, totally screwed.

Micah glanced at me again, hope lighting up his face. I tried to make my expression neutral, but he looked disappointed I didn't seem more excited about his plan. I turned my gaze to the ground.

As we reached the shuttle, Riley rushed forward, his eyes bouncing between me and Micah. He was attempting to hide his nerves, but I could see them edging out ever so slightly.

Riley had told Micah he couldn't find the humans. Yet they were right around the corner, less than a mile away. I seriously doubted Riley wouldn't be able to find a target less than a mile away. Not unless he didn't want to find them.

The thought comforted me only slightly as we piled into the

shuttle. Riley might not be interested in killing humans, but he was still playing along.

The dead humans were placed in the middle of the shuttle with the supplies and I took a quick look at them. The boy was maybe fourteen or so, surprisingly well fed, with plump cheeks. The girl was tall and probably pretty, but it was hard to tell with her eyes all dead like that. They were still human, dull and a light shade of green.

I turned away and caught Riley staring at me as we lifted off the ground.

"How long has it been?" Micah asked.

"Fifteen or twenty minutes," Jules replied.

I stared at the humans as we rode in silence. I'd never seen a human Reboot. The process was long over by the time a Reboot got to HARC, and I'd never been allowed to stick around a dead human long enough to see them Reboot.

I watched them out of the corner of my eye for a long time, until I heard Micah suck in a breath.

"Look at the girl."

My gaze flew to her, but I wasn't sure there was anything different. Her human eyes still stared at the ceiling vacantly. I leaned a bit closer.

Her hand twitched.

"What time are we at?" Micah asked.

"Fifty minutes or so?" Jules asked. "We're going to need a death timer to tell if she's under sixty or not."

Her hand twitched again and I gripped the bottom of my seat, holding my breath.

Her body convulsed, a huge gasp escaping her mouth as she slammed her chest into the air, then back to the floor.

She was still again, but her eyes were closed.

Riley slowly unbuckled his seat belt and edged onto the floor between her and the boy. He sat next to her still body.

She gasped twice more, her body jerking like she was having a seizure.

"Is this normal?" I whispered.

"Yes," Riley said without turning around.

Her eyes flew open. The dull light color was gone, replaced by bright green.

A strangled noise escaped her throat, like she was in pain. Was Rebooting painful? I frowned, trying to remember, but there was nothing to that memory but the screaming and panic.

She bolted upright, her head whipping from side to side. She didn't appear to see any of us. She was panicked, tears starting to stream down her face. She screamed.

Riley clamped his hand over her eyes and circled his arm around her waist, pulling her to the other side of the shuttle. He turned so she was facing the wall and held tight as she struggled and screamed.

"Don't look, okay?" he said softly. "Everything's okay, but you don't want to look."

I glanced over at the other human, still motionless on the

shuttle floor. Riley spoke softly to the girl as she began to sob in his arms, her whole body shaking.

"She'll be fine," Micah said, his voice full of sympathy, like he wasn't the one who'd killed her.

I pushed my hands underneath my thighs for fear of reaching out to choke him. I took a deep breath, closing my eyes briefly.

"Wren," Micah said.

I ignored him.

"Wren."

I slowly opened my eyes, trying not to let the hate shine through.

"She's better now," he said. He gave me a nod, like he needed me to agree. "We made her better."

I clenched my hands into fists beneath my thighs.

We had to get away from these people. Immediately.

SEVEN

CALLUM

I RAN FOR THE GATE AS SOON AS I SPOTTED THE SHUTTLE IN THE sky, my heart pounding loudly in my chest. It landed several yards away and a tall, muscular guy got out first, a girl wearing a blood-soaked T-shirt in his arms. He was followed by Jules, who was also carrying a dead human, then Micah, and, finally, Wren. She was pale, her face hard as stone. Micah said something to her but she walked right by him.

I couldn't breathe. I hadn't been able to breathe since Addie told me the hunt was actually for humans. Since she told me Micah and his friends had been slowly killing all the humans they could find and bringing back the ones who Rebooted.

Wren's face made it worse. I'd forced myself not to panic,

to be calm and rational even though I wanted to scream at all these crazy people. I had to wait and see what Wren's reaction was, to gauge how much trouble we were in.

Apparently we were in "everyone panic, we're screwed" trouble.

"Wren!" Micah called to Wren's back.

Her face hardened and she threw a look over her shoulder that made Micah stop in his tracks. I swallowed as I watched his face change, the excited, friendly expression he'd been wearing around her slipping away.

She offered me her hand as she approached, relief splashed across her face. Even through my panic, I felt a twinge of happiness that she was relieved to see me. I laced my fingers through hers and squeezed.

"Come with me," she said, pulling on my hand as she kept walking.

"They told me what the hunt was," I said under my breath as we strode across the compound.

Her eyes flicked to mine and she swallowed, nodding slightly. I held her hand tighter.

We walked across the reservation and through the back gate. A thick band of trees was in front of the lake, and Wren didn't stop until we were right in the middle of them. She released a rush of air as she dropped my hand and turned to me.

"We need to leave. Now."

I hesitated, taking a quick glance back at the reservation.

Addie might have been on board with that plan, given how upset she was earlier, but the rest of the Austin Reboots? We couldn't leave them here.

"Callum, they're going to kill all the humans in the cities."

My eyes widened as Wren relayed Micah's insane "we're more evolved" plan. Visions of my mom and dad and David flashed through my brain.

"He could just free all the Reboots and leave," I said when she finished, though I could tell by the look on her face that Micah wasn't that rational.

"I told him that." She rubbed her forehead, frowning at the dirt. "He said it wasn't wrong to kill the humans because they'd kill us if they had the chance. That's what he told me about killing those unarmed humans today. That doesn't make any sense, right? That's very much the wrong thing to do?"

"Yes." I stepped forward, putting my hands on her arms. I needed for her to know how right she was about that, how much she needed to hold on to that feeling. "That is very much the wrong thing to do."

She nodded. "Okay. We need to go, then. I don't want anything to do with this."

I dropped my hands, running one down my face. There was no way I could leave now, even if all the Austin Reboots agreed to come with us. I couldn't leave my parents and brother and all the humans I ever knew to die.

"We just dropped a hundred more Reboots in their laps," I

said slowly. "If we leave, all those humans will die."

Wren pressed her lips together. "Maybe not. The humans won before."

"HARC trained us in combat," I said with a humorless laugh. "This isn't like before."

She gave me a pleading look. "If we stay, there's a very good chance one or both of us will end up dead in a war we care nothing about."

"I care," I said quietly.

Her face shifted into the emotionless stare she did when she didn't want me to know what she was thinking, and I tried to replicate it. I didn't want her to know I was disappointed she didn't care. I wished her first instinct was to help, not to run.

I tried to push the feeling away. I couldn't totally blame her for not wanting to jump back into a war when she'd just risked her life several times to save me.

"What do you want to do?" she asked a bit nervously.

I stepped closer to her, lowering my voice. "I'd like to stay long enough to find out how many Reboots will help us. Most of the people from the Austin facility are going to have family or friends in the cities. We can try to get word to the rebels about what Micah is planning. And then, when it looks like the time is right, we can split off from Micah and go to the cities."

She blinked. "To help the humans."

"And free the rest of the Reboots. That was the rebels' plan anyway, to get them all out of the city."

"So you'd like us to go *back* to the cities, rescue all the Reboots, *and* save the humans."

It sounded kind of hard when she put it like that. I winced. "Yes."

"I'll get right on that," she said dryly.

She seemed annoyed, but at least she wasn't furious and pointing out why my plan was stupid. It probably *was* stupid, but I couldn't leave. If I left, it was the same as killing that man in Austin. Except I'd be killing everyone I'd ever cared about as a human. Even though Wren claimed emotions faded some as a Reboot, mine were still all there, same as always. It sort of sucked sometimes, to be honest.

I turned at a rustling sound to see the big blond guy who'd been on the shuttle with Wren walking through the trees toward us. Micah was right behind him.

Wren's amused expression faded, and she looked between Micah and the other guy, crossing her arms over her chest.

"Riley," the blond guy said as he approached, extending his hand to me.

The name sounded vaguely familiar, and I searched my brain as I shook his hand. "Callum."

"One-fifty-seven," Wren explained. "My trainer at HARC."

Wonderful. Was it wrong that I was a little disappointed he wasn't actually dead? Of all the Reboots *not* to be dead, it had to be this guy? The guy who shot Wren repeatedly to make her tough?

"Did you come from the Austin facility?" Riley asked.

"No, I escaped with Wren from Rosa."

"Oh." His face brightened as if he liked this about me, and he grinned as he looked from me to Wren.

"I'd like to speak with you," Micah said to Wren, giving Riley a frown like he didn't approve of him making small talk with me.

She just stared, and I began to get nervous. Silence from Wren was bad. She might have been plotting exactly how to rip Micah to shreds.

"I'd like a chance to explain," he said, and I furrowed my eyebrows in confusion. Explain? How was he going to explain genocide?

Wren met my gaze for a moment, then turned to Micah with a sigh. "Fine."

I started to protest, but she shot me a warning look. Micah had his "I will pound you with my fists" expression turned toward me, and it occurred to me that maybe open defiance wasn't the smartest move. We were outnumbered by the reservation Reboots. Not to mention that we were stuck in the middle of nowhere with them and their arsenal of weapons.

She started to follow Micah, and Riley did the same, nodding at me. "It was nice to meet you." He took a few steps, and when he turned around he had a grin on his face. "Good job getting Wren out. I was worried she was a HARC girl forever."

Wren didn't even glance back at that statement, but I had

to resist the urge to tell him he was a dumbass. Anyone with half a brain could have seen that Wren was brainwashed and traumatized by HARC. She was certainly not their "girl."

"She got me out," I corrected with a frown.

He chuckled. "But I get the feeling you had a little something to do with that." He gave me another approving look before he jogged to catch up with Micah and Wren.

EIGHT

WREN

I FOLLOWED MICAH ACROSS THE RESERVATION AND TO THE BIG tent. He pulled back the flap and turned to Riley, who still looked amused by meeting Callum. Riley had known me as the type of girl who didn't think twice about romance.

"You mind checking on that new Reboot, Riley?" Micah asked.

"Sure." Riley glanced at me.

"You can take a minute," Micah said, before disappearing into the tent. I almost rolled my eyes. How nice of him to give us his permission.

I faced Riley. He was almost smiling, but his eyes were serious.

"I'm glad you're here," he said quietly.

I wasn't sure I was glad to be here anymore, so I just stared at him.

"You did a good job on the hunt today," he said. He put a hand on my arm, locking his gaze on mine. "Very calm and rational."

"When you don't know what to do, you keep your mouth shut." Riley's words from our first week of training echoed in my head. *"Calm and rational keeps you alive. Panic makes you dead."*

I nodded, still feeling that small spark of pride I used to get when he praised me.

His serious look faded as he stepped back, replaced by a half smile. "And I see what it takes to get you out of HARC. Who knew you were such a softie?"

I rolled my eyes at him and he laughed as he walked away. I took a deep breath as I faced the tent, arranging my face into a neutral expression before I stepped inside.

The tent was empty, nothing but Micah and the guns lining every wall. He sat at the long table in the center and I sank into a chair across from him. The air felt tense, and I had the sudden urge to grab my gun. I pushed it back and cleared my throat.

"You're upset." He folded his hands on the table.

I narrowed my eyes at him. "Let's say confused."

A corner of his mouth twitched. "Okay. Confused."

"You killed unarmed humans." I chose my words carefully, aware of the weapons on every wall around me. The hundred-plus Reboots outside were more likely to back him up than me.

"Yes."

"And you don't . . ." I shifted in my chair. "Do you feel guilty?"

He shrugged. He looked younger suddenly, closer to twenty than thirty. He was letting down his guard for me. "I don't know. I did, at first. But, you know." His eyes met mine. "After a while the guilt goes away."

"Yeah," I said softly. It did. Callum had made me more aware of that than ever. "But revenge. That didn't go away."

"No." He leaned forward, resting his palms flat on the wooden table. "I was only seven when I died. I had to spend five years in a holding facility, and for a couple years I got to be part of a special group they experimented on. They've been shooting us up with drugs and running crazy tests from the beginning, you know."

I shook my head. "I didn't know."

"They had some nasty stuff in the works. Stuff to make us weaker, crazier, all kinds of shit. Half the kids there didn't even make it to a full facility. It was worse than the large-scale experiments they're doing now."

"My friend died from one of their experiments," I said quietly.

His face softened. "The recent one meant to diminish brain-power? Make us more compliant?"

"Yes. It almost killed Callum, too."

"And that still doesn't make you want revenge?"

I paused, truly considering it. "Maybe."

"I always wanted to get even. I used to stare at Suzanna every day and plot how I would kill her, down to the last detail."

"Suzanna Palm? The HARC chairman?"

"Yeah. We spent a lot of time together."

"You did?" I asked in surprise. I'd only seen the chairman of HARC a handful of times during my five years at the Rosa facility. I'd known she was in charge of all HARC operations, but was never totally clear on her role.

"She runs most of the important experiments herself. She's the controlling type, can't delegate." Micah leaned closer to me, his face serious. "You can't even imagine the things they're working on, Wren. And I've been gone for years. Those drugs they were developing, they're probably further along now. Or ready."

"What were they working on?" I asked.

Micah sighed. "I got a little bit of everything. One of them slowed my reflexes down to where I could barely move. One made everything I saw purple. One made me want to eat humans alive. One slowed down my healing so much it was hours before a wound closed."

I swallowed. I'd never considered how lucky I was to have died at twelve, and not earlier. I'd never bothered to ask the other Reboots what they did all those years in the holding facility.

"So, after I escaped, I decided it needed to stop. We can't

trust the humans. Even those rebels who claim to be helping us are just using us so they can get rid of HARC. I mean, they made it pretty clear they didn't want us hanging around after they helped us escape, right? Who cares if we had families or lives in the city before? Now that we're Reboots, we're just supposed to leave and never come back."

I nodded. *"I'm not dying for them."* Desmond had said it to me a couple nights ago, when he tried to convince the other rebels not to help us.

"I didn't come to this decision lightly," he said. "When I got here, I tried to focus more on the reservation, to let go of my anger, but the human attacks were constant. Not even just from HARC. Human stragglers in the area would try to raid the reservation and kill as many as possible. They weren't scared of us out here like they were in the cities. They hadn't seen what we were capable of. We put up those signs to deter them, to warn them, and they didn't listen. The Reboots who left, the older generation? They didn't want to fight HARC. That's why they left. They wanted to go live somewhere peacefully and leave the humans alone." He ran a hand over his face. "And HARC killed every one of them, because they could. I moved the reservation out here so they would know we weren't hiding or running, but it wasn't an aggressive move. They showed up and attacked us anyway. They won't stop, Wren."

I focused on the table, a frown crossing my face. The rebels were a small group of humans. The majority had been just fine with HARC imprisoning Reboots and killing us at will.

Micah scooted closer, touching one of my hands. I slid it from his grasp. "I understand that not all humans are bad. I really do."

I met his eyes. He was being serious.

"Tony? That one human who's the leader of the rebels? He's always been really nice to me. He talks to me like I'm an equal. I had an older brother in New Dallas who might still be alive. Maybe he grew up to be a nice human." He clasped his hands together. "But a few exceptions aren't enough. A few humans who can tolerate us are not enough to convince me that all Reboots will be safe. By letting them live, I risk all the Reboots. I made a really difficult choice, but I truly think it was the right one." He took in a breath. "Do you see my point?"

I absolutely saw his point. It was logical. He'd decided he wanted to save his people—the Reboots—and he was willing to take risks and make terrible sacrifices to do it. Hadn't I done the same thing with Callum? Hadn't I let Addie come into the HARC facility with me, even though I knew it was dangerous? Hadn't I risked my own life, as well as those of at least twenty human rebels, to save one person?

Hadn't I known that if we succeeded, plenty of human guards would be killed by the freed Reboots? Hadn't I decided that was acceptable?

"Wren," Micah said quietly.

I swallowed, looking up to meet his eyes. "I see your point."

NINE

CALLUM

I STOOD BEHIND THE CROWD AT THE FIRE PIT THAT EVENING, watching as a group of young Reboots pulled out instruments and began playing a lively song. People gathered around and started singing and dancing. It seemed odd for the mood to be so jolly when a few of their own had just gone on a killing spree.

Some of the Austin Reboots had joined in the festivities, the firelight flickering off their happy faces as they grabbed hands and laughed, but the majority sat in groups apart from the crowd, their faces grim. Word had spread among our group about Micah's plans, and most of us were not pleased.

Wren stood not far away with Micah, her face tight as she nodded at something he said. His expression wasn't as openly adoring as it had been, but they were clearly civil and she hadn't emerged from his tent earlier that day with his head on a stick.

She caught me staring and widened her eyes slightly, like she was annoyed at being stuck with him. I laughed and a small smile started to form on her face. I gestured for her to come over, but she nodded at Micah, who was talking rapidly, and rolled her eyes.

Something caught her attention behind me, and I glanced back to see Isaac walking toward the tent at the entrance of the reservation with a plate of food in his hands. The new Reboot was still in that tent, the one they'd killed earlier.

"I don't understand why they put up with this."

I turned at the quiet voice to see Addie standing next to me. I shrugged, because I didn't know, either. I scanned the crowd around me. I wondered how many had been killed by Micah's hunting teams.

I glanced at Isaac again. *"Just lucky, I guess."* That's what he'd said when I asked how he came to live at the reservation. He said he wasn't born here.

"No one tried to put a stop to it?" Addie whispered.

"Maybe they don't care," I murmured, gesturing for her to follow me. "Come on."

Isaac stopped when he saw us coming, hand poised to pull back the tent flap. A flash of nervousness crossed his features and he scanned the area behind us.

"I'm not sure you guys should come in," he said.

"Why not?" Addie asked.

"Micah likes to introduce new Reboots slowly. You know, so they're not overwhelmed."

"You don't think they've already been overwhelmed by the whole being-murdered thing?" I asked.

Isaac gave me a look like he didn't think that was very funny, and I quickly shut my mouth. I had a feeling my suspicions about his cause of death were correct.

"I'm going to give this to her," he said. "She's not talking right now anyway." He disappeared into the tent.

Addie crossed her arms over her chest, shivering in the chilly night air. "Have you talked to Wren?"

"A little."

"Beth told me she heard Wren sewed up their gunshot wounds while they were still dead so there would be less scarring. I thought that was nice." Addie shrugged. "Like she did the only thing she could, you know?"

I looked back in surprise to where Wren was, but she and Micah were gone. She hadn't told me that. I was pretty sure I would have panicked and exploded at Micah if I'd been on that hunting trip. But Wren was able to keep it together well enough to sew up a dead person's chest. That never would have even occurred to me.

Isaac emerged from the tent, hands in his pockets, shoulders hunched like he was trying to disappear. "Do you guys need something? Do you want to go get some food?"

"Is that how you died?" I asked quietly, nodding at the tent.

He cleared his throat, glancing around as if searching for an escape. "I can't really talk about it."

"What do you mean, you *can't*?" Addie asked, her brow furrowing.

He took a step closer, ducking his head. "Micah doesn't like it. We're supposed to let go of the past."

Let go of the past? Was that code for "You're not allowed to be mad we murdered you so just shut up and act happy"?

"Were you with other people?" I asked. I didn't care what Micah liked. I was going to talk about it. "Did they kill your family, too?"

Isaac hesitated. "Yeah," he finally whispered, releasing a rush of air like he was relieved to have said it. "My parents died when I was young, but I was with my older brother and a few people who were basically family. They all died."

"How old were you?" Addie asked, her voice full of horror.

"Fourteen. It was a year ago. They came in and shot us all, and I woke up on the back of a motorcycle with Jules." His words came in a rush now. "And then they brought me here and it was basically like I was supposed to be grateful."

"You mean you *are* grateful."

I jumped at the words coming from the side of the tent, and Micah stepped out, his face hard and angry. Isaac paled, almost tripping over his own feet as he took a step back from us.

"Y-yes," he stuttered.

I hadn't seen that kind of fear in a Reboot's eyes since leaving HARC, and Isaac's panic made dread unfold in my chest. Why was he so scared? Why would he stay here if Micah had killed him and everyone he knew?

Micah looked into the distance, pointed down at Isaac, and in seconds Jules was by his side, a frown on her face.

"We'll discuss this further in my tent," he said.

The way Isaac's eyes rounded with fear told me I didn't want to know what went on in Micah's tent.

Jules grabbed Isaac's arm and I stepped forward, attempting to block her.

"Stop," Isaac said, giving me a wild look and shaking his head. "Leave it."

I opened my mouth to protest as Jules yanked him to her. Micah watched the scene with his arms crossed over his chest, a menacing presence that didn't have to lift a finger.

"Callum, leave it," Isaac repeated, throwing me a pleading glance over his shoulder.

I let out a defeated sigh and moved back so I was next to Addie again. She was motionless, fear plastered on her face.

Micah took a step forward, furious eyes darting between Addie and me. "There are rules here."

"No one told us any rules," Addie said.

Micah's jaw moved, like he was trying to control his temper. "Isaac told you at the beginning of the conversation that we don't talk about our lesser human lives."

Lesser human lives? Was this guy for real?

"But I know you're new, so I'm cutting you some slack." His tone lightened enormously, which gave me the impression he was completely out of his mind. It was like he flipped a switch from "I'm going to kill you" to "Let's be friends."

I took a small step back. I didn't want to be friends.

"But I suggest you mind your own business and stop interfering in things you don't understand."

Which part didn't I understand? He killed people. He controlled them. He scared them. Seemed pretty basic to me.

Addie and I didn't say a word, which appeared to please him. He gave us a slight nod and turned to walk to his tent.

"That seems really bad," Addie breathed when he was out of earshot.

Yeah. It did.

I returned to our tent that evening to find Wren already sitting on the mattress, her legs pulled to her chest and an arm wrapped around them. She turned to me with a worried expression as I shut the tent flap.

"How's Isaac?" she asked. "Did you find him?"

I nodded. I'd filled her in earlier, then gone looking for Isaac. It was quiet outside, most of the Reboots already in their tents, and I lowered my voice when I spoke. "Micah didn't have him for long, and he seems fine. He wouldn't talk to me, though."

"Micah could do whatever he wanted to them," she said

with a sigh. "They'd just heal a few minutes later and no one would know."

I winced at the possibility. "Lovely." I sat down next to her and ran a hand down my face. "I can't understand why they would all just go along with him being their leader."

"He makes some good points," she said quietly. "They want to survive, and he's providing them with a good plan."

I raised my eyebrows. "A good plan?"

"A logical plan," she corrected, avoiding my eyes.

I pushed back a burst of annoyance at Micah being called "logical." That was the last word I would have used to describe him. I gave her a confused look.

"He's doing the only thing he knows how to do to protect everyone here. His experience has shown him that humans and Reboots can't live together. So he had to make a choice."

"The choice to kill everyone?" I asked.

"Everything isn't black and white, Callum," she said quietly.

I paused, deciding not to tell her I thought murder *was* black and white. You chose to kill people or you didn't.

Unless HARC made you insane and you accidentally killed someone. I paused, a pang of guilt zipping through my body. Maybe it wasn't *totally* black and white.

"But that wouldn't have been your choice," I said.

"No," she said immediately. "But I see his rationale."

I scrunched my face up. I didn't see how anyone could make a decision that involved murdering an entire species. I could barely handle that I'd killed one person.

"I made choices like that," she said to her lap.

I slid my fingers between hers. "How do you mean?"

"I went into the Austin facility knowing that humans were going to die. That maybe some Reboots would die. I decided that was an acceptable sacrifice to save you. Micah has decided that all the humans are an acceptable sacrifice to save the Reboots."

I held her hand tighter. "That isn't the same. You never *wanted* to kill anyone. You did it because you had to, or because you were protecting yourself or me. You're not committing mass murder because you can. You see the difference, right?"

Wren squinted, like she was thinking about it. It freaked me out when she gave serious thought to things that seemed simple to me. She really had to think that hard about it?

She caught the look on my face and immediately slipped her hand out of mine, her cheeks turning pink. "Yes," she said. It was an obvious lie, said to make me feel better.

She looked embarrassed now, and I wrapped an arm around her waist, pulling her closer. I didn't appreciate her seeing any of Micah's points, but I felt guilty for making her uncomfortable.

"Hey," I said, running my hand to the back of her neck. "They said you sewed up the kids Micah killed."

She nodded, her fingers closing over the collar of her shirt. I tried not to look. I didn't want to tell her that by not showing me her scars, she'd made me even more curious about them. But

I couldn't come up with a way to ask about them that didn't sound like *"I really want to see your boobs,"* so I kept my mouth shut.

"That was a nice thing to do," I said, gently removing her fingers from her shirt and taking her hand.

She shrugged. "I would have liked someone to do that for me."

I nodded, giving her an understanding look when she met my eyes. I leaned down and brushed my lips across hers, holding her tighter.

TEN

WREN

I MET MICAH OUTSIDE THE RESERVATION THE NEXT DAY, IN THE grass near the lake. Most of the reservation was already there, milling around as they waited. Micah had explained to me that everyone capable of fighting participated in sparring/training sessions several times a week. I'd volunteered right away when he mentioned it, and I was happy for the distraction this morning.

My heart took a dip as I found Callum in the crowd. He stood next to Isaac, arms crossed over his chest, and when his eyes met mine he smiled. I returned the smile, trying to push last night's conversation out of my head. I kept seeing his face after I told him Micah was logical, like he was horrified I could ever think that.

I'd known it was a mistake the moment I said it. But what was I supposed to do? Lie? Micah wasn't insane; he was strategic. He was making decisions based on logic and experience and he wasn't letting emotions get in the way. The results were kind of horrifying, and I hadn't lied when I said I wouldn't have made the same decisions, but to dismiss him as insane wasn't smart.

"You all right?"

I jumped, quickly turning away from Callum to find Addie next to me, a concerned expression on her face.

"Fine."

She frowned and made a face like she was going to say something, but Micah was strolling in my direction, Riley next to him. Addie squeezed my arm gently and I shook her off, not wanting to encourage her to talk to me. I didn't want another person looking at me like I was crazy.

"Good morning." Micah smiled at me as Addie walked away. "You ready?"

"Yes."

"I'd like for you to take whoever seems like they need the most help. I'm thinking only a couple weeks until we go in to the cities, at most. We need to kick it into high gear."

I swallowed. That was soon. I expected more time to figure out what to do. Leaving was risky, given what happened to the group that split off. Staying meant going along with Micah's plan, and dealing with Callum trying to recruit the reservation

Reboots to help the humans. Staying also meant training with the reservation Reboots, many of whom would turn around and use those skills to kill humans.

My eyes darted over the crowd I was supposed to train. So many of them looked young. Many were around eleven, twelve years old.

"They look young," I said, pointing.

"Everyone twelve and up is participating," he said.

By "participating" he meant "ordered." Twelve was also the HARC age for training. I glanced at Riley, who also seemed uncomfortable.

I couldn't keep my mouth shut about this one.

"Sixteen," I said.

Micah raised his eyebrows. "Sorry?"

"Sixteen and up, not twelve."

"I think twelve is fine."

"I died when I was twelve and was put into HARC training right away. I don't think you realize what that's like," I said, realizing too late that of course he understood. I wasn't used to dealing with an authority figure so similar to myself.

"I died when I was seven, and also started at twelve, so I understand fine," he said. "The training process won't be the same here anyway."

"I'm not training twelve-year-olds for war."

Silence fell over the crowd, and many Reboots stared at Micah nervously. One girl vigorously shook her head at me behind Micah's back, fear plastered on her face.

I took in a small breath, watching the faces of the rest of the crowd. Callum was right about them being scared. And not just in the way they were scared of me. What exactly did they fear from him?

Micah's jaw moved as he studied me. "Thirteen."

I caught Callum's eye and he gave me a look I thought meant he was proud. Next to him, Isaac winced.

I whipped my head back to Micah. "Fifteen."

"Fourteen."

"Fifteen." I'd trained too many young kids in my time at HARC. I wasn't doing it again.

He paused, narrowing his eyes at me. The silence stretched out between us for so long I saw Jules start to shift uncomfortably behind him.

I scanned the rest of the group behind Micah. Kyle stood with them, as well as Riley, and about fifteen others. They were apart from the rest of the Reboots, mostly One-twenties or close, and none of them appeared to be scared of Micah. In fact, a few were glaring at me.

"Fine. Fifteen." Micah's face relaxed and I could almost feel the crowd doing the same.

"Everyone under the age of fifteen, back to camp," Micah said. He cast a quick glance back at me. "For today." He cocked his head like he dared me to say something about that. I stared at him.

I turned and headed in Callum's direction. Maybe I'd train Under-sixties. I could use some of their optimism and talkative-ness today.

"So." Micah's voice made me stop and when I turned around, he clapped his hands together and grinned at me. "Want to do a demonstration first?"

"A demonstration?" I repeated.

"Could be fun, right?" he asked, a challenge behind every word. "Show them how it's done?"

Excitement zipped through my chest as I met his gaze. It had been a long time since I'd sparred with a Reboot so close to my number and skill. Not since Riley left.

"Of course," I said. Micah's smirk grew bigger, but I could see the gleam of satisfaction in his eyes. He was sure of his abil-ity to win. I pushed back a smile of my own.

He pulled off his sweatshirt and to reveal a T-shirt under-neath, and the Reboots immediately began to move back. They left a huge, wide space for us.

"No weapons, no neck breaks," Micah said. "Everything else is fair game. We go until one of us is down for five sec-onds."

I nodded, taking a quick scan of the crowd. There was a hint of excitement in the air, but several Reboots looked wor-ried. They couldn't have been worried about us getting hurt, so it was something else bothering them.

Micah walked closer to me. Some of the excitement was

gone, his brow set in a hard, firm line. He was serious about this challenge.

For a moment, I considered letting him win. He clearly needed to solidify his place as leader in the reservation, and proving he was a better fighter than me would go a long way toward that goal. It might even help me gain some of his trust.

But I'd never let anyone win. I'd rarely lost at all.

I stretched out my fingers and then balled them into fists. I didn't want to lose today, either.

"Riley? Want to count us down?" Micah asked without looking at him.

"Three . . . two . . . one. Go."

Neither of us moved. I'd been waiting for him to rush me, so I could sidestep him and possibly grab an arm to break. A corner of his mouth turned up. He'd been waiting for the same thing.

"It's not a staring contest," Riley said from behind me, his voice tinged with amusement.

Micah took a swing at me, like he thought I'd be distracted by Riley's voice. I smiled as I easily ducked it.

He took a step back before I'd even had a chance to fully straighten. His strength wasn't his speed or force, it was his patience and ability to assess the situation. He hadn't underestimated me because of my size.

I took one quick step forward, throwing my left hook into his face and heading for his stomach with my right fist. He blocked the former and let out a slight wheeze as I connected with his gut.

His hands were up and he began throwing punches hard and fast, matching mine. I ducked and blocked and almost hit the dirt when he connected with my cheek. He had the second-hardest punch I'd ever felt. The number one honor still belonged to Riley.

He dove suddenly and wrapped his arms around my legs. I hit the ground with a grunt and Micah slammed my shoulders down with his hands, easily pinning me down with the full weight of his body.

I'd always hated being pinned.

I kicked him dangerously close to the crotch and he flew off of me with a gasp. I darted from his reach before his hand could close around my ankle. A few people cheered and I took a quick glance back at the crowd. Had they cheered for Micah? I hadn't been paying attention.

He was already charging for me as I sprang to my feet and I almost laughed. Apparently his patience didn't last long. I ducked as he swung, whipping around to smash a punch into his side. His rib made a noise as it cracked.

He stumbled slightly and I swung again, cracking his nose this time. He blinked like he was disoriented, but I knew as soon as I felt his foot slam into my knee that he wasn't, not even a little bit.

It was broken, and I hopped away on one foot before placing

the other back on the ground and pushing back the pain that screamed up my left leg.

Micah paused, looking from my knee to my face. "Damn," he said with a chuckle.

I grinned, gesturing with my head for him to come to me.

"Why don't you hop over here?" he said with a smirk, taking a step back.

I laughed despite myself. I'd never fought without HARC watching my every move to make sure I wasn't having fun. It was strange, especially since I wasn't sure I liked Micah any better than I'd liked most of the HARC humans.

Micah laughed and I bolted forward, dragging my bad leg slightly behind me. His eyes widened in surprise but I already had his arm in my grasp. I swung him around and yanked the arm back as quickly as I could.

I sort of liked the sound of bones breaking. It was like home.

He wasn't smiling anymore and I caught the hint of anger on his face as he began swinging again. It was quiet as we moved around the circle punching and dodging.

When I saw the opportunity to get him on the ground I took it. I swept his legs out from under him and he gasped as something cracked as he hit the dirt. He scrambled to his knees and I punched him as hard as I could, the moment he was on his feet.

He bounced up again before I could blink. He swung at me wildly and I took a small step back before aiming for the exact place I needed on his legs. I dove forward, my leg screaming in pain as I landed on my knees in front of him. I drove my palm into the spot where he was already injured, and while he screamed, slammed my foot into his other knee.

He collapsed on the ground. His fingers dug into the grass and he pulled himself halfway up before collapsing again and waving a hand. He let out a giant breath. "I give."

It was silent for a few seconds before a few nervous giggles broke the tension. I turned to see Callum doing something between a wince and a smile. I wiped at my mouth and came away with blood.

"I told you," Riley said, appearing next to me and putting his hands on his hips as he looked down at Micah. "Didn't I say you'd get your ass kicked?"

"Next time you're doing the demonstration," Micah said, pointing at him. He managed a chuckle.

"All right. That's fine, I'm used to Wren kicking my ass."

I rolled my eyes at him. He'd actually won plenty of times. Okay, maybe not plenty. Like, ten percent of the time. Still, not bad.

I turned around to see Callum in front of me. His face scrunched as he lifted up his shirt to wipe off my face. He gave me an amused look as he swiped the garment across my mouth.

"What about you?" Riley asked, squinting at Callum. "You want to do a demonstration next time? You're probably used to Wren beating the crap out of you."

Callum laughed softly, his gaze on me. "I think I'll pass."

I smiled at him and he leaned down to kiss my cheek. Training felt like a hundred years ago, and my stomach twisted uncomfortably at the thought of hitting Callum. I still felt a little sick whenever I thought about the time I'd beaten him up.

"You care if I skip out on this?" he asked softly. "I think they could use some help back at the reservation today."

I shook my head. "No, go. You don't need any more training."

He gave me a grateful look and leaned down to kiss me before heading back toward the reservation.

"All right," Micah said, grunting as he got to his feet. "Pair off." He nodded to me. "Let's get to work."

Riley was waiting for me when we finished later that afternoon, letting the crowd file back to the reservation without him as I pulled on my sweater and tied my hair in a ponytail.

"I'm glad to see you're still being difficult and pissing people off," Riley said with a grin as I approached him.

"I was never difficult," I said, a smile playing on my lips.

"No? I seem to remember a 'I'll stop punching you when you start ducking faster' conversation not long before I left."

"It's not my fault you got slow in your old age." Old age being nineteen, as he was only twenty now.

He laughed, which was still a weird sound to me, coming from him. He must have been so unhappy at HARC. I'd never really noticed.

"You could've at least let me know you weren't dead, by the way," I said. "I was actually kind of sad about that."

His expression softened. "That's a pretty incredible sentiment, coming from you."

I frowned at him in response and he sighed.

"I'm sorry. Honestly, I wasn't a hundred percent certain you wouldn't rat me out."

"Thanks for that."

"You know how it was. You were their girl. You did everything they said, without question. I thought you even kind of liked it there."

"I did," I said softly. "I wouldn't have ratted you out, though."

He studied me for a moment. "I apologize, then."

I sighed as I slid my hands into my pockets. "It's all right. I can't totally blame you. Things were different before Callum." And Ever. But my throat closed every time I said her name aloud, and I didn't think Riley would remember her anyway.

"So, Callum, huh? You trained a Twenty-two?"

"Yes."

"May I ask why? Or did you start picking all your trainees based on level of cuteness?"

I shot him a look. "He asked me to."

"He asked you to? Well, shit. If I'd known that was the way to get you to do things, I would have tried that a long time ago."

I covered my mouth with the backs of my fingers as I tried

not to laugh, but one came through anyway. "It wouldn't work as well coming from you, Riley."

He grinned. "Awww, you've become all soft and mushy. It's cute."

"I'd be happy to show you how soft and mushy my fist is *not*, if you'd like a reminder."

"I'm going to pass on that offer, but thank you."

I smiled at him, watching as the Reboots over his shoulder disappeared inside the reservation walls. Everyone was out of earshot, and Riley glanced around as if noticing it, too.

"You like it here?" I asked quietly.

He cocked his head, his face becoming more serious. "In a way. It's better than HARC."

No argument there. "Micah. He's . . . intense."

"He is." Riley seemed to be choosing his words carefully, studying my face as he considered each one. "You guys don't seem to be getting along terribly well."

"We're civil. I did notice that some of the Reboots here seem sort of scared of him."

"I guess they are." Riley squinted. "I mean, yeah, they are. He kind of rules with an iron fist. Thinks it's the best way to keep us safe."

"You agree?"

"Sometimes." He glanced behind him, then back to me. "You heard about the group that split off and got killed last year?"

"Yeah."

"That happened right after I got here. I arrived at the reservation and it was chaos. A bunch of them got together and decided they were tired of the way Micah was running things. They stopped returning their hunting weapons and staged a revolt one day."

I lifted my eyebrows. Micah had conveniently left that part out.

"Yeah," Riley said, noticing my surprised expression. "We're not supposed to talk about it. In fact, if you could not mention to Micah that I shared I'd appreciate it."

I nodded in agreement. They weren't allowed to talk about it? That was weird. "What happened?"

"The revolt didn't really go that well," Riley said. "They were mostly the older generation and kids, people who'd never been at HARC, and a bunch of the higher numbers who'd escaped from HARC or Rebooted here immediately backed up Micah. So they left instead."

"And Micah just let them go?"

"At that point, yeah. They weren't exactly welcome anymore, you know? Then it's only a few weeks later, we're on a hunt over in one of the old cities and we find them all dead, along with a few bodies of HARC officers. After that, no one was going to risk speaking out against Micah." He gestured to the reservation. "This is really the only safe place for us."

That might have been true, unfortunately.

"You're sure it was HARC?" I asked. "Micah wouldn't . . ."

Riley shook his head. "It was definitely HARC. And Micah hates them way too much to tip them off. He planned on finding the group again after the humans were taken care of."

At least that was something. The thought had been in the back of my head since Callum had told me how scared Isaac was of him.

"I think Micah's pretty terrified of you and all the new Reboots, to be honest," Riley continued.

"Why's that?"

"Because you're challenging everything." He gestured to me. "You're refusing to train kids and asking questions and Micah doesn't really appreciate that. Since the revolt, everyone has done exactly what he says."

"You included?" I asked. "Or do you often have trouble finding humans that are only half a mile away from you?"

The edges of his mouth twitched. "I often have trouble, yes." He ran a hand through his light hair. "I don't like doing it. It reminds me of being at HARC."

"I don't blame you." I studied him. "So when the time comes to kill all the humans in the cities . . ."

He shrugged, scrunching his face up. "I don't know. Part of me hoped it would never happen. But now with all these new Reboots, I don't think it can be stopped. Micah's getting a group together for a trip to Austin tonight, which means he's about ready to go in. He arranged a meeting with Tony and Desmond to get some fuel. And apparently they have information for us."

"Tony and Desmond do?" I asked in surprise.

"Yeah."

"How do you guys communicate with them?"

"Radio," he said.

"And HARC doesn't listen in?"

"They very well might. But we use codes."

Guilt zipped through my chest and I let out a small sigh. I hated feeling indebted to Tony and Desmond, but I felt ill at the prospect of letting Micah use them like this. Maybe Callum was right about one part of his plan—we needed to try and warn them.

"The trip to Austin," I said, trying to sound casual. "Micah will take a few people with him?"

"Yeah. I'll go. Probably Jules as well. Why? Do you want to go?" He snorted. "I'm not sure that will go over so well with Micah, but I could ask."

I hesitated. It would look suspicious if I asked to tag along. Micah would be watching my every move. The best option for warning Tony was probably slipping him a note, since conversation would be difficult with Micah around, but that would be impossible if I couldn't even get near him.

"Pass," I said, making a face as an idea occurred to me. "I just came from Austin, and given the state the shuttles are in, you guys are going to get stuck and have to walk a few hundred miles."

"It'll be fine," Riley said. "We've fixed shuttles before."

"You should ask Callum if he'll come along," I said. "He is great with machinery. And he could teach you guys how to use the navigation systems."

Riley cocked his head, studying me. "Callum."

"Micah seemed impressed with his work on the shuttles." I shrugged. "Just a suggestion."

"I could take one of the Reboots who've been here for a while. We've had several people work on shuttles." His eyes bore into mine, like he was daring me to tell him the real reason I wanted Callum to go.

"You could." I didn't trust Riley with that information. Warning humans about a Reboot attack basically made us traitors, and he might take Micah's side in that situation.

His lips twitched. "Say 'please, Riley.'"

I tried to glare at him without smiling. "Please stop being a pain in the ass, Riley."

He chuckled. "I'll see what Micah says. You do realize I know you're up to something, right?"

"I don't know what you mean."

"I feel hurt you don't trust me."

I punched his shoulder as I passed him. "Payback's a bitch."

ELEVEN

CALLUM

"DUDE, YOU'RE INSANE."

I grunted as I pushed the round piece of wood into the ground to make the last side of the tent and straightened to face Isaac. I squinted in the setting sun, watching as the Reboots in the distance transported water to the food tent. We were in the corner of the reservation, far enough away so that no one could overhear our conversation, but I still spoke quietly.

"Why am I insane?" I asked. I pushed back a brief moment of panic as the image of the human I killed slid into my vision. Isaac hadn't meant "insane" in that way.

"They imprisoned you!" Isaac gave me a baffled look, a rope dangling from his fingers. He'd stopped working on the tent and was just staring at me.

Addie cocked an eyebrow at me as she hammered a post into the ground on the other side of the tent. I'd suggested we start feeling out the reservation Reboots, seeing if they all wanted to kill the humans. My idea to partner with them to fight off Micah didn't seem to be going over so well with Isaac, my first test subject.

"And they tried to kill you!" he continued, stepping closer to me and lowering his voice. "And they would have killed you for sure when you reached twenty. And you want to go in and save them now?"

"HARC did that. I can't blame all the humans for what they did." I cocked my head. "Do you know why HARC does that? Kills Reboots at twenty?"

"It's supposedly a population-control thing. They don't need that many Reboots. Also they apparently found that nineteen or twenty was the age they started getting restless in the facilities. Doing crazy things like thinking for themselves."

"The horror."

"And yet you want to go back!" Isaac said with a laugh before casting around a furtive glance. "Maybe I shouldn't say that so loud. You probably don't want word of that plan getting out."

"You seriously want to kill all the humans in the cities?" Addie whispered, her hands on her hips as she walked closer to us.

He squished up his face. "Well, not particularly. But I don't really have a choice. My money's on Micah in that battle, and I don't want to be the one who deserted. Kind of seems like a bad choice, long-term."

"But if we got together enough Reboots to help the humans—if we saved the Reboots in the facilities and convinced them to join us—Micah wouldn't stand a chance. He'd be way outnumbered," I said.

Isaac shook his head, tossing the rope he was holding to Addie. "Listen, I know you guys are new, but that kind of talk is going to get you strung up."

"Strung up?" Addie repeated, horrified.

"Yeah. I'm lucky I didn't get to experience that last night." He took a step back. "I'd can it, if I were you." He turned to go, almost breaking into a run to get away from us.

"Well, that went well," Addie said with a sigh.

"What do you think 'strung up' means?"

"I think it means Micah's an asshole."

I snorted. "Yeah. I already figured that one out. What about the Austin Reboots? Have you talked to any of them?"

"Yeah, Beth and I have been testing the waters. Lots of them still have human families, so they're not jazzed about Micah's plan. They're also not pumped to run back to HARC cities, but a lot of them would at least help us save the Reboots in the facilities. We were talking about maybe swiping the schematics Micah has in his tent at some point before we leave. So that's something."

That *was* something. Not as much as I was hoping for, but at least we weren't getting outright refusal.

A blond head caught my eye, and I squinted to find Wren walking across the reservation with Riley. She scanned the area around her, splitting off from Riley when she spotted me. She strode straight to me and rose up on her toes like she was going to give me a kiss, which seemed strange, since she'd been a bit awkward around me since last night. I was trying not to show I was still freaked out by her deciding Micah was logical, but it seemed I was failing.

But she didn't kiss me. She leaned close to my ear, placing a hand on my chest. "If they ask you to go to Austin, say yes. Don't seem too excited. I think you'll have the opportunity to slip Tony or Desmond a note."

She pulled back, giving me a quick smile before turning to walk away. I wanted to grab her hand and tell her thank you, but I got the impression she wanted to keep our interaction brief. Riley was watching us from outside the big tent.

"What was that about?" Addie asked.

I shook my head. "Nothing."

"Callum!"

I turned at the sound of a voice to see Riley waving me in his direction.

"Come on, we need you!"

I shot a grin at a confused Addie and jogged across the dirt, coming to a stop in front of Riley. He gave me this look I didn't understand, like a cross between amusement and annoyance.

"Do whatever you have to do. We're leaving in half an hour."

"What? For where?" I figured playing dumb was probably the best option right now. Riley rolled his eyes.

"Austin. We're getting fuel from the rebels. Micah expects you to show him how to use the navigation system as we travel."

"Sure."

"Meet me back here. I'll get some weapons ready for you."

I nodded and took off for the tent used as the school. It was empty except for a Reboot who was probably almost in his forties. He was one of the only older Reboots I'd seen here, and I rarely saw him outside of the school tent. I couldn't really blame him. It must have been annoying to be the only old person around.

"Do you mind if I have some paper and a pencil?" I asked.

He gestured at a cabinet. "Go ahead. Not too much."

I took one piece and a pencil and shot him a grateful look. "Thank you." I jogged back to the tent I shared with Wren and found it empty, so I plopped down on the ground and scribbled out a quick note to Tony. I tried to keep it from sounding terrifying, but maybe two "don't panic"s would have the opposite effect.

The tent flap opened as I was folding the note and sliding it into my pocket, and I smiled as Wren peered inside.

"Hey," I said. "I was just going to look for you. We're leaving for Austin."

"Now?" She blinked in surprise as she crawled inside and sat down on the mattress.

"Yeah. Thank you for getting me a spot on the shuttle. That was good thinking."

A small smile crossed her lips. "You're welcome."

"Did you tell Riley why?"

"No. He's knows something's up, but it seemed kind of risky. Not that he's totally on team Micah, but still, what we're doing wouldn't sit well with a lot of Reboots."

I raised my eyebrows. "You don't think so?"

"We're sort of taking the humans' side."

"We are?" I asked. "Are you okay with going to the cities to help them?"

She pressed her lips together, turning to look at the side of the tent. "If you're going, I guess I'm going."

Not exactly the enthusiasm I was hoping for. Annoyance flared in my chest, and I took in a deep breath. "You really don't want to help them at all?" It came out more judgmental than I'd meant it. Or maybe I did mean it that way.

She brought her knees to her chest with a sigh. "You were right about warning Tony and Desmond. They helped us, so we should return the favor. But no. I don't have a burning desire to go help people who hate me."

"They don't all hate us. You don't give humans enough

credit." My anger started to seep through and I clenched my fingers into fists. She was willing to write off humans, but she defended Micah?

"And you give them too much! It hasn't even been a week since a bunch of them tried to kill us both. And your parents—" She stopped suddenly, swallowing.

"No need to remind me about my parents," I said tightly. "I remember just fine."

"I know you do." Her eyes were on the ground. "So I don't understand why you're so eager to rush back and help them."

"And I don't understand how you can turn your back when we have the opportunity to help. Not just humans, but Reboots, too. You saved everyone in the Austin facility with one other Reboot. *One*, Wren. Can you imagine what you could do with a hundred?"

She frowned at me and didn't respond.

"They're all dying in there and you don't even care?" It was getting harder to keep my voice steady. "Look at what they did to me. To Ever. We can stop that."

She looked like I'd slapped her, and I wished I hadn't mentioned Ever's name. Maybe I'd done it because she'd brought up my parents.

"It is not my responsibility to save everyone." She glared at me.

"Whose responsibility is it, then?"

"You're the one who wants to save everyone so badly! You

do it." She spoke barely above a whisper, but her words were furious.

"I want you to help me. I want you to *want* to help me."

She paused, staring at me for so long I began to get uncomfortable. Finally she spoke quietly. "I don't. I don't want to help." She shook her head as she crossed her arms over her chest. "Maybe you need to take a look at who I am, instead of who you wish I were."

I blinked, taken aback.

"Maybe you don't like who I actually am." She shrugged. "I wouldn't really blame you."

I reached for her arm but she shook me off, leaning out of my reach. "That's a terrible thing to say. Of course I like who you are."

"Why?" She met my eyes. "Why are you distraught about killing one human but you don't mind that I've killed dozens? Why are you okay with my lack of guilt about it? About the fact that I followed orders without question at HARC for five years? I did things I haven't even told you about, yet you put your foot down within weeks of getting there. Why are those things okay for me but not for you?"

"I . . . I don't . . ." I fumbled for words, but I didn't have any.

"Just think about it," she said softly.

I didn't want to think about it. I wanted to pull her into my arms and tell her of course I liked her and I didn't care about any of that.

Did I care about any of that?

She ducked out of the tent and I didn't try to stop her from going. I sat on the ground, blinking as I tried to process everything she'd just said to me.

I knew Wren had killed more people than I wanted to count. She'd killed some of them right in front of me, to save me, and I hadn't faulted her for it. It was self-defense. She never wanted to kill anyone.

And neither did I. Yet I had. And if I started judging her for something she had to do, shouldn't I start judging myself?

"Everything is not black and white, Callum." Her words to me yesterday suddenly made more sense. I didn't think I saw as much gray as Wren—not even close—but maybe I could see why she'd likened herself to Micah. Why she'd been confused about how the way she killed was different than the way he did.

Or maybe it wasn't different. Maybe Wren and Micah and I were all the same. We'd all killed. I bet if a human looked at the three of us they wouldn't see much of a distinction.

I sucked in a breath at that thought as I shakily crawled out of the tent. I tried not to think about how humans saw Reboots, because sometimes I still felt like a human. But I couldn't help but think, for a moment, that Wren had a point about them not wanting our help.

TWELVE

WREN

I PROBABLY PICKED THE WRONG MOMENT TO ASK CALLUM THOSE questions. In fact, now, as I sat alone in the tent listening to the sounds of dinner being served, I thought I should have kept those questions to myself forever.

But we would have ended up here eventually, me wondering why he liked me when he seemed to despise so many of the things I'd done. Perhaps it was best for him to consider it now.

I swallowed, terrified of the conclusion he would come to.

The sounds of laughter drifted in from the fire pit, and I reluctantly pulled back the flap of the tent. I wanted to avoid people entirely, but I'd missed lunch and couldn't ignore the rumbling in my stomach.

As I approached the fire pit, I saw two figures standing not far from the food table, gesturing wildly with their hands.

"Just because I think my own father isn't a bad guy, doesn't—" Addie yelled, but Kyle cut her off.

"That kind of human-lover talk is going to get you dropped real quick!"

"What the hell is 'dropped'?" She made an annoyed sound. "You are all—"

"Whoa." I grabbed her wrist before she could say something that would get back to Micah. I didn't know what "dropped" meant, either, but I couldn't imagine it was good. Reboots around them stared worriedly, and I was reminded of the scared look the girl had given me when I stood up to Micah. He was obviously implementing some pretty serious punishments.

"You need to get your Reboot under control," Kyle snapped at me, his massive chest heaving up and down.

Anger flared in my chest, mixing with my lingering frustrations with Callum. "I'm sorry, I didn't realize Addie was under my *control*."

She snorted, quickly covering her mouth with her hand as Kyle glared at me. The area around us quieted, and he stared at me a beat longer before stomping away.

"That was awesome," Addie said.

"You're being a pain in the ass."

She laughed, following me to the dinner table. "How so?"

"I think you're supposed to be more discreet in your human-love. Not to mention the fact that I've seen Jules watching you since you called her out about the birth-control thing."

"I can't help it if the chick's crazy."

I gave her an annoyed look and she sighed. "All right, I'm sorry. I'll be more discreet." She grinned as I speared a piece of meat and plopped it on my plate. "Look how well you got me under control."

I almost laughed, but the weight sitting on my chest wouldn't allow it.

Her eyes flicked over my face, concern in her expression. "You okay?"

"Fine." I ducked my head and headed for an empty spot on the ground. She sat down next to me, and a few Reboots to our right watched us. Isaac was with them, as well as the new Reboot. Her dark hair was pulled back and she looked like she hadn't slept in two days. She noticed my gaze and a smile barely tugged at her mouth. She nodded. I returned my attention to my food, unsure what to make of that.

"Can I ask where you stand with helping the humans?" Addie whispered.

"I'd rather not," I said flatly. "But I do agree with warning Tony and Desmond. Callum is trying, tonight."

"That's awesome. I thought he might be." She glanced at me. "But you're not angry? My dad risked his life to get us to the reservation. And then it's run by a crazy guy who wants us to have a bunch of babies and kill everyone. It sucks."

"You're really pissed about that baby thing, huh?"

"It's total crap. I haven't been having sex at all because I'm worried they snuck in at night and took it out without me knowing."

Amusement played on the edges of Addie's lips and I laughed. "That seems a little extreme."

"They're all total nut jobs, so I wouldn't put it past them. Have you checked yours? Did Micah harass you to take it out?"

I shook my head. "No. Not that it matters."

"What does that mean?"

"I've never . . ."

Her eyebrows shot up. "Never? Not even with Callum?"

"No." I brushed my fingers over my shirt where my scar was. I'd thought about having sex with Callum, more than once since we'd been at the reservation. I'd been thinking about what he said, about how he wanted to see my scars if we had sex, and how maybe that wouldn't be so bad. They were just scars, after all.

A lump formed in my throat again when it occurred to me that it might not happen at all now. I quickly pushed the thought away.

"Why not?" Addie asked.

"I'm, you know . . . weird."

She laughed harder than I would have expected. "You really

are." Her smile faded to a more serious expression. "Is everything okay? With Callum?"

"Fine," I said, taking a bite of meat and avoiding her eyes.

"He's crazy about you, you know," she said softly, like I
hadn't just told her things were fine. "I see other girls looking at
him sometimes, and he doesn't even notice. He only sees you."

I blinked as tears threatened to spill over, and cleared my
throat.

"Sorry," Addie said. She waved her hand and gave me a
sympathetic look. "None of my business."

I ate a bite of meat and dropped my fork on my plate. Part of
me wanted to escape to my tent, but the other part of me liked
having someone to talk to again. I hadn't even realized that was
something I liked about Ever until she was gone.

"You and Micah spend a lot of time together," Addie said
quietly.

"I guess."

"Has he told you his plans?"

"Not really. He doesn't trust me. He creeps me out and I'm
pretty sure he knows it."

Addie snorted. "Yeah. I don't think I could keep it together
the way you do. I'd go off on him." She gestured to something
behind me. "But he lets you into his tent. And he keeps his plans
in there, doesn't he? Schematics of all the facilities?"

I nodded slowly. "That's what he told me."

"Maybe you could grab them one day? Like when we're

about to leave? I think it would be helpful."

I gripped my fork and started moving the remains of my meat around the plate. "Maybe," I said softly. I didn't want to talk about Micah's plans to kill the humans, or my role in stopping it. It made me think about Callum.

Addie sighed like she was disappointed. I felt like telling her to join the club.

A figure blocked the heat of the fire and I looked up to see Isaac standing in front of us. He was rubbing his fingers over one arm like he was nervous, and he cleared his throat before kneeling in front me.

"It occurred to us"—Isaac tilted his head to the group of Reboots he'd been sitting with—"that there will be a bunch of new Reboots after we kill all the humans."

I blinked at him, not sure what to make of that statement.

"They'll wake up just like we did, with their families gone and a bunch of crazy-ass people wanting to be their best friends," he whispered.

I almost laughed, but Isaac's expression was serious. Addie and I exchanged a look, her face full of hope.

Isaac leaned a little closer to me. "So if the Austin Reboots are going to do something to stop it, we're with you."

THIRTEEN

CALLUM

THE SHUTTLE BEGAN TO DESCEND AS WE NEARED AUSTIN, AND Micah turned off the lights so we wouldn't be spotted. I sat in the back next to Riley, and Micah and Jules talked quietly in the pilot's section.

I leaned my head back against the metal wall and closed my eyes.

Why are you distraught about killing one human but you don't mind that I've killed dozens?

Wren's words kept circling my brain, demanding my attention.

Why are you okay with my lack of guilt about it?

I'd always thought deep down she did feel guilty. I just

thought she didn't show it. Maybe she did feel guilty, and she didn't even realize it?

Maybe you should take a look at who I am, instead of who you wish I were.

I ran my fingers through my hair. It was true that I liked Wren the way she was, but it was also true that I thought she'd change the longer we were away from HARC. I thought she'd have more interest in other people. I thought she'd be excited to use the skills HARC taught her to help, instead of to kill.

I glanced at Riley next to me, and it occurred to me for the first time that he might know Wren better than I did. He'd known her for years, since she was a newbie.

He noticed me staring at him and gave me a weird look.

"What was Wren like as a newbie?" I asked quietly.

"Tiny. Quiet." He paused, thinking. "Terrified."

"Terrified?" I repeated skeptically.

"Definitely," he said with a laugh. "Everyone was making a big deal about her number and she was so young. And she was so freaking traumatized by how she died that every loud noise made her this huge, shaky mess. She was always trying to hide in corners and under tables."

My chest twisted around until it was hard to breathe. I couldn't imagine her like that. Even at twelve, I couldn't see her ducking under tables, terrified.

"I almost didn't pick her," Riley continued. "I wanted the highest number, but I was worried I couldn't be hard enough on her. I felt too bad for her."

"I can't really imagine," I said quietly, dropping my eyes.

"Sure you can," Riley said. "You were there."

"Yeah, but I was seventeen. And I didn't have to train any-one. I just did everything Wren said."

I still did everything Wren said. I realized a big part of me was waiting for her to jump on board with saving the humans, and tell me exactly how to do it.

But she was right. I was the one who wanted to save them, who needed to save them, so I had to be the one to take charge. If I didn't step up, we were all going to end up following Micah to the cities to kill everyone. That wouldn't be on Wren, it would be on me.

I returned my attention to Riley, a frown crossing my face. "If she was so terrified, why did you shoot her all the time?"

A flash of irritation crossed his features. "*Because* she was so terrified. Man, she would have been dead in six months if I hadn't gotten rid of her fear of guns. HARC wasn't giving her a free pass because she was twelve. I couldn't, either." He shrugged. "Would you really want to be the one who did such a crappy job training the twelve-year-old that she ended up dead? I couldn't . . ." Riley shook his head and cleared his throat. "I couldn't handle that."

I leaned back in my seat with a sigh. Now I felt like an ass. When he explained it like that it sounded like I should be thanking him, not be angry with him.

"She's entirely different from when I left," he continued. "The Wren I knew never would have escaped."

"You don't think so?"

"No. She liked it there. Not just accepted it, but *liked* it." He shook his head. "From what I gathered, her human life was pretty bad. HARC actually looked good in comparison."

Wren had never told me much about her human life. I'd pried a few details out of her, but I'd come to the same conclusion as Riley. It hadn't been that great.

He leaned back against the wall, closing his eyes. "She must have really liked something about you to leave." He opened one eye. "I don't see it."

I laughed softly. I forgot sometimes that Wren considered HARC her home, and I realized suddenly that she hadn't used that against me yet. It would have been easy for her to remind me that she'd saved me—more than once—and maybe I owed her. I did owe her.

I ran my hand over my face as the shuttle touched down on the ground. Micah killed the engine and I unbuckled my seat belt and got to my feet. I had a gun strapped to either hip, but I was the only one who didn't pull it out as we got off the shuttle.

We were about two miles from Austin, in the trees Wren and I had used for cover on our way from Rosa. We walked in silence toward the city, Micah and Jules several paces ahead of us, and Riley lifting his gun every so often as he scanned the area. He had the same sort of alertness as Wren, half his brain always on something I couldn't see or hear. It was strange that people who were so observant couldn't pick up on the emotions of others or feel sympathy.

When the Austin skyline came into view, I turned my gaze to the ground. I'd been excited last time I saw it. Full of hope about seeing my parents again, wondering if they even knew I'd Rebooted. I'd worried about scaring them at first, but I'd imagined they would get over it and hug me and beg me to stay with them instead of going to the reservation.

Maybe if we succeeded in helping the humans fight off Micah and HARC, I'd pick a different city from Austin to live in. Maybe I'd go to New Dallas or take off to see the death state with Wren. Sticking around Austin no longer appealed to me.

As we got closer, I could hear the soft hum of the HARC electrical fence. I recognized the area immediately, and easily spotted the leaves covering the tunnel the rebels had built that allowed secret access to and from Austin.

"We wait here," Riley said, pointing to the tunnel entrance. "They should be here soon."

No one sat, or relaxed, or lowered their guns, and I shifted from foot to foot, uncomfortable. The note sat heavy in my pocket, and I carefully slipped it out, keeping it folded inside my palm.

I jumped at a rustling sound behind me and whirled around, hand poised over my gun. The others did the same,

Riley stepping up next to me as the sound of footsteps echoed through the quiet.

I sucked in a breath as a dark head appeared from behind tree branches, and a smile spread across Tony's face when he spotted me. He was a big, solid guy, with streaks of gray through his dark hair. He was carrying large, plastic fuel containers in either hand and seemed genuinely happy to see us. Riley lowered his gun, followed by Jules, then Micah.

"Jesus, Tony," Riley said, letting out a breath. "You scared the crap out of us."

Tony grinned. "Apologies. We didn't need to use the tunnel this time."

Desmond walked up behind him, also carrying fuel. My memories from our time with the rebels were still fuzzy, but I remembered that he hadn't looked at me in the same way Tony did. Tony regarded me like I was still a seventeen-year-old human, not a Reboot.

"Oh, good," Desmond said dryly. "They brought the one who tried to eat us."

I winced. "Sorry about that."

Micah chuckled, holstering his gun. He shook Tony's hand, and I tried not to cringe at the entirely fake smile he was giving the human.

"Why didn't you have to use the tunnel?" Jules asked suspiciously.

Tony beamed again. He was exceedingly happy about

something, and I felt bad about having to crush him. I clenched my fist tighter around my letter.

"The fence is only half-staffed most days now," he said, nodding back to it. "HARC's having a hell of a time controlling the population in Austin. They've got to keep a lot of officers inside."

"What do you mean?" I asked, my eyes flicking to the skyline.

"The facility is still a mess," Tony said. "They don't have it running yet, which means no Reboots. They want to ship in some from Rosa and New Dallas, but it's too risky to leave those cities with so few Reboots. They don't even have enough staff. A good amount of officers quit after that night. They all think One-seventy-eight will be back and they don't want anything to do with it."

My eyebrows shot up. I'd thought releasing all the Reboots in Austin was only a temporary setback for HARC. I'd assumed they'd have Reboots back in the facility in twenty-four hours, minimum.

"There are no Reboots in Austin?" Riley asked. "At all?"

Tony made a zero sign with his hand. "None. People in the slums are hopping the wall to the *rico*. No one cares about curfew. We managed to get so many weapons in our raid, we've armed half the city." He turned to Micah. "I think now's the time."

Micah rubbed a hand over his chin. "You may be right."

I swallowed, looking from Tony to Micah.

"HARC's had to divert officers from other facilities to cover Austin," Tony said excitedly. "They're all weaker right now. Wren's already done it once, with barely any support. With her, you should be able to attack all four with no problem."

A flash of irritation crossed Micah's features and I pressed my lips together to hide a smirk. I loved how annoyed he was that Wren was the better Reboot. Better in so many ways, actually.

Micah twisted his face into a smile again and it struck me that Wren could have turned out like him. He was the second-highest number I'd ever heard of. He had similar skills and abilities and that same calm, cool demeanor. I wished she were with me, because I would have squeezed her hand and told her how much better she was than him.

"I think we're probably looking at days," Micah said. "Everyone is trained and ready and, thanks to you guys, we have enough fuel to get everyone there."

I winced, which Desmond noticed, and a slight frown crossed his face. I was sort of glad I didn't have to tell them the bad news in person. He might shoot me.

"I'll radio tomorrow and let you know when we're think-ing," Micah said. "Most likely day after tomorrow. We want to hit Rosa first, then the other three directly after. Keep the momentum going."

"Sounds like a plan," Tony said, vigorously shaking his hand.

Riley and Jules grabbed the fuel and started to walk back the way we came. I quickly stepped forward as Tony began to turn away.

"Um, I wanted to say thank you." I extended my hand, the letter pressed into my palm. "For helping Wren get me the antidote."

"You're welcome, son," Tony said, taking my hand. His gaze darted down when he felt the paper and when he looked at me again some of the excitement had drained from his eyes.

I slowly dropped my hand and he quickly put his own in his pocket, the letter safely in his palm. "I hope I can return the favor someday," I said quietly.

He nodded, and I turned around to see Micah watching me, his face expressionless. His eyes followed me and a flash of nervousness raced over me.

"Here," Riley said, shoving a fuel container at me. I took it and picked up my pace to match his.

Micah took one of the containers from Jules, a smile creeping over his face. "It's finally time."

FOURTEEN

WREN

I TURNED AT THE SOUND OF A SHUTTLE, RELIEF FLOODING MY chest. It must have been almost dawn, and I hadn't been able to sleep after my fight with Callum. Part of me knew he was well trained and fully capable of taking care of himself, but the other part of me was upset I hadn't gone with him so I could make sure.

He pulled back the tent flap a couple minutes later and looked at me in surprise. "Hey," he said softly as he crawled inside. "You're awake."

"Couldn't sleep. Did it go okay?"

He nodded as he took his place next to me. "Fine. I gave Tony the note." He studied me for a moment, his face serious, and I swallowed as I prepared for the worst.

He ran his hand beneath my hair and tilted my head up, planting a soft kiss on my lips, and I took in a surprised breath.

"I was thinking tonight that maybe it's unfair for me to tell you how to feel," he said quietly.

I pressed my hand to his chest, playing with the fabric of his shirt. I didn't know what to say to that, so I kept quiet. Maybe it was unfair.

"And I like you because you're funny and strong and different and—"

"Stop," I said, ducking my head closer to his chest as my cheeks started burning.

"You're the one who accused me of not liking who you are," he said with a laugh. "I'm listing what I like."

"I know. I regret it now."

He chuckled as he put a hand under my chin and tilted my face to his. "Fine." He kissed my cheek, then pulled away to look into my eyes.

"I don't care about you killing people because you did it because you had to," he said. "The first time you were presented with the opportunity to kill innocent people, you were horrified. You don't give yourself enough credit. I was looking at Micah tonight, thinking you could have turned out like him. But you didn't." He smoothed my hair back. "Not at all."

I swallowed and opened my mouth to ask if he was sure,

but his lips were on mine and I wrapped my arms around his neck and pressed my body into his.

"I'm sorry," I said, barely breaking away from the kiss. "You know I'll stay and help you, right? I know it's important to you." It wasn't important to me, and I could feel the weight of that still hanging between us. But if what he said was true, that he didn't want to tell me how to feel, maybe that was okay.

"I know," he said. "Thank you for that." He kissed me again, more urgently this time, and I ran my hands into his hair as his body slipped over mine. This was a nightly routine, but it felt different this time, my heart beating fast with relief and some leftover sadness.

His fingers traced down my cheek and to my neck, and I didn't bother to tense like I usually did when he came near the collar of my shirt. But he didn't touch my shirt or my chest—he never did, because I knew he was waiting for the okay from me—and instead wrapped his arm around my back and pulled me close.

I buried my face in his neck, letting out a long breath as I closed my eyes and melted against him.

I woke to Callum still sleeping, which was so rare I didn't dare move for fear of waking him. The sunlight coming through the cracks in the tent was bright, and I suspected we'd slept until almost noon.

Callum stirred about half an hour later, his arms finding me, like they did every morning.

"I'm glad you're here," he said sleepily in my ear.

"Where else would I be?" I asked with a laugh.

He placed his palm flat against my back, sending shivers down my spine. "Nowhere. I just thought you should know. I'm always happy you're here."

A smile slowly spread across my face, and I leaned forward to kiss him.

Yelling and running footsteps suddenly exploded all around us and I jerked into a sitting position. Those were bad yells. Panicked yells.

I scrambled out of the tent and pulled on my shoes, Callum right behind me. Reboots were all running in the direction of the fire pit, and Beth sprinted by me, her face furious.

"What's going on?" I yelled, breaking into a run.

"It's Addie!" she called over her shoulder.

My insides twisted around, the day Ever died flashing through my vision. It had been like this, with people running and panicking, and by the time I'd gotten there it was too late.

I broke into a sprint, passing other Reboots as I rounded a corner of tents.

I stopped.

It was Addie. Strung up in the middle of the compound. Her wrists were tied to a wooden beam by rope, her feet dangling above the ground. Her shirt was covered in blood, her head slumped down toward her chest. A crowd of mostly reservation Reboots had gathered around her, their faces grim. But no one made a move to help her.

Micah stood right in front of her, Jules at his side with a long stick in her hand.

My heart was pounding in my ears. Was she dead?

Her head moved and the relief was so sudden and powerful it almost knocked me over.

"What the—" I turned to see Beth running toward Micah, fists clenched.

"Back!" Micah stepped in front of Addie, his face hard and furious. Beth quickly stopped and he stared her down as he pointed to the crowd. "I said, back."

She glared at him for a couple seconds before retreating, muttering something to the Reboots next to her. They were spreading a message between them rapidly, bodies poised like they were ready for a fight. Even some of the reservation Reboots were inching forward, their faces hard and angry.

"Keep those wounds open!" Micah yelled, whirling around to face Addie. Jules nodded and lifted a giant stick. She struck Addie so hard I heard a crack.

Anger exploded inside my chest and I shoved the Reboots in front of me out of the way. I'd spent five years taking orders and watching people I liked get hurt or killed. I wasn't doing it anymore.

Micah saw me coming and his eyes narrowed. His shoulders

straightened. He was ready for a fight.

I stopped directly in front of him, drawing in a breath before I spoke. "Why is she up there?" I kept my gaze on Micah, afraid I would lose it and rip off his head if I looked at Addie again.

"I don't tolerate talk of rebelling and saving humans," he said evenly. "Recruiting Reboots to save humans is unacceptable."

I scanned the crowd. Someone she'd trusted had ratted her out. My eyes found Isaac, but he looked horrified, the group around him furious. They hadn't been lying about being with us.

I turned back to Micah and cocked my head. "You don't tolerate *talk*? Really?"

His jaw twitched. "Yes. Betraying fellow Reboots is the worst thing I've seen at this reservation. I'm not even sure this punishment is sufficient." He waved a hand in Addie's direction.

Guilt pressed against my chest as I thought back to my conversation with Addie last night. I'd blown her off when she asked me about those schematics. I'd shown no interest in helping her and Callum approach people, even though I knew they were risking Micah's wrath if they were discovered. Why hadn't I helped them at all? How much trouble would it have been, really? The Austin Reboots had been looking to me for direction when we first got here. I may have had more sway with them.

A breeze blew through the silent reservation as I spoke quietly. "Let her down."

"No."

"You've made your point. Let her down."

He took a step closer to me, so I had to lift my chin to meet his eyes. "I said no. Perhaps I should put you up there as well?"

"Please try. I'd love to see that."

Out of the corner of my eye, I saw the Reboots move forward slightly in a show of support. Of me. Micah saw it, too, and anger crept up his face.

He cast a glance over his shoulder. "Hit her again."

My vision was red as I launched myself at him and slammed my palms into his chest. He hit the ground with a yell and I jumped as he tried to grab my legs. He was already trying to get to his feet so I slammed my knee into his chin and he stumbled, blood spewing from his mouth.

I leaped on top of him and wrapped my hand around his neck, pushing his head into the dirt. I leaned closer. "I'm taking her down," I said loudly. "And you're going to sit here and let me, or I will put you up there instead."

I released his neck and he gasped as I got to my feet. I marched to Addie, the edge of my vision catching restless Reboots fingering their weapons. I barely shook my head, and they backed off.

Jules lifted her stick as I got closer but Micah waved her off.

"Let her take her down," he said.

I let my fingers fall out of fists as relief washed over me. I took a quick glance back at Micah to see him sitting in the dirt, wiping blood from his mouth. His face was serious but not angry, and it made me nervous.

I swallowed as I turned back to Addie and pulled a knife from my pocket. None of her recent injuries had healed yet, and she could barely open her eyes as I came closer. One of her shoulders was obviously dislocated, and the back of her shirt was nothing but tattered threads, old blood crusting on it. She'd been like this for a while, perhaps beaten in private somewhere before being dragged out for display. Her wrists were red, the wounds from the ropes probably opening again as soon as they closed. They'd tied them too tight; her hands were purple from lack of circulation.

I pulled over the stool they must have used to get her up there, circling one arm around her waist as I tugged the knife across the rope. She stirred, taking in a sharp breath as I freed one of her hands. She collapsed against me as I cut down the other rope and I quickly wrapped my other arm around her back to steady her.

"Thank you," she whispered into my shoulder, sobs beginning to shake her body.

I turned at the sound of footsteps and found Callum standing beside me. His face was full of anger and concern, but something else I didn't see very often. He was proud of me.

"I can take her," he said, easing his hand around her waist. I stepped back and he whisked her into his arms.

I hopped off the stool and followed Callum toward the back

of the reservation, where Addie's tent was. I glanced behind me to see a trail of Reboots led by Beth following us. Micah was still on the ground, one arm slung across his knees as he watched me. His expression was hard, his chest heaving up and down as he fixed a hard glare on me.

FIFTEEN

CALLUM

I STOPPED IN FRONT OF THE TENT ADDIE SHARED WITH A FEW other people and slowly lowered her to the ground. I pulled back the flap and offered her my hand to help her inside, but she ignored me and gestured for Wren to put her arm back in the socket. I winced as she did it, but Addie barely made a peep.

She nodded in thanks to Wren and pulled her legs to her chest. The wounds on her wrists were closing up, but she started crying, dropping her forehead to her knees.

"Here," Beth said, holding out a clean, wet towel to Wren. She took it, hesitating for a moment before kneeling down next to Addie and wiping at the blood on her arms.

Some of the other Reboots were lurking in the distance, talking quietly. Some were running in between tents, clothes and supplies in their arms. It looked like our time at the reservation was over.

Addie sniffled and, as the only Under-sixty in the general area, I started to say something comforting.

"I'm sorry," Wren said quietly, clenching the bloody towel in her hand. "I should have . . ."

I snapped my mouth shut and looked at her in surprise. I wasn't sure what she had to be sorry for. I'd almost cheered when she attacked Micah and took Addie down.

Addie shook her head, wiping at her eyes. "No, it was stupid. I talked to too many Reboots about our plan. I got excited after Isaac approached us."

Footsteps sounded behind me and I turned to see Riley, his face alarmed. "What is going on? Micah has Jeff and Kyle stationed in front of his tent and it looks like the Austin Reboots are about to attack."

"Beth, can you start spreading the word that we're leaving?" I asked, glancing at Wren for confirmation. "Wherever we go, I think we have to leave now."

She nodded in agreement. I hadn't even told her about Austin, about how now could be the perfect time for us to go to the city and drive HARC out.

A shot sliced through the quiet reservation and I jumped, whirling around to see where it had come from. Beth sprinted in the direction of the noise, dirt flying behind her, and Wren jumped to her feet, pulling her knife from her pocket.

She helped Addie up and pointed at her tent. "Are you good? Can you get your stuff together real quick?"

Addie nodded and disappeared into her tent.

Wren turned to Riley. "You coming with us or are you staying with Micah?"

"I'm coming with you." He said it without hesitation, and a smile tugged at Wren's lips.

"Then start figuring out a way around Kyle and Jeff so we can get some of the weapons in that tent." She turned to me as Riley took off. "Where are we going?"

I almost opened my mouth to ask Wren where she thought we should go. But if I left it up to her, we'd be running as far away from humans as possible. And I would not blame her for that. I couldn't ask her to step up and lead us into a battle she had no interest in fighting.

I took a deep breath. "I . . . I have one idea."

"What's that?"

"Since Tony said there are no Reboots in Austin we could probably fly a shuttle right in and fight off HARC with little trouble. And if the humans helped . . ."

Wren raised her eyebrows at me like she doubted that.

"I know you don't want to go back to the cities, but—"

"No, let's go," she interrupted, taking off in the direction of our tent.

I blinked, jogging to catch up with her. "Are you sure? Because—"

"Callum, there's one person here who has a plan," she said, casting an amused look at me. "And it's you. So, go. Start getting it together. I'll pack up our tent and help Riley with the weapons."

I grinned at her, excitement rushing through me as I swooped down for a quick kiss. "I'll find you in a few minutes."

SIXTEEN

WREN

I'D ONLY JUST LEFT CALLUM AND STEPPED INTO THE TENT WHEN
I heard the rustle of noise behind me. A hand on my neck.

Then the crack.

And everything went numb.

My eyes were covered with something and I opened my
mouth to yell but someone wrapped a cloth around it and tied
it tightly behind my head.

I tried to struggle, or reach out, but my body wouldn't move.

The sliver of light peeking in from my blindfold disappeared
suddenly, and my face was pressed up against my knees and I
was being jostled against some kind of material.

I was in a bag. I tried to scream, but then I couldn't breathe.

I tried to suck oxygen in through my nose but it wouldn't come, and the beginnings of panic started to set in.

Everything went black.

"Can you kill a Reboot from lack of oxygen?"

I tried to blink but my eyes weren't cooperating yet.

"No." It was Micah's voice. "Trust me, I've been through that experiment."

I sucked in a breath suddenly and Micah chuckled.

"See?" he said. "She's fine."

"I wouldn't have been heartbroken if she were dead," Jules replied.

"Micah doesn't kill Reboots. He's superior to humans in that way." It was Addie's voice, dripping with disdain.

I knew the sounds around us. The rush of air, the hum of an engine.

I blinked open my eyes. We were in a shuttle.

Micah and Jules sat in the Reboot seats, guns in their laps. Addie was on the floor across from me, a rope tied around her chest.

I looked down. My own arms were bound tightly to my torso, but someone had taken the gag off my mouth.

I glanced back at Addie. She was keeping her panic under control, but her chest rose and fell too quickly, her eyes wide as they met mine.

Callum. I twisted around, trying to see the rest of the

shuttle. Empty. It was only the four of us and whoever was piloting the shuttle.

"I told you living at the reservation was a privilege," Micah said.

I managed to struggle up to a seated position, leaning back against the shuttle wall. "We were leaving your stupid reservation."

"I figured that. Lucky you, I'm going to help you out."

I tried to twist my body against the rope but it was no use. Micah knew not to take any chances with me.

I met his gaze. "Callum?" I'd tried to keep my voice steady but it shook, just slightly.

Micah raised one eyebrow. "Do you see him in here?"

"Did you hurt him?"

"By 'hurt' I'll assume you mean 'killed,'" Micah said. He leaned forward, putting his forearms on his thighs. "As your friend here pointed out, I don't kill Reboots. Your boyfriend is fine. I'll deal with him when I get back."

Why wouldn't he bring Callum along? I saw no reason to trust Callum, since he'd made it clear he was on my side.

Maybe because I was the only one who'd been openly defiant of him? Micah seemed to have an odd moral code, one he felt strongly about. Maybe Callum hadn't warranted this kind of punishment yet.

I took a deep breath and forced myself to believe that.

"Where are we going?" I asked.

Micah smiled as he leaned back in his seat.

That was all the answer I got.

We flew for a long time. Too long. Hours. If we were headed south, we were to the cities, if not past them. If we were headed north, I had no idea where we were.

My stomach clenched at the thought. Finding my way back was going to be hard. Maybe impossible.

The shuttle had slowed and Micah walked to the pilot and murmured something before returning. He nodded at Addie, and Jules sprang out of her seat and grabbed her by the hair.

Micah yanked me up by the ropes binding my arms and spun me around to look at him. Behind me, a sudden whoosh of air blew my hair into my face.

My eyes slid to the shuttle door, where Jules held Addie perilously close to the edge. Outside was nothing but blue sky. The ground was small beneath us, dotted with trees.

Were they going to drop us out of the shuttle? I tried to take a steadying breath but the panic was beginning to spread into every limb.

Micah dragged me to the edge by my shirt collar.

"Say hello the humans you love so much for me," Jules said to Addie, a crazed smile on her face.

I felt something on my fingers and found Addie's hand fumbling for mine. I grabbed it and held tightly, trying to meet her panicked expression with calm. I wasn't sure it worked.

Micah pulled me close to him, so he could stare straight at me. "Don't hit your head," he hissed.

He released my collar and slammed his hands against my chest.

I shot out of the shuttle with Addie, my fingers tightly wrapped around hers.

SEVENTEEN

CALLUM

OUR TENT WAS EMPTY. OUR CLOTHES AND BLANKETS WERE STILL piled in the corner.

There was no sign of Wren.

I pulled my head out of the tent and straightened, squinting in the sun as I scanned the reservation. Kyle and Jeff were still stationed in front of Micah's tent, and they'd been joined by about fifteen other reservation Reboots, most of them Over-one-twenties.

Many of the Austin Reboots were scurrying to Beth, who was standing near the fire pit, hands on her hips. They appeared to be getting into some sort of formation, their faces tight with fear and anticipation.

Riley split off from the front of that crowd and jogged over to me. He was tense, constantly turning his head to scan the area around me.

"Where's Wren?" he asked.

"I don't know. She was going to find you."

"I haven't seen her." Our eyes met and a hint of concern crossed his face. "How long—"

"Callum."

I turned to find Isaac leading a group of at least thirty reservation Reboots. The new Reboot Micah had just killed was with them, as well as most of the Under-sixties.

"What's going on?" Isaac asked.

"We're leaving," I said quietly. Wren had said Isaac had come around, but I still felt a flash of fear that they would rise up against us and go join the Reboots in front of the tent. "We're going to Austin."

"I'm sorry, we're going *where*?" Riley gave me an incredulous look.

"We're going to Austin," I repeated, my eyes on Isaac's. "HARC's losing their grip on the humans there. We're getting the weapons so we can take over the city." I glanced at Riley. "You still have the fuel for the shuttles?"

"Yes." He was still confused.

"We'll fuel two shuttles and fly there." I took a deep breath and looked at the crowd behind Isaac. Thirty or so behind him, and we already had a hundred Reboots from Austin. Together, we could take down the One-twenties, even if they were armed. "Will you help?"

Isaac paused for a beat. "When we get to Austin, can the Reboots leave if they want? Or do we all have to stay and fight?"

"You're all free to do whatever you want," I said, though I hoped they'd choose to stay and help.

"All right. I'm coming with you."

I blinked at the quick decision. "Really?"

"Yeah." He jerked his head at the Reboots behind him. "I don't know about them, but I'll explain what's happening and let them decide."

"If they want to help have them join Beth and the other Austin Reboots," I said, smiling at him.

"Got it. You have someone fueling the shuttles?"

"Not yet."

"I'm on it." He faced Riley. "Where's the fuel?"

Riley gestured for Isaac to follow him as he headed for the reservation gate, casting a glance over his shoulder at me. "Tell me when you find Wren, okay?"

I nodded and jogged toward Addie's tent. Several Reboots regarded me warily as I passed, and I noticed the girl who was always carrying the baby around was frantically packing her tent with a few friends. I slowed, thinking they were coming with us, but she shot me a withering stare and I backed off.

I stopped at Addie's tent, pulling back the flap to reveal a young Reboot shoving clothes into a bag.

"Have you seen Addie?" I asked.

"No." He looked at me. "Not since One-seventy-eight saved her."

I dropped the flap, worry beginning to creep into my chest. Wren had said she'd help Riley. It wasn't like her not to be where she said she would be.

I took off running. I went up and down every road in the reservation, asking anyone I found if they'd seen Wren or Addie. No one had.

By the time I headed back to the fire pit, the rock in the bottom of my stomach was growing by the second.

Riley and Isaac were standing next to Beth, and my heart skipped a beat when I saw the crowd behind them. It was all the Austin Reboots, and enough of the reservation Reboots that we had maybe a hundred and fifty. It was more than I had hoped for.

Kyle and Jeff stood firm in front of the weapons tent with the other One-twenties, guns out and ready. They were all trying to maintain calm expressions, but I could see the fear seeping through some. They were outnumbered, and Micah was nowhere to be seen.

I turned back to Riley, my breath catching in my throat when I saw the grim expression on his and Isaac's faces.

"What?" I asked as I sprinted over and stopped in front of them.

"Micah and Jules are gone. No one has seen them." Isaac ran a hand through his hair with a sigh. "And a shuttle is gone."

My whole body went cold, and I tried to keep my voice steady. "He took them."

"I think so," Riley said.

"Where?"

"I don't know." Riley frowned in thought, then gestured for me to follow him. "Come on." He looked at Beth. "Hold position for a minute, okay? I'll give you a signal."

Beth nodded and my heart pounded in my chest as I hurried beside Riley. Wren wasn't supposed to be the one in trouble. Nothing was ever supposed to happen to her.

"Here." Riley held a handgun out to me. "Take it. I could only arm about ten people with what I had, but it should be enough."

I didn't argue as I wrapped my hand around the barrel of the gun.

"It's already loaded," he said. "You may need it shortly. I think things are about to get ugly."

I nodded as I slipped it in my pocket. If Micah took Wren, things were about to get *very* ugly.

Riley and I stopped in front of Kyle, who had beads of sweat on his forehead despite the chilly wind blowing through the compound. He gripped his gun tighter as he pushed back his massive shoulders, eyes darting to the large group of Reboots behind us.

He ignored me, his attention focused on Riley. As the higher number, Riley was probably sort of his superior. I swallowed down the urge to grab him by the neck and demand he tell us everything.

"There's a shuttle missing," Riley said.

"Yeah," Kyle replied.

"What are Micah and Jules doing with it?" Riley kept his voice even, calm.

Kyle sort of winced. "Micah will be back by tonight."

"After he does what?"

Kyle stared at us blankly.

"A drop?" Riley asked quietly.

I looked at him quickly. What was a "drop"?

"Yes," Kyle said, his lip curling as he sneered at me. "I mean, it's sort of expected, right?"

Riley ran his hands through his hair, his face worried. "Micah's dropped bad Reboots in bounty-hunter territory before. But it's been years. I heard it made people around here antsy."

"What? Where is that?"

Riley turned to Kyle for the answer and he shrugged. "Micah said he was going to look for them from the sky. He wasn't sure."

"They're usually near Austin," Riley said. "Because the majority of escaped Reboots come from there."

"Yeah," Kyle agreed. "And with the human situation in Austin . . ."

HARC probably had bounty hunters all over the place, to deal with the humans trying to escape.

Riley glanced at me, but I was still glaring at Kyle. He'd known Micah was taking Wren and he hadn't tried to stop him.

I took a step forward, narrowing my eyes at him.

"What happens when he drops Reboots in bounty-hunter territory?" I asked slowly.

"Bounty hunters deliver Reboots back to HARC," Kyle said, meeting my gaze. "But I couldn't say for sure. None of them ever come back."

I took a small step back. Clenched my fist. Swung.

Kyle hit the ground and a brief pain radiated through my hand and up my arm. I'd never hit anyone that hard before.

He was on his feet in seconds and I ducked his attempt at a punch. Wren was five times faster, and he missed by so much he stumbled. I clocked him under the chin and he hit the ground again.

I turned to see Riley's eyebrows raised, barely masking his surprise. He motioned with his hand and I heard the sound of over a hundred Reboots running.

I wanted to hit Kyle again, but instead I took a deep breath and tried to pull the panic away from the logic in my head. That's what Wren would have done. She would have been rational about it. Calm.

I pulled my gun out and raised it as I heard the Reboots stop behind me. I fixed my eyes on Kyle's.

"You're going to want to get out of my way."

EIGHTEEN

WREN

I COULDN'T MOVE.

Judging by the pain radiating through my body I'd broken more bones than I could count. I suspected one of them was an important neck- or backbone, given the paralysis. Out of the corner of my eye, I could see one of my legs bent at a funny angle.

The sun was directly in my line of vision, low in the sky. It was late afternoon. It was somewhat warmer than it had been at the reservation, which made me think Micah had taken us south. Or west?

I swallowed back panic as I squinted and tried to find Addie in my limited view. I was on a road, broken bits of asphalt and gravel surrounding me. A plain white building was to my right, a brick building to my left, and both were taller than any building I'd ever seen. Had Micah dropped us in one of the cities?

"Addie?" I yelled. "Addie!"

Silence answered me and I took a deep breath and closed my eyes. Maybe she'd fallen too far away to hear me.

The pain was reaching a scream-worthy level, which must have meant I was about to start healing. I sighed and tried to concentrate on anything else. Callum. Addie. Bashing Micah's face in.

I was suddenly able to move my hands again, and I struggled to a sitting position against the rope still tied around my chest. The impact had loosened it and I squirmed my arms free and yanked my leg back into its normal position.

I frowned at the scene in front of me. I was in the middle of a street, tall buildings with trees in between them lining either side down the block. But it was totally deserted. Micah had said, *"Say hello to the humans you love so much for me,"* implying he was dropping us in an area he knew was full of humans.

But I didn't see any. I didn't see any signs of life, actually.

I could stand a minute later, and I whipped my head around as I looked for Addie. Considering she was a Thirty-nine, I doubted she'd healed at the same speed as me. She was probably still on the ground somewhere.

Not dead. Definitely not dead.

The thought of Addie being dead made panic grip my

stomach. She couldn't be.

"Addie?" I called, turning in a circle. If she'd landed on top
of a building maybe she'd be able to see me down here. I waved
my arms as I turned around again. Something that looked like
a HARC shuttle caught my eye at the end of the street, and my
heart jumped, my fingers searching for a weapon.

I squinted. It was the wrong color to be a HARC shuttle.
All HARC vehicles were black, and this one was red, and the
front end was completely smashed.

It was a car. But HARC had banned all cars when they
built the Republic of Texas. I cocked my head, turning around
slowly. Were we in one of the old cities?

A head popped up suddenly and I almost laughed with relief
as Addie raised one arm to wave at me. I ran to the corner of the
brick building and sank down on my knees next to her, taking
a quick glance down at her body. She was dirty, her black pants
covered in dust and pieces of a tree it appeared she'd taken
down with her. She cradled one arm like it was still broken, and
her face was bloody, a giant lump on one side of her cheek. She
pointed to her face and shook her head.

"Broken jaw?" I asked.

She nodded. I let out a tiny sigh of relief and got to my feet,
putting my hands on my hips as I surveyed the area. I was going
to have to guess which direction—

A HARC transport van was headed toward us.

A real one this time.

It sped over the hill and zoomed in our direction, dodging giant potholes as it made its way down the street.

"Get up!" I grabbed Addie's arm and hauled her to her feet. She stumbled a bit and winced as she put pressure on one leg. Her eyes widened as she spotted the vehicle.

I took off for the intersection in front of me, Addie at my side. I whipped my head both ways as we reached a wide street, but I saw nothing but tall buildings and a few abandoned cars. Hiding in one of the buildings seemed like a shortsighted plan, and a quick pat of my pockets revealed that Micah had taken my gun and knife.

We rounded a corner as the van swerved to my right as it raced toward us. If they jumped out maybe I could overpower them. If I could get one of their guns I might—

I gasped as something sharp hit my neck. Addie made a similar noise as a needle sank into her neck.

The van was right next to us now, the side door open. Two men hung out the opening, weapons poised.

Beside me, Addie yelped, and I turned just in time to see her hit the ground, a rope wrapped around her ankles. I barely dodged a second rope, blinking stars out of my eyes. What had they given us?

I snatched the needle out of my neck and tossed it away as one of the men jumped out of the van, gun pointed at my face.

The world spun as I grabbed the barrel of the weapon, thrusting it up so quickly it slammed into his chin. I turned it around and fired it in his general direction. Fog was beginning to invade my brain, and I could no longer see him clearly.

I caught a glimpse of Addie's motionless figure on the ground as something crashed against me. I hit the pavement so hard I could hear my arm crack. A hand grabbed for my neck, my weapon, and the darkness was starting to seep into the corner of my eyes.

A human face floated across my vision and I pushed a hand against his stomach, aiming the gun directly for his chest.

His body made a thump as it fell. Then, silence. My eyes drifted closed.

I woke to the sun barely peeking out from behind one of the buildings. I had to open and close my eyes a few times before they cleared, and I immediately felt the pressure of something on my leg.

My arm ached as I tried to prop myself up on my elbows, and a quick glance revealed it was still broken. My neck burned from where the needle had punctured it, and I looked at the sun in confusion. It was much lower in the sky. I must have been out for at least an hour.

The pressure on my leg turned out to be a dead human collapsed on me, and I squirmed out from under him. The other human lay dead beside the van, and I quickly found Addie a few feet away. Her leg was bent at a funny angle, but it looked like her jaw had healed. I poked her shoulder, but she didn't move.

I jumped over the potholes in the road and wrenched open the back of the HARC van. The driver had run straight into a building and was slumped over the steering wheel, dead. Otherwise, the vehicle was clear of humans.

There were two shotguns inside, and I slung them over my shoulder and walked to the humans. They each had a handgun and one had a knife, so I relieved them of everything.

My arm still burned as I slid the weapons into my pockets, and I frowned as I rubbed at the needle mark on my neck. What had Micah said about those drugs HARC had given them?

I winced as I remembered him mentioning one that slowed his healing time. Great. Why hadn't I asked him more about that? Like how long "slowed" really was. Why hadn't I had a conversation with him about what kinds of HARC drugs I should be on the lookout for?

Because he's an insane person and I didn't want to spend time with him. I sighed in annoyance. No excuse.

I ran a hand down my face as I looked at Addie again. No telling how long she'd be out, but I couldn't sit around and wait for her to wake up. HARC might have been tracking that van.

I looked up, searching for some hint of where we were. A big, white sign hung askew on the building the van had hit, with only the letters *S* and *W* remaining. At the top of the sign was a *P*, surrounded by a whole slew of colors. It looked like it used to have bulbs all over it—I couldn't imagine why—but most of them were broken or gone now.

I turned to the other side of the street, where an elaborate three-story building stood. It had big windows and columns, and it was nicer than any building I'd seen in the slums. The next building was smaller, but they continued down the street, right next to one another like these humans had to make use of every bit of space.

I squinted at a black sign with white letters on one of the buildings. *Silhouette Restaurant and Bar.*

Well, that was no help.

I turned and faced north. My eyes widened. That, on the other hand, was very helpful.

It was the Austin capitol. The original one.

NINETEEN

CALLUM

MY WORDS HUNG IN THE AIR FOR A MOMENT—*"YOU'RE GOING TO want to get out of my way"*—until Kyle took a step forward, gun pointed at my chest.

"Make me."

I lunged at him and both our guns went off, pain screaming down my left side as the bullet tore through skin. The Reboots around me yelled as they charged forward, and shots rang out from the One-twenties guarding the tents.

"Stay back!" someone yelled. "Don't make us shoot you!"

Kyle's fist slammed across my jaw and I hit the dirt. More bullets zipped through the air around me as the Reboots ignored the warning of the One-twenties, and my chest tightened in fear. I paused on the ground, catching myself as I started to look for Wren to help me out of this situation.

Kyle kicked me in the ribs as I attempted to get to my feet, and I let out a grunt.

"Get on your feet and put your arms up. Block the next one." Wren's voice was in my head as I rolled away from his boot, poised for another kick, and sprang up.

He aimed his gun for me and I realized I had lost mine when I hit the ground. He fired a shot into my shoulder but I swung at him anyway, ignoring the sharp pain that radiated down my arm.

"Confuse me. Surprise me."

I gripped the barrel of the gun as Kyle fired again. He blinked, giving me a baffled look as I kept it steady with my shoulder. I winced as the bullet tore into flesh that hadn't healed yet and yanked on the gun so hard Kyle stumbled. I got a grip on it and tried to swipe it across his face, but he moved out of the way too quickly.

"What have I told you? Fast."

He made a move for the gun and I slammed my head into his so suddenly he gasped. He stumbled backward and I blinked through the sparks in my vision to grab him by the collar. I punched him once, twice, three times, until he hit the ground and tried to scramble away.

I grabbed his foot and hauled him back, glancing up at the sound of my name. Riley tossed cuffs in my direction and they landed in the dirt next to me. I scooped them up and slapped them around Kyle's wrist. He sat up and kicked wildly at me, and I pressed my foot into his chest, shoving his back on the ground.

A scream made me turn and I caught sight of the tent just as it collapsed. The support beams folded in and the crash echoed through the reservation as everything went down.

"Move!" Riley pointed a gun into the face of a Reboot and she reluctantly raised her arms, chest heaving up and down.

"Micah's going to kill you," Kyle muttered, glaring at me from the dirt.

I raised my eyebrows, glancing at the scene around me. The One-twenties were on the ground, most of them cuffed as the Austin Reboots pointed guns at them. It looked as though Micah was going to be seriously outnumbered when he returned. I didn't think he was going to get a chance to kill anyone.

The wind whipped across my face as I caught myself looking for Wren again, checking to make sure she was okay, waiting for instruction. I took in a shaky breath as I lowered my eyes to Kyle again.

"Not if I kill him first."

The shuttle landed outside the gate as the sun started to set.

I tightened my grip on the gun in my right hand and scanned the Reboots around me. Some of our group was pretty beat up, and I cast a worried look at Beth as she finished taking inventory of the Austin Reboots.

Kyle and the rest of them sat tied up or handcuffed a few feet away. We'd positioned the twenty or so Reboots so Micah would have a clear view of them.

The rest of the reservation Reboots appeared to have split in two groups: some were hiding in tents or packing their bags, hoping to avoid all the drama. They had no interest in going to the cities with me or with Micah. The others were with us.

"Two dead," Beth said quietly, twisting her hair around her finger as she took a spot beside me and stared at the landing shuttle.

I winced, taking a quick glance around. I probably hadn't known them, but I felt guilty all the same.

"That's better than I would have expected," Riley said from my other side.

The shuttle door opened and my heart pounded in anticipation. Wren could still be in there. She could have overpowered Micah or he could have changed his mind.

Micah stepped out, followed by Jules.

Then nothing.

My heart sank.

I released a slow breath. Calm. What chance did a few human bounty hunters stand against Wren? She'd probably already taken them all out and was halfway to Austin by now.

I stepped away from the group and strode toward Micah. The smug, self-satisfied look on his face intensified as he met my eyes, but I could see a flicker of doubt as he took in the crowd of Reboots behind me and his tied-up cohorts beside us.

I stopped in front of him. "Where's Wren? And Addie?"

Micah pushed his sleeves up his arms. "I explained that there were rules here. Wren and Addie broke them, so I had to deal with it."

"You dropped them in bounty-hunter territory."

He smiled at me. Smiled, like he was so proud of himself. Like he'd won. Everything in my body shut down for a split second and I couldn't move or breathe or think.

I slowly took a step back. The gun felt heavy in my hand suddenly and I gripped it harder.

"Get in," I called over my shoulder.

There were suddenly Reboots all around me, rushing for the shuttle, yelling. Isaac ran past me with fuel containers in both hands and immediately started refueling the shuttle Micah had returned in. A few reservation Reboots formed a circle around him, protecting him as the rest piled inside.

"Stop!" Micah yelled.

No one even paused. Micah glanced at Kyle and his other loyalists tied up on the ground again, and rage flashed across his features.

He lunged for me and I quickly ducked, darting out of the way so fast he hit the ground. He jumped to his feet and I lifted the gun. Clicked off the safety.

His face was tight with fury, his eyes focused on me.

"Go ahead," he said, taking a step closer, so the barrel of

the gun was almost touching his forehead. "Please. Prove to everyone you're no better than a human." He jerked his head to the reservation. "You're already doing a bang-up job of killing us all anyway."

I slowly lowered the gun. He'd taken Wren and he was a murderer and a psychopath and he deserved to die.

But a weight lifted from my chest as I realized I wasn't going to kill him. Maybe I would have liked to. Maybe it would have made me feel better.

I still wasn't going to do it.

"We took all the fuel out of the other shuttles," I said as I clicked the safety back on. "And told the rebels what you were planning." I nodded at the meager crowd of defeated reservation Reboots behind me. "So there won't be any further communications with them."

The shuttles roared to life and I glanced over my shoulder to see Riley waving for me to get on.

I met Micah's gaze as I took a step backward. "Did you really think you could just get rid of her and everyone would listen to you?" A smile started to form on my lips. "Do you really think you killed her by handing her over to a few humans?"

I ducked as I stepped onto the shuttle, grasping the edge of the door as I looked at him. "There's no way Wren is dead," I said as the shuttle began to lift off the ground. "I'd be scared, if I were you."

TWENTY

WREN

I TRIED TO START THE VAN AGAIN, BUT APPARENTLY HAVING A DOOR in its engine wasn't a good thing. I didn't know the exact distance from old Austin to New Austin, but it wasn't too far to walk. Twenty miles, maybe. Once Callum found out what Micah did, he'd head straight for the cities to find me. We'd been planning to go to Austin, and it was our home, so I felt pretty confident he'd go there first.

I left the shotguns and put one handgun in my pants, one in Addie's. I emptied the vehicle of ammo before I left, but they didn't have much extra.

I walked to Addie and knelt beside her. "Addie," I said quietly, shaking her shoulder. I didn't know why I was being quiet, because as far as I knew, old Austin had been deserted for over twenty years. The streets were quiet, empty, the only sound the wind rustling the trees.

"Addie!" I shook her harder, but she didn't stir.

I let out a long sigh as I looked at the HARC van. It was possible they would send someone to check why it had stopped in the middle of old Austin.

I squinted ahead at the capitol. That was north. New Austin was northwest, but I wasn't exactly sure *how* west. I ran my hand down my face as I tried to remember the old maps of Texas. I couldn't picture the new cities mixed with the old. I needed a map, even an old one.

I grabbed one of Addie's arms and hauled her over my shoulder. I groaned under her weight as I stood. Hopefully she'd wake up soon. I didn't know how far I could carry her.

My leg burned as I limped forward, and I kept my broken arm close to my chest. I steadied Addie with my right arm, hooking it around her neck to keep her in place.

The capitol really was so much bigger. I'd heard about it, and I knew the one in the New Austin *rico* was nothing more than a small knockoff, but I hadn't realized by how much. The huge, round dome was on top of a massive base, and there appeared to be a statue of a person at the very top. They'd missed that detail in the new version.

I glanced at the buildings on either side of the wide road as I walked. I'd hoped to see one of the old cities with Callum, and it was too bad he wasn't here now. He probably would have known more about the city than I did.

There were still cars parked on either side of the street, rusting and missing parts. Some were even abandoned in the middle of the road.

It must have been nice to have access to something with wheels all the time. That would have been really helpful right about now.

I hobbled to the end of the street and turned to look at the capitol as I headed west on the street that ran in front of it. Part of me wanted to go inside, see what was left of it, but I didn't think going in any building was particularly safe. Nothing was sturdy, and the last thing I needed was to be buried alive in the middle of a dead city.

I turned north again when I reached a street that was somewhat clear. The buildings were huge on this street, twenty, thirty stories tall with hundreds of windows.

There was some destruction, some streets that were more rubble than buildings, but overall it wasn't as bad as I'd been led to believe. I thought Austin was gone, mostly destroyed, but it was more like it was deserted. Had all these people died of KDH?

It seemed sad they'd rejected Reboots. Micah was right on one count—we had a found a way to survive. Maybe if the humans hadn't panicked, we could have stayed in this city. Humans or Reboots could have lived in these buildings instead of tents and thrown-together houses.

But HARC had always been about control, so maybe starting their own cities and fencing the humans in was more appealing. Or maybe it really was the only way to contain the virus and keep humans safe. What did I know?

It was just getting dark when my leg finally started to heal and Addie moaned. She squirmed on my shoulder and I stopped and slowly kneeled down as I slid her off onto the concrete.

She blinked at me, rubbing one of her arms. The gashes on her arms and legs were still open, and one of her legs was broken. Given how many hours it had taken me to heal, she had quite a ways to go.

I estimated I'd barely made it two miles, maybe less, and we'd stopped in the middle of the road. A big, redbrick building was to my right, and on my left a gray building with big windows and a blue sign that read *Kerbey Lane Café*. She looked left, then right, then left again.

"Where are we?"

"Austin," I said. "The original."

Her head tilted up as she surveyed the building next to us, her eyes wide.

"And those guys in the van?" she asked.

"They tried to grab us."

She gave me an amused look. "Obviously that didn't work out so well for them."

I plopped down in the middle of the road with her. "It did not."

She examined the area around us, wincing as she moved. She rubbed her arm and inspected the long gash.

"They slowed our healing time," I said. "It took me a few hours."

She moaned. "If it took you a few hours, it's going to take me a week."

"Probably not quite that long," I said with a smile.

"And so you hoisted me on your back and carried me . . ." Addie glanced behind her. "Have we been going for a while?"

"Only a couple miles."

"Oh, only a couple miles." She rolled her eyes, grinning as she bumped her shoulder against mine. "Is it awesome being you? Do you just sit around and revel in your awesomeness?"

I gave her a baffled look, not entirely sure how to respond to that. She laughed, pushing her dark hair behind her shoulder.

"Thank you," she said more seriously.

"You're welcome."

She paused for a moment, rubbing her fingers across her forehead. "I'm sorry I got us into this."

"I don't think it was you who pushed us out of a shuttle."

"But it was me who talked to too many people at the reservation about the plan. This wouldn't have happened if it weren't for me."

"I don't know about that." I shrugged. "I could have left you up there to get tortured. It's not like it would have caused any lasting damage."

She snorted, which turned into a full laugh. "Uh, yeah. I guess you could have. But I think I prefer it this way." She ran her hands over her hair. "I was losing my mind there."

"You and me both." I hopped to my feet, extending my hand to her. "Can you walk? We should probably find somewhere to stay for the night."

She took my hand and stood slowly, putting all her weight on her left leg. She tried to step forward and winced.

"It's still broken," she said. "I could drag it, or—"

"Let's go in there," I said, pointing to the café. "The windows are still mostly intact. Looks like it's not about to cave in."

She gave me a grateful look and I gestured for her to lean against me. She hobbled across the street slowly with me.

The door had been broken a long time ago, and what was left of it swung open and closed in the wind. As we walked inside, a small animal scurried across the floor and Addie moaned.

"I hate rats."

"They don't taste too bad."

"Oh my God, never tell me that story."

I shut the door and pulled a chair in front of it to keep it closed. The inside had likely once been bright green, but now the paint was peeled off the walls. Tables and chairs were scattered everywhere, and a row of booths ran along one wall. The plastic was cracked, the stuffing torn out in some places. I decided not to tell Addie there may very well have been more rats living in those seats as I gently placed her down in one.

I sat down on the other side, brushing cobwebs off the dirty table.

"Where are we going?" Addie asked, scooting back in the booth and leaning against the wall. "Austin? The real one?"

"Yes. If we can find it." I raised my eyebrows at her. "I don't suppose you have a map of Texas in your head?"

"Nope, sorry." She squinted out the dirty window. "Surely we could find a map around here somewhere? At one of those old fueling places maybe? They used to sell, like, a whole bunch of stuff there. I bet back during the war people took the food and left the maps."

"That's a good idea, actually."

"I'm going to pretend you don't sound all surprised about that."

I laughed as I pulled my knees to my chest and rested my head on them. "Sorry."

"You think Callum and the Reboots will still go to Austin?" she asked.

I nodded, rubbing my finger across a crack in the table. "They wouldn't stay at the reservation. And Callum knows Austin's the first place I'd go to look for him."

"Agreed. Maybe he murdered Micah when he found out what happened, and took over everything."

I gave her a skeptical look. "Callum isn't really the murdering type. He has morals."

"Morals shmorals. I bet when he finds out what Micah did he'll lose it." Addie leaned her head against the wall. "The only reason he's all high and mighty about killing people is because he was only at HARC for a few weeks. He doesn't understand what we went through."

I nodded, trying to hide my surprise. "Did he talk about it with you?"

"Not really. Mostly I just noticed it with you guys. Sometimes I wanted to be like, 'Dude, chill. You're so uppity sometimes.'"

I laughed, quickly covering it with my hand. I cleared my throat. "He's not uppity. He's stubborn."

"Whatever." She waved her hand in the air. "I think it would bug me, having to be the bad one all the time."

I shrugged. "I'm used to it."

"Whatever you say." She shifted, wincing as she pulled her broken leg onto the booth. "Thank you for not leaving me there."

"I'm going to pretend you don't sound surprised about that."

Addie grinned. "I'm a little surprised."

"Don't sugarcoat it."

"Come on. You would barely talk to me at the reservation. It was like you're antifriend."

"I'm not antifriend," I said softly, playing with dangling threads on the edge of my pants.

"Just didn't like me, then?"

"I only ever had one friend," I said, not looking at her. "HARC killed her not long before I escaped with Callum."

"Oh." She was quiet for a moment. "Why?"

"She was a Fifty-six, and was on her first round of those crazy drugs. She kept getting worse and worse. I think she sort of lost hope. She was upset about attacking me every night. We were roommates." I swallowed. "She went on a rampage, killed a bunch of guards, and then basically gave herself up to HARC."

Addie let out a long breath. "Crap. I'm sorry."

I leaned back against the wall and stared at the sagging ceiling. "I already knew that Reboots escaped," I said quietly. "Leb had told me at least a week before she died, and I didn't do anything to help her."

"You would have been in the exact same position you were with Callum if you'd helped her," Addie said. "On the run with a crazy Reboot who needed the antidote."

"I got it for Callum," I said softly. "I could have gotten it for her, too."

Addie was silent for a moment. "I sort of doubt she would want you carrying around this kind of guilt."

"She wouldn't."

"Then what can you do to make it better?"

I turned to her. "Nothing. She's dead."

"Yeah, she is. But there are other things you could do to make it better, aren't there?"

"Like what?"

"Like what would she have wanted you to do? Would she have wanted you to mope and never have friends and—" She stopped suddenly and winced. "Promise not to hit me until this drug wears off?"

I let out a soft laugh. "Yes."

"Would she have wanted you to run off with Callum and leave all the Reboots in the cities to fend for themselves? Did she have a family? Would she have wanted you to abandon the humans?"

"She had four sisters in New Dallas," I said quietly.

"Then what would she have wanted you to do?"

I stared at the table as her words sank in. I didn't think Ever would have expected me to save everyone or fight a war on behalf of the humans. She wouldn't have expected it, but I could almost picture her face if I told her that's what I was doing.

She would have been proud.

TWENTY-ONE

CALLUM

IT WAS DARK WHEN AUSTIN CAME INTO VIEW.

I sat in the passenger's seat next to George, the small Reboot who was piloting the shuttle. He looked about fourteen years old and seemed entirely comfortable in the pilot's seat. He explained to me that Micah had all kids learn to drive when they turned ten, because it would be where they were most "useful." I'd laughed, sort of hysterically, and George hadn't said much to me since.

The other shuttle was behind us, following our lead. It was full of mostly reservation Reboots, and I'd worried they'd take off in a different direction, abandon our plan to go to Austin. But they'd stayed right behind us the whole trip.

Riley walked up to the doorway, arms crossed over his chest. "I instructed everyone back here to put on their helmets since we're close."

"Thanks."

"Jeez." George's eyes widened as he blinked at the Austin skyline. The buildings of the city were alight and they must have appeared huge to someone who'd been living in tents his whole life.

I turned away, staring into darkness instead. I couldn't stop thinking about Wren, and how her current situation was entirely my fault.

Why had I made her stay at the reservation? Why hadn't I listened when she begged me to leave? She'd said it to me: *"One or both of us could end up dead."* Even though she'd said "both," I hadn't even heard it. I'd thought she was just worried about me. Why had I assumed she was invincible? Why hadn't I considered that by making her stay I risked losing her?

"Callum."

I looked up to see Riley and George staring at me. Riley cocked his head toward the pilot. "You need to tell him where you want to land."

"Oh." I turned to the Austin skyline. "Veer east. We'll land in the slums, near the schoolhouse. I'll point it out as we get closer."

"Right in the middle of the slums, huh?" Riley said skeptically.

"Unless you have a better plan." I suspected Riley thought my entire plan was bad. He hadn't said much to me since I laid it all out for him on the ride over.

He slid his hands into his pockets as he leaned against the shuttle wall. "If the humans in the slums and the city join HARC, we're screwed."

"Why would they do that?"

"Because they're scared of us. Because you just told Tony that Micah was planning to kill them all. They may not be on our side anymore. If they ever were."

I strapped my helmet on. "Then we show them there's nothing to be scared of. Try not to kill anyone."

He gave me an amused look. "I'll give it a shot." He tilted his head to the Reboots behind him. "I think you might want to explain that to them, too. Maybe tell them what to do when we get there?"

I nodded and slid from my chair. Riley moved farther into the shuttle, and the Reboots quieted as they turned to me. Even Beth and the other Over-one-twenties had largely left this plan up to me, and I shifted beneath the gaze of so many people.

I wondered if Wren felt this way. She'd always seemed confident in her plans, even if they'd been conceived five minutes prior. I knew that she didn't particularly enjoy being the center of attention, being the person everyone turned to for help, but I wondered if she was ever nervous. Did having the weight of so many lives on her shoulders stress her out?

I cleared my throat. "When we land, I'm going to Tony's house. It's not far, maybe a ten-minute walk. You guys stay here. A team of the best shooters should form a line outside the shuttle. I don't know whether to expect an attack from HARC or not."

A few faces grew eager, but for the most part no one looked excited about the prospect of a HARC attack.

"It's really important that you don't kill any humans unless you have to," I said, my voice low. "If you're under attack, I understand. But we want the humans in the slums on our side. If we're going to get Wren and Addie and all the Reboots still under HARC control back, we can't do it alone. If humans approach you, lower your weapons. Explain that to them."

"And if they don't listen?" Beth asked.

"Don't get confrontational. If things escalate, aim to wound, not kill." My eyes skipped over the crowd. "Do any of you have family in the Austin slums?"

Zero hands went up. I guess that was to be expected, as almost all the escaped Reboots were from the Austin facility and HARC didn't assign Reboots to their hometowns.

"What about Rosa?" I asked.

A bunch of hands went up.

"Okay. Good. As soon as we find Wren and Addie and get HARC out of Austin, anyone who wants to go to Rosa is welcome to join us. We're going to follow Micah's original plan to free the Reboots from HARC's control. Anyone who doesn't want to do that or thinks they can't stand being around humans is welcome to leave when we touch down in Austin."

A blast rocked the shuttle and I stumbled, grasping at the wall for support. We veered left and the Reboots slid sideways.

"Fence guards are firing!" George yelled, swerving us hard to the right.

I ran back to the pilot's chair, peering over his shoulder in time to see him swing to miss a shot from the ground.

"Do you need us to return fire?" I asked, gripping the back of his chair tightly.

"Nope," he said, increasing speed as we dove for the ground. "They weren't expecting us. They've got no one in the air."

I nodded as I scanned the sky, pointing to where I could see the top of the schoolhouse. "There. You should be able to land on the road."

"Got it."

"Any chance of a soft landing? I'd like you to be able to pilot this thing out of here if you have to."

He gave me a baffled look. "Are you kidding?"

I wasn't sure which way to take that until he swooped lower to the ground and placed us very gently on the road in front of the schoolhouse. The area around us was deserted, quiet, the patchy grass in front of the schoolhouse giving way to the dirt road we were parked on. In the distance were the outlines of houses and buildings, but there wasn't a human in sight.

"Stay here, okay?" I said to George. "If things get really bad while I'm gone, you feel free to take off. Don't wait for me."

He nodded. "Got it."

The shuttle door slid open and Beth stepped off with me, Riley right behind us. The second shuttle landed next to the first and the door opened. Isaac peered around the side, then motioned for the Reboots to follow him.

"I'm coming with you to Tony's," Riley said, sliding his gun from his waistband.

"I just told George to take off if things get bad here," I said. "You'll be stuck."

"So will you."

"I'm not leaving until I find Wren."

He nodded, glancing at Beth. "You hear that? If you have to leave, don't worry about us."

I turned to the sky. No HARC shuttles yet and no one on the ground. If the humans had heard something, they weren't investigating yet.

"Which way?" Riley asked.

I pointed. The directions were fuzzy in my head, but I remembered the general area. I knew what the house looked like.

I stole a glance over my shoulder as Riley and I took off running. The higher numbers had formed a line in front of the shuttles, weapons in hand but pointed at the ground. If they died or if something went wrong, that would be on me. Sure, I'd given them a choice, but it was my plan that put them here.

"They'll be fine," Riley said, tugging on my sleeve and making me face front again. "It's a good plan, Callum."

I wasn't sure he meant that, but I gave him a tight smile anyway. I turned right on a familiar road and increased my pace until Riley and I were running top speed down the slum roads.

The sound of gunfire cut through the night as we turned onto Tony's street. My chest tightened as I turned to look at the sky. Two sets of lights. HARC was coming.

Tony was already on his porch as we approached, a gun in his hand as he searched for the source of the commotion. Desmond ran out the door behind him, his eyes flashing with anger when he spotted us.

"Get away!" He jumped off the porch and strode across the lawn, gun pointed at my chest.

"We're here to help," I said, lifting my arms in surrender. Riley took a step forward and I quickly shook my head, motioning for him to stay put.

"Like hell!"

Tony walked closer to us, pushing Desmond's gun down. His face wasn't nearly as friendly as it had been last night.

"Is Micah here?" he asked, gesturing to the HARC shuttles in the sky.

"No. We left him at the reservation. The Reboots we brought want to help."

Desmond snorted. "What a relief. Are we supposed to trust everything you say now?" He glared at Riley.

"I'm on your side here." My voice rose as I looked between him and Tony. "And I brought the Reboots to do what you wanted." I pointed in the direction of the schoolhouse. "They're over there right now, fighting off HARC so you can take the city back."

"Then where will they go?" Tony asked, crossing his arms over his chest.

"There's nowhere for us to go," Riley said.

"We'll stay," I said with a nod. "I'm waiting for Wren and we'll need human allies if we're going to rescue Reboots in the facilities."

"So you saving us is more like you occupying us," Desmond spat.

I clenched my fists, trying to control my anger. Wren had said I was giving the humans too much credit. Maybe she was right. Maybe we should have left and let the humans solve their own problems.

"What do you expect?" I asked, trying to keep my voice controlled. "That we roll in, protect you, and then leave? We're not here to serve you, we're here as partners."

An explosion lit up the sky and I instinctively ducked, as did Tony and Desmond.

"Reboots are at the schoolhouse," I said. "Instructed to fight off HARC but to harm as few humans as possible."

"What did you mean, you're waiting for Wren?" Tony asked.

"Micah betrayed her and dumped her and Addie in bounty-hunter territory," I said. "You don't happen to know anything about bounty hunters, do you?"

"No, they're a whole different part of HARC. Mostly criminals given a second chance." He rubbed a hand over the back of his neck. "Addie, too? Leb's going to kill me."

"She'll be fine," I said tightly. "I'm sure the bounty hunters are no match for Wren."

"And we need to deal with this first," Riley said, pointing to where two more shuttles were flying in. "We could use some support."

Tony and Desmond glanced at each other, and the anger started invading my chest again. I'd counted on them helping. I'd counted on them being grateful and accepting us and being happy to work together.

"We'll see what we can do," Tony said, which didn't sound promising.

I whirled around, half expecting Tony to shout something more encouraging after he'd seen my angry face. But there was nothing but silence as I broke into a jog. Riley appeared beside me, and we turned to go back in the direction of the school-house.

"You and Wren were right," I said, glancing at him.

"I don't know, that went better than I expected. They didn't try to kill us."

I shook my head, biting back anger at the humans as we

rounded the corner. A HARC shuttle lay in two pieces on the
ground, and someone had tied an officer, bleeding but still
alive, to one of the halves. I almost laughed. At least they were
listening to my "only kill if necessary" suggestion.

Humans started coming out of their houses, trickling into
the street, and Beth was in the distance handing off a gun to a
teenage human who looked vaguely familiar. I squinted at his
slight frame and curly hair. Gabe. He'd been there the night we
first met Tony. A tiny sliver of hope wiggled into me among my
disappointment. At least someone was willing to help us.

He spotted me and waved, but a shuttle zoomed overhead
and a blast of gunfire blew up the dirt around me. I ducked
and ran, passing Isaac and three other Reboots returning fire
from the ground.

I stopped next to Beth, and she pointed at something behind
me. "Look."

I turned. A group of at least twenty humans ran toward
us, some of them armed. Their faces were tight with fear and
worry, but when they aimed their weapons, it wasn't at us. It
was at HARC.

TWENTY-TWO

WREN

"HOW BAD DO YOU THINK IT WOULD BE TO EAT THIS CANDY?"

I looked at the dirty pink package Addie was holding up. "Worse than eating rats, I think."

She examined it. "I disagree. I'm intrigued. They're advertising 'sour' like it's a good thing."

"I think there's a reason that's the only food left in here," I said, stepping over the mess of broken shelves and empty bottles. We'd found a fueling station not long after leaving the café, but it looked like it had been picked over many times before.

Something white and blue caught my eye, and I grabbed the edge and pulled out a giant bound book with the words *Map of the US* on the plastic cover.

"Got it," I said, flipping to the end of the book and finding Texas. I located the lake at the edge of New Austin, Lake Travis, and traced the route up with my finger. "There's an old Ranch to Market Road that goes straight there. If we find it and follow it, we should be fine." I glanced at her. "We might want to be careful, though. I wouldn't be surprised if HARC uses that road."

She nodded and we hopped over the debris on the way to the door. It was sunny and cold, and my leg was frozen where my pants were torn. The night had been quiet, not a human in sight, and now that Addie was fully healed, we could probably make good time to New Austin.

Addie crossed her arms over her chest as she emerged from the store. "How far is it?"

"Not that far. Fifteen miles, maybe." We were still in the middle of the city, crumbling buildings on either side of us.

"Cool." She gave me a worried look. "When we find Callum, we're going to go to Rosa, right? To rescue everyone? I know you weren't exactly wild about the idea, but you and Callum know Rosa."

"Yes," I said. "I told Callum I would." And maybe the idea was slightly less annoying than before. If Ever were still in there, I wouldn't have hesitated to go back for them. So what about all the others? The trainers I knew? The Under-sixties getting shot up with drugs? It didn't seem right to leave them.

"Good," she said with a smile. "Besides, I'm sure no one

really thought you were dead. They're probably expecting you."

"Why would they think I wasn't dead?"

"Not everyone was as brainwashed by HARC as you, Wren. Some of us were sort of suspicious when Reboots mysteriously went missing, especially the high numbers."

"I was not brainwashed."

"Yeah. Sure you weren't."

"I wasn't!"

Addie rolled her eyes like she seriously doubted it. "Anyway. They are probably expecting you to come back for them. Or at least hoping."

"That's wildly optimistic of them."

Addie punched my shoulder. "Stop acting like you don't care. You totally care. You're like a big ball of caring."

"Yes," I said dryly. "That's just the way to describe me."

"But my point is, the Rosa facility is the biggest. It has the most badasses like you. We release them, we get them to help us with the rest of the cities, run off HARC, save all the humans. Boom."

"Boom?"

"Yes. Boom. Done. Easy."

I raised an eyebrow at her.

"Okay, maybe not easy," she conceded.

"Maybe not." I tucked the map under my arm. "One step at a time, okay? I'm not doing anything until I find Callum. And then I wouldn't mind strangling Micah."

"I'm down with strangling Micah. Then let's push him out of a shuttle. Then let's chop his head off."

I laughed and she grinned at me.

"I'm not kidding," she said.

"I know you're not."

After a few miles, the big buildings of the city began to disappear and the road became narrower. It was also in better shape than most of the other roads in the city, confirming my suspicion that HARC used it for travel, but the homes lining it were in shambles. It looked like the entire area had been heavily bombed. This had probably once been a wealthy area, but now the houses lay in ruins.

When we turned onto the Ranch to Market Road to find a wide, empty street in decent shape, I scanned the sky warily. I pointed to the trees on the left side of the road.

"Maybe we should walk in the trees," I said. "I'm not sure being out in the open on the road is the best idea."

"Sounds good to me." Addie followed me across the black asphalt and to the trees. They didn't provide as much cover as I would have liked, as many of them had started to lose their leaves. The river that wound all the way to New Austin was right beneath us, the trees giving way to rocks and a steep incline.

"Where are you going to go when all of this is over?" Addie asked.

"I don't know," I said, leaves crunching under my boots as

we walked. "Callum and I had talked about it a little. He'd like to see the ocean."

"That would be nice."

"You?" I asked. "If the rebels manage to get rid of HARC, would you want to stay in the city with your family?"

"Maybe. If they wouldn't mind me staying with them. I miss Rosa."

"Oh yes. The smell, the trash, the lovely people. What's not to miss?"

She cast an amused glance at me. "I liked it."

"I'm sure your family wouldn't mind," I said. "Leb went to a lot of trouble to get you out. I assume he did that because he was hoping to see you again."

One side of her mouth turned up. "Yeah."

A familiar noise made my head whip around, and Addie froze in her tracks.

A shuttle.

I darted behind a tree, and Addie did the same. I slowly pulled my gun from my pants and clicked off the safety.

The shuttle made a banging sound as it hit the ground, and I let out a slow breath. It wasn't that far away. Not much more than fifty yards.

I glanced at Addie to see her face tight with fear, her fingers wrapped around her gun. I gestured for her to stay put and she nodded. The ground was littered with leaves and crunchy brown grass. If we ran now, they'd definitely hear us.

Silence followed the shuttle landing, and I wondered if they'd gone in a totally different direction. What were the odds they were searching for us anyway? It had been less than twenty-four hours since I'd killed those HARC guys.

Footsteps dashed my hopes. Several different footsteps. Coming toward us.

Addie met my eyes as we listened. As the footsteps got even closer, I peeked around the tree to see the corner of a black-clad shoulder. Then another.

I lifted my gun and nodded at Addie.

I ducked out from behind the trunk just in time to see HARC officers step off the road and head straight in our direction. I lifted my gun, my finger beginning to pull the trigger.

I paused.

They'd come prepared for us. They were in helmets with hard plastic covering. Each of them held a long black shield in front of them.

One of the officers darted forward when he spotted us, and I fired off two shots in his direction. They bounced off his shield.

I whirled around, grabbing Addie by the wrist. We took off as the officers began to fire, and bullets bit at my shoulders and legs.

Something wrapped around my ankles and I gasped as I went down. I kicked my legs, but the wire circled tight around them, digging into my skin.

Addie skidded to a stop and reached for me, but a blast rocked the earth and I only saw the outline of her as she hit the ground.

Someone snatched the gun out of my hand and I grasped his arm so loudly he yelled. But there was another officer there, holding my neck down.

Both my guns were gone. I managed to squirm from the officer's grasp, breaking a few of his fingers in the process. Addie was a few feet away, throwing punches at a HARC officer, and I caught him by the ankle and knocked him to the ground.

She leaped over him and grabbed me under the arms, but the wire was attached to something in the distance.

Two humans hit her at the same time and she fell with a grunt. I crawled for her, but humans had me by the arms and then the waist. There were four of them holding me, and all the twisting in the world didn't loosen their grip.

Defeat began to creep in as I watched two officers haul Addie to her feet.

"Radio in that we got One-seventy-eight," one of the officers said.

They didn't mention Addie. Of course they didn't. I was the one they wanted. And they wanted me alive, given the fact that I still didn't have a bullet in the brain.

My eyes met Addie's. I looked over her shoulder, at the empty space. The steep incline leading to the river.

Using the officers for leverage, I lifted my legs off the ground and slammed them into Addie's chest. She yelped as she flew backward.

One officer let her go, but the other dove for her arm, screaming as he started to fall down the incline. He quickly dropped her, scrambling to find his footing on the rocks. The other officer grabbed his jacket and yanked him back.

Addie disappeared over the side.

TWENTY-THREE

CALLUM

"ALL HUMANS EVACUATE IMMEDIATELY. PLEASE HEAD TO THE nearest HARC gate and exit now. A shuttle will be there shortly. I repeat. All humans—"

"Yeah, yeah," Isaac muttered as the announcement blasted from every HARC tower around Austin for the hundredth time. "We get it."

"I could shoot out the speakers in all the towers," Beth said, shotgun swung over her shoulder.

I shook my head, brushing dirt off my pants as I stood. "Don't. Let the humans leave who want to leave." I glanced at the humans milling around the area. The schoolhouse was still standing, but many of the homes were destroyed.

A family of three ran through the street, bags swinging, and I did a double take. *Not my family.* Would they be one of the groups sprinting for the nearest exit, or would they stay?

It appeared that most humans were staying. Many weren't talking to us, they were congregating in their homes or just outside. But they weren't running, and they weren't fighting us.

A few Reboots lifted their hands in a wave, bags slung over their shoulders, and I swallowed as I watched them go. That made almost fifty who had decided they didn't want to remain in Austin. Many who didn't have families couldn't be convinced to stay and help after we lost a few more Reboots last night, and our numbers would be maybe a hundred after they were gone. Riley was still working on getting an accurate count. Whatever it was, it was far less than I'd hoped.

Tony and Desmond stood at the end of the street, past a mess of shuttle parts, and I stepped over the debris as I headed in their direction. The humans around them stopped talking as I neared, but Gabe smiled at me.

"This is Callum," Tony said, clapping me on the back. "Twenty-two. He's the one who arranged everything." Tony's attitude toward me had improved tremendously when HARC retreated before sunrise and the humans reclaimed the city. Desmond still mostly scowled.

The humans visibly relaxed at the mention of my number. I didn't know whether I liked that reaction. If Wren were here, it would have been the opposite. They might even have run away in fear.

"I've been asking around, but I've got nothing on the bounty hunters yet," Tony said before I could ask. "And my connection to HARC is gone now, obviously."

"I just checked; the gates aren't live anymore," Gabe said. "If she wants to get in, she won't have much trouble."

I swallowed, trying to push back my fear. It was midmorning and still no sign of her. I wanted to hop in a shuttle and start circling the perimeter, but it was too dangerous. We'd run HARC out of Austin but they were setting up shop elsewhere, preparing for a fight. One shuttle on its own beyond Austin was sure to be shot down. Not to mention the fact that Wren would hide at the first sight of a HARC vehicle.

Riley came to a stop next to me, a frown on his face. "We should put some people at the HARC watchtowers. We'll want to know when they're coming back. And they can keep an eye out for Wren and Addie."

"I know a few who wouldn't mind," Gabe said, bouncing on his heels.

"Can we put people on the city side, too?" I asked. "Chances are Wren will try to enter on that side. She'd go back to the area where the tunnel is first."

"I haven't been over to the *rico* yet," Tony said. "You might want to do a quick sweep of the area, see how many humans are left and what kind of attitude they have."

"I'll go," I said. I looked down at my clothes, smeared with dirt and grime. I had a few things in the backpack slung over my shoulder, but maybe I could stop by my old house and grab more before it was blown up or something. Some of the Reboots were going through the slums, searching for empty homes to crash in. It wouldn't be long before they moved on to the city.

Tony held out a hand com. "Channel three," he said. "Don't say anything you don't want HARC to hear; this is their equipment. But I'll radio and tell you to come back if Wren shows."

I nodded and slipped the com into my pocket. Gabe found two humans to go with me, and three Reboots trailed behind us, Beth leading them. They didn't appear to want to talk to one another on the walk over and I didn't try to push it. Our alliance with the humans seemed tenuous at best.

The wall was unguarded, quiet, and I dug my fingers into the brick and hoisted myself to the top. I offered my hand to a human on the ground. He glanced over his shoulder, as if considering going back instead.

"The death doesn't rub off on you, I promise," I said as the other Reboots jumped over the wall. One of them snorted.

The human reddened and took my hand as he started up the wall. I pulled him to the top and held his hand as he found his footing on the other side of the wall. I did the same with the next one and then hopped down myself.

"Thanks," the younger guy said, his eyes flicking over me

for a moment like he was looking for something but didn't want to be too obvious.

We walked straight through the city and down Lake Travis Boulevard. There were a few humans out, sitting in front of stores, casually talking or eating like nothing was wrong. It appeared HARC hadn't touched this side of town, because everything was still pristine. I wasn't really surprised.

I nodded to one of the humans. "You want to talk to people over here, tell them where to go on the slum side to get instructions if they're staying?"

"Sure." He jogged away and I stopped, squinting in the sun at the part of town where I used to live.

"You guys going to the towers by yourselves? Things look pretty dead here." I pointed in the direction of my old house. "I'm headed that way. I'll comb the residential areas, see if I run into any humans."

"Yeah," Beth said, lifting her com. "We'll radio if we get into trouble."

The wind was chilly as I turned away from them, and I pulled my jacket tighter across my chest. I wondered if Wren was outdoors. If I was cold, she must have been freezing.

I took a quick glance down at my com, willing Tony's voice to come through any second. Part of the reason I'd volunteered to come over was to have something to do, something to stop me from exploding, but now I sort of wished I was back there, angling for a shuttle or making a lap around the Austin fence.

I turned onto my street and upped the volume slightly on the com. If I couldn't go search for Wren, this was the next best thing. Staying busy. It's what she would have told me to do.

I glanced at Eduardo's house as I approached it, looking for signs of life. He'd been one of my best friends, and willing to help me even after I Rebooted, but I wasn't sure how his parents felt. The swing in front of their white house moved with the breeze, but it was the only sign of life on the whole street.

I'd always been aware I lived in one of the poorest areas outside of the slums, but I'd liked my neighborhood. The guy who lived in the blue house across the street used to tell me I was "growing like a weed" every time we ran into each other. Even if he'd just seen me the previous day.

My house still had the auction sign in front and I took in a deep breath as I stepped onto the front porch. I hadn't locked it when I left a few days ago, and the doorknob turned easily when I tried.

It was empty, exactly as I'd left it. The kitchen cabinets were still open from where I'd hunted through them for food.

I trudged down the hallway to my room. The door was cracked slightly and I pushed it open.

I hadn't made the bed before we left, and it was the first thing my eyes found. The sheets were rumpled, one of the pillows half hanging off the bed. My chest tightened. I'd barely slept that night, the first and only time I'd had a girl in my bed, and the memory of the way Wren had curled up against me while she slept hurt suddenly.

I took in a ragged breath and tried to stop my brain from going down that path. A corner of my mind was trying to prepare me for the fact that she might be gone, and I refused to listen. Giving in for even a second was so painful I had to squeeze my eyes shut and focus on something else.

I yanked open one of my drawers and started shoving clothes into my empty backpack. I finished and meant to head for the door, but instead I found myself plopping down on the bed. The bag slid to the ground and I swallowed as I closed my eyes.

What was I supposed to do if she was gone? Lead the Reboots into Rosa? Find the bounty hunters and exact revenge?

That night we'd spent at Tony's, I'd told Wren she should help the humans and keep fighting if I died. I was pretty sure I wasn't going to live another day, and I was also pretty sure she had no intention of helping or fighting anyone. She'd tried to reassure me, but I could see in her eyes that she didn't mean it. I understood that now. The thought of jumping back into the fight if Wren was dead was exhausting. I would probably still do it, though, if only for vengeance.

I rubbed a hand across my forehead. If she came back—*when* she came back—we'd do whatever she wanted. Leave, stay, fight, whatever. Maybe she'd been right about staying out of it. Maybe I'd already done enough for the humans and we should leave. Taking charge of the Reboots and leading them to Austin had been easy. Getting humans to side with us? Not so much. Maybe I needed to focus on saving the Reboots, and let the humans solve their own problems.

The sound of the door opening made my head pop up.

Someone was in the house.

I jumped to my feet and swung my backpack over my shoulder. Would my parents come back? Why hadn't I considered that? HARC was gone; they could come back and reclaim their house if they wanted. Or had Wren found me? My heart soared for a moment, until I remembered that someone at the gate would have radioed to let me know. Everyone knew I was waiting for her.

"Callum?"

I blinked at the sound of my younger brother's voice from the front of the house. How did he know I was here?

Footsteps headed in my direction as I pulled open the bedroom door and strode into the hallway. David stopped short a few feet away, jumping when I emerged from my room.

"Hi," he said.

It had only been a few weeks since I'd died, but he looked older, different even than when I last saw him after tracking my parents down in the Austin slums with Wren. He was almost fourteen, but the dark circles under his eyes and tight expression on his face made him appear closer to my age.

"Hi," I said hesitantly. I'd often pictured his face when I came to the door that night. My parents had been horrified, but David's expression was more one of shock. I'd clung to the idea that maybe he didn't hate me as much as they did, and I found that my hands were shaking now that I was faced with him again.

He swallowed, shifting from foot to foot. We'd been close before I left, friends even, and I'd never seen him nervous around me. I took a small step back, trying to hide my own nervousness.

"I talked to some of the Reboots in the slums," he explained. "They said you'd come over to the city side. I figured you'd come here."

I tightened one hand around the strap of my backpack. "Do Mom and Dad know you're here?"

"No." He shrugged and sort of laughed. "They're holed up in the apartment. I snuck out. When I heard there were a bunch of Reboots in town I knew it was you."

I cocked my head. "How'd you figure that?"

"Because you came to our place and then, like a day later, the whole city explodes and all the Reboots are gone. Then the city explodes again and all the Reboots are back." He grinned. "You kinda bring trouble with you."

"Hey, that first time wasn't my fault. I was basically unconscious." I smiled at his perplexed expression. "It's a long story." Relief started to wash over me, and I pushed back the sudden urge to hug him. We weren't really the hugging type when I was a human, so now seemed like a weird time to start.

He nodded, clearing his throat. "You probably have a lot of stories, huh? You were at HARC?"

"Yes."

"What's your number?"

I held up my bar code. "Twenty-two."

He raised his eyebrows. "You're, like, practically still human."

I almost laughed, almost opened my mouth to tell him that was what all the Reboots thought, too, but I hesitated. Was I practically still human? I would have said yes last time I saw him, but now everything felt different. I'd killed someone and I'd been fully prepared to kill Micah, too. I hadn't, but I certainly never threatened to kill anyone as a human. On the other hand, I wasn't the monster my parents thought I was, either.

I shrugged, still not sure how to respond, and his gaze slid down to my waist, like he was noticing the two weapons there for the first time. "Mom and Dad feel bad about what happened. They just weren't expecting . . ."

I started down the hall, walking past him into the living room. "It's fine. Other people had warned me about what could happen if you drop in on your family. I should have listened." I kept my face turned away from him, not wanting my expression to betray how much that had hurt.

"No, you shouldn't have," David said, following me as I headed for the front door. "We didn't even know you Rebooted. Personally I'm glad you're alive. I mean, again."

A smile crossed my lips as I reached for the doorknob. "Mom and Dad are going to freak out when they realize you're gone, you know."

"Like I care."

I opened the door and turned to him. He was thinner than last time I'd seen him. We'd rarely had enough to eat, but he looked worse now, and it occurred to me that I must look better. I'd gained some weight and muscle at HARC, faster than I would have if I were a human. I'd never considered it before, but maybe I was the lucky one.

"You should tell Mom and Dad to come back, reclaim the house," I said. "You don't want someone else moving in."

"You could come tell them yourself."

I stepped onto the porch. "I'll pass on that."

"I think they want to see you."

"Then they can come see me. I'll let you know where I'm staying in the slums." I frowned as I headed to the auction sign in the front yard. "I should figure that out, I guess." I threw the auction sign on the porch and glanced at David. I didn't want him to go yet. I wanted to talk to him, to make sure he knew that even though I was different, I wasn't a monster.

I jerked my head toward the street. "I'm doing some rounds, letting the humans on this side know where they can meet with people in the slums. Want to come? Sometimes people run away when they see a Reboot coming. Might be helpful to have a human along."

He cocked his head. "Are you sure it's because you're a Reboot? It could just be your face."

I smiled as I tried to hold back a laugh. "Do you want to come or not?"

"Yeah, all right."

Two hours later, I headed back to the slum wall with David. There had been more people than I expected in the cities, ignoring HARC's order and curious to find out what the Reboots were doing. Tony and the rebels had done a good job of spreading the word about their partnership with Wren and Addie, and the human attitude toward Reboots seemed to be more one of cautious hope than fear. Luckily the rebels hadn't had time to explain about Micah, and I decided to keep it that way.

"Have you ever been shot?" David asked, continuing his endless stream of questions.

"Yes. A lot, actually."

"Stabbed?"

"Yes. And burned. And electrocuted. And I've had a lot of broken bones."

"Electrocuted?" David asked, mouth hanging open.

"On the Rosa HARC fence. It wasn't actually that bad. Getting burned is the worst, I think."

He kicked the dirt as he frowned at the ground. "So I know HARC said you were all bad or whatever, but obviously they were wrong. Do you think that maybe you're actually all better? Like, maybe they should be trying to make us all Reboots instead of fighting with you."

"I don't know about that."

"Why not? We'd all be practically invincible."

"And we'd all be the same. I think we should all just be who we're supposed to be."

David shrugged. "I guess."

I stopped as we approached the slum wall and cocked my head toward it. "Go ahead. I'm headed to one of the watchtowers for the night."

"Why? Are you making sure HARC doesn't come back?"

"Among other things." Thinking about Wren out there somewhere made my stomach churn.

"All right." He started to hoist himself over the wall, turning back to me. "I'll come find you again tomorrow, okay?"

A smile spread across my face. "Okay. Be careful, though. Tell Mom and Dad where you're going next time."

He snorted as he started to climb. "Yeah, right."

"David."

"Fine, whatever." He grinned at me before disappearing over the side of the wall.

TWENTY-FOUR

WREN

THE OFFICERS PUT SOMETHING OVER MY HEAD.

My vision was black as they dragged me across the dirt to where the shuttle was humming. It was getting increasingly harder to breathe through the bag, and I clenched my fists as I wriggled my hands in my handcuffs. They were too tight.

"Secure her legs before she gets on this shuttle. You can't take any chances with this one."

I took in a tiny breath at the sound of Officer Mayer's voice. He sounded so pleased with himself.

Someone shoved me to the ground and I kicked my legs, coming in contact with nothing but air.

"Give her one of the shots. I'm serious about keeping a short leash on this one, boys."

A needle pricked my neck and I pressed my lips together, stuffing back the urge to scream.

The world went dark.

My eyes wouldn't open right away. I was awake, and I could hear the bustle of humans around me, but my lids were glued shut.

"She's coming to, I think," an unfamiliar voice said.

"Is everything secure?" Officer Mayer asked.

"Yes." There was the sound of jiggling chains, and I felt them rub against my wrist. "All set."

I took in a sharp breath and tried to blink, letting in a tiny portion of light. The bag that had been over my head was gone. My left leg ached, and I squinted down to find the knee smashed, blood soaking my already-dirty pants. *Lovely.*

We were in a shuttle. I lay on the metal floor, handcuffed to a bar on the side by my wrists. Someone had chained my ankles together as well. Officer Mayer sat in the seat in front of me, an expression of supreme satisfaction on his face.

They hadn't killed me. I met his eyes as I realized this fact. Was I still valuable to them, after I'd caused all this trouble?

I shifted slightly and Officer Mayer watched my face closely. He looked down at my leg, which clearly was going to take hours to heal from those drugs they'd given me. Longer, if I wasn't able to put the bone back in the right place. He was almost eager as he searched my face.

"Does it hurt a little, One-seventy-eight?"

I snorted. Was he kidding?

The shuttle began to descend and I tried to twist around to see where we were. The pilot's door was closed.

We landed and the shuttle door slid open to reveal four guards, weapons pointed at my chest. Suzanna Palm, chairman of HARC, stood behind them, her face excited.

"All four of you," Officer Mayer said, gesturing to the guards. "Two carrying her and two keeping a gun on her at all times. You can't let her out of your sight, even for a minute."

One side of my mouth hitched up into a smile. It was flattering, how scared they were of me.

A guard unchained me and handcuffed my wrists together. He grabbed me underneath the arms, hoisting me to my feet, and the pain screamed through my leg. Another guard snatched them up and I had to clench my fingers into fists to keep from crying out.

The guard holding me by the boots wrinkled his nose, turning his face away from me. I was cold to him, dead and gross.

For a moment, I saw Micah's point about getting rid of them all.

They carried me out of the shuttle and I twisted in the human's arms, trying to catch a glimpse of where they were taking me. I didn't recognize the large, brick building. It wasn't Rosa. Or Austin.

As we passed through the entrance, the cold artificial air hit me and I shivered. The floors were white tile, the walls a nice cream color.

"Downstairs," Suzanna said. She glanced back at Officer Mayer. "Is she prepped already?"

"She is."

"Good. Put her in the cell for now."

The guards took me inside an elevator and we dropped several floors before the doors slid open again.

It was not as nice down here.

Rows of empty cells stretched out in front of me. HARC cells were usually glass and white and sterile, but here they were dirty little rooms with bars.

They dropped me on the floor of one in the middle, and I pressed my face into the concrete floor to distract myself from the pain.

The bars slammed shut behind them and I struggled to a sitting position. There wasn't even a bed in the cell. Just a toilet in the corner. The cells in front of me were empty, and silence engulfed the room.

I scooted back against the wall and looked around the tiny space. No windows anywhere. There was no way to tell what time of day it was. And judging by how many floors we'd dropped in the elevator, we were well hidden.

My heart sank as I took a deep breath. If I accepted I was going to die here maybe that would make it easier. Only a few weeks ago, I'd lived with the possibility that I could die at any minute and would certainly die within three years. I needed to get back to that place.

But that place was gone, apparently. That place was taken up with Callum, and my chest kept tightening as I wished I'd given him a better good-bye. I had no idea what that good-bye would be, but the one we had seemed inadequate.

I moved my legs slightly, forgetting that one was still broken. I closed my eyes against the blinding pain, trying to push it back to where I couldn't feel it. It was getting harder the longer I went without healing. I wasn't used to having to deal with broken bones for more than a few minutes. Even in training, when Riley had broken multiple bones a day, I'd had a short recovery period between each one. This pain was constant, and I didn't like it.

I leaned back against the wall, examining my mangled leg. What if it never healed? What if they figured out how to stop healing altogether one of these days? What if each shot was worse, and that leg healed all wrong and ugly? It would probably look worse than my chest.

I started laughing, a hysterical laugh that got louder as the panic began to fully set in.

TWENTY-FIVE

CALLUM

THE AREA BEYOND THE WATCHTOWER WAS QUIET ALL NIGHT, AND still except for the occasional swaying tree. I found the tower closest to the rebels' tunnel and paced alone in the small space all night. When morning came, I trudged past the fence and scouted the area, but there was nothing.

It was time to go find her.

"Leaving my post," I said into my com. "Coming in."

"*Got it,*" Riley's voice replied.

I headed over the hill and past the outskirts of town to the slum wall. The city was starting to move, and there were a lot more humans out and about today. Their attitude seemed to be one of avoidance, like they were going to ignore the Reboots and pretend none of this was happening. Whatever worked for them.

I hoped my parents and David had come back last night to the house; otherwise it was probably in the process of being claimed by someone else.

I reached the wall and hopped over, landing softly on the other side, then I started down the dirt path in the direction of the schoolhouse. I wondered how much equipment HARC had left in the Austin facility. Any transport vans or shuttles? Maybe I could snag one and head out to look for Wren and Addie. Screw what everyone said about it being too dangerous. She would search for me, even if there was a high likelihood of HARC spotting her.

A Reboot ran across my line of vision, and then another. I frowned, turning to see where they were headed.

I could see nothing but houses and trees, but beyond that was the HARC fence.

I broke into a jog.

There were no shuttles, no shooting, no panicking. It wasn't HARC at that fence.

"*Reboot at the south fence.*" Riley's excited voice came through my com.

I ran faster as a clump of Reboots came into view. They were standing in front of the fence around someone. I couldn't see who but—

I stopped. It was Addie. And she was alone.

* * *

I rubbed a hand across my forehead and tried to breathe. The air was stuck in my chest, unable to get past the lump in my throat.

Wren had been captured.

"She pushed me over into the river to save me," Addie said, pulling the blanket one of the Reboots had given her tighter around her shoulders. She sat on the grass in the middle of a circle of Reboots, not far from the fence where she'd come in. I was across from her, trying not to panic. I was not succeeding.

She looked at me and swallowed. "I'm sorry."

I shook my head. "Don't be. It's not your fault." That sounded exactly like Wren, actually. In the midst of fighting for her life, she saw an opportunity to save Addie so she took it. I cleared my throat to push back the sudden urge to cry.

"I tried to get here as fast as I could but I walked the wrong way for miles and had to circle back."

"Did you recognize the HARC officers?" I asked.

She shook her head miserably.

"But they wouldn't kill her, right? If they wanted to kill her, they would have done it then," I said. "They had an opportunity, didn't they?"

"Definitely." She nodded. "They were holding us, and the guy told someone he had her."

Hope bloomed in my chest as I turned to Riley. "Where would they take her?"

"My first guess would have been here. Suzanna Palm uses the Austin capitol as a place to interrogate criminals. But with the way things are now, they're not going to risk flying a shuttle into the city."

"So Rosa, then. Right? That would be their next choice."

"Maybe," Riley said. "But Tony said they're taking all the Austin refugees to New Dallas. HARC could be setting up shop there."

Addie squinted at something behind me and I turned to see Tony and Gabe running for us, excitement on their faces.

"Oh, thank goodness," Tony said with a sigh when he spotted Addie. "Your dad would have killed me." He took a glance around. "Where's Wren?"

"A group of HARC officers captured her." I got to my feet, running a shaky hand through my hair. I wanted to freak out. I could feel the urge starting to close in, making it hard to think, and I looked around wildly for someone to step forward with an idea.

Riley frowned in thought, but everyone else was staring at me, clearly having already decided *I* was the one who was supposed to know what to do.

And they were right. If I wanted Wren back, I needed to step up and organize everyone before it was too late.

"We need to find out which facility she's in," I said, turning to Tony. "Can you get word to Leb in Rosa? Do you have someone in New Dallas?"

Tony nodded. "We're already trying to communicate with the other cities about what happened here. I don't have many people in New Dallas, but I can try."

"Do you know what they would do with her?" Addie asked. "That could help, right? If we know what they want?"

Tony cleared his throat, dropping his gaze to the ground. "HARC has always wanted to know why some kids take so long to Reboot. Why they're strong like Wren. I'd say it's likely they're going to experiment on her." He winced and spoke softer. "There may not be a lot of time to find her in, um, one piece."

My stomach lurched into my throat and I tightened my hand into a fist. The thought of them taking Wren apart and dissecting her made the world swim in front of my eyes.

"And if I were going to guess, they took her to Rosa," he continued. "We never had much of a rebel presence there, and they might know that."

I took a deep breath, trying to push my worries about Wren under the surface for a moment. That's what she would do. She'd launch into action and then get upset about it (maybe) later, in private.

"You think you can maybe find out for sure?"

"I'll do my best."

I gave him a grateful look and turned to Riley. "Let's start getting a group together to go after her. We'll wait until tomorrow to see if we can get confirmation of where Wren is, but I'm heading out either way. I can't wait anymore."

TWENTY-SIX

WREN

I WOKE UP STRAPPED TO A TABLE. I HAD A HARD TIME OPENING MY eyes again, but when I did the lights on the ceiling were too harsh and bright after my dark cell.

I wiggled my ankles. They were chained to the metal table, like my hands, and there was no way out of them, even though my leg had healed. How long had it been? I didn't even remember someone coming into the cell and giving me something to knock me out, but they must have.

I turned at the sound of voices beside me. It was Suzanna and Officer Mayer, heads bent close as they talked to each other. Suzanna gestured to me and the commanding officer straightened. He still had that smug expression on his face I so desperately wanted to wipe away.

I scanned the room. It looked like a smaller HARC medical lab. I was on a table in the middle of the room, a tray of sharp instruments to my left. A computer hummed in the corner, next to a cabinet of vials filled with liquid. Maybe they were going to make me crazy like Ever.

Suzanna crossed her arms over her chest and squinted at me. Maybe not crazy. Ever had seemed stronger when she was crazy, and I couldn't see that situation ending well for them. I swallowed as my eyes flicked over the equipment. This seemed bad.

Officer Mayer pulled a chair up next to me and sort of smiled. It wasn't a real smile. He'd actually given me one before, when I'd completed a mission to his satisfaction. He'd even liked me, in a way. Maybe that was part of the hate I saw in his eyes now. I'd let him down.

I smiled back.

Suzanna shuffled around the room, picking out a few vials. I cursed myself again for not asking Micah more about the experiments he'd been through at HARC. What had he said about them? There was one that made everything look purple?

I'd already encountered the one that made me heal slower. That one was not fun.

Suzanna was at my side suddenly, and something sharp pricked my neck. The liquid she pressed in burned, a little at first, and then so badly I clenched one of my hands into fists.

The burn started to scream down my entire body and I swallowed hard, resisting the urge to yell.

Instead I closed my eyes. They'd never specifically trained me to withstand torture, but they might as well have. Perhaps I hadn't realized it before Callum, but what they did to all Reboots was a form of torture.

When I opened my eyes, Suzanna was above me, her face crinkled in confusion. "Which expression means she's in pain?"

"That's the only expression she has."

"Hmmm . . ." She cocked her head, her gaze skipping down my body. She pointed at my clenched fist. "Oh, that looks like she's in pain. Good." She gestured at something. "Hand me the next one."

"Suzanna . . ." Officer Mayer sounded stressed as he got up from his chair.

"What?" she snapped.

"Let's . . ." He turned his back to me and lowered his voice. I heard him anyway. "Let's kill her. Let's kill them all."

It sent a chill down my body and I swallowed down a wave of panic.

Suzanna glared at him. "Killing every Reboot who steps out of line is shortsighted. With the right drug combination, we'll be able to wipe out the defiant part of their brains." She gestured to me. "We can put our best Reboots back in the field, even if they were once determined to rebel. Get this one back to her old obedient self."

I clenched my fingers into fists, pushing down the urge to thrash against the cuffs. I didn't want to be their mindless slave again. I didn't want to return to taking orders and killing people when they told me to.

"If you—" Officer Mayer started.

"When I want your opinion on my Reboots, I will ask for it, Albert," Suzanna snapped.

She pulled the computer over and positioned it next to me. She squinted at the screen. "Let's get started."

I grunted as the guard dumped me onto the hard concrete floor. He didn't bother to take the cuffs off my hands and feet before he slammed the door, and I had to wriggle around to get into a sitting position.

I leaned against the wall and closed my eyes against the spinning. I'd been on that table for hours, and the spinning had been constant since about the second shot.

I think I would have preferred death to sitting in here like a lab rat. I would have even preferred death to being "fixed" with their drugs and put back in a facility.

I tucked my face against my knees as Callum's face popped into my head. When I pictured him, it was always that day at HARC when I made him punch me, and we were standing in front of his room, his arms wrapped around me, so close I almost kissed him. The look he had that night was my favorite expression of his—amusement mixed with attraction and a healthy dose of annoyance. I would probably never see that look again. Or any look from him.

I wondered if Addie made it back and found him. If the situation had been reversed, I would have marched straight into the first HARC facility I could find and started searching for him. I suspected Callum's reaction would be the same.

A smile crossed my lips.

TWENTY-SEVEN

CALLUM

"NEW DALLAS," I REPEATED, LOOKING FROM TONY TO DESMOND. "You're sure?"

"Yes," Tony said. "I just got word back from one of the officers there. They've got her locked away from the other Reboots, in the old human cells."

"I thought Rosa was more likely," Riley said, stepping up next to me.

Tony leaned back in his chair. We were in his kitchen, surrounded by about twenty humans. A group of them sat with us at the table; the rest milled around the living room and spilled out onto the porch.

"They're setting up a command center in Rosa," Tony said.

"Sending all HARC personnel from Austin there. It's basically the human base of operations now, and they didn't want One-seventy-eight anywhere near it, especially given how familiar she is with the Rosa facility. And New Dallas is better equipped for prisoners. They did a lot of experiments on adult Reboots there."

Addie looked at me excitedly. "Then we can go tonight, right?"

"Yes. Definitely." I turned to Tony, swallowing hard. "Did they know anything about . . . her condition?"

"All he knew was she was there. I'm sorry. I got nothing else."

"That's all right." I sighed with relief. If she was there, she was probably alive. She had to be alive. It had only taken Tony about twenty-four hours to find out where she was, and I had to hope that was fast enough.

"I'll start getting the Reboots ready and prep the shuttles," Riley said. "We'll need to leave some people here to guard the city." He nodded at Tony. "How do you want to split your men up? How many will come with us?"

A long silence followed Riley's words, and my heart dropped at the uncomfortable expression on Tony's face.

"No humans are going to New Dallas," he said quietly.

"Why not?" Addie asked. "If we're going in, we're going to try to free all the Reboots there, too, right?" She looked at me for confirmation.

"That's what I was hoping." I turned to Riley and he nod-ded in agreement.

"You can ask around, but I've talked to a lot of people," Tony said, folding his hands on top of the table. "We're not doing another rushed raid into a HARC facility. We don't feel like it's the best use of our resources right now."

I stared at him for a moment. "You mean rescuing Reboots isn't the best use of your resources. Rescuing Wren."

He dropped his eyes. "It's not."

I cast an angry look between him and Desmond. "None of this would have even happened without Wren! The HARC facility here would still be running and you'd all still be screwed if it wasn't for her!"

"We were part of that raid, too," Desmond said, though a guilty look crossed his face. "She didn't do it alone."

"And neither did you," I said.

"Do we at least have some human support in New Dallas?" Riley asked. "A way into the facility?"

"I can tell you where the Reboot rooms are and where the control room is," Tony said. "I have a guy inside who agreed to leave the door on the roof open, so you can get in that way. You'll probably be able to make it past the fence in a shuttle no problem. Apparently there are HARC shuttles coming in and out of all the cities right now." He sighed. "But that's it. It's too risky for any of the humans to help you."

Addie made an annoyed sound and threw her hands in the air.

"Oh, come on," Desmond said. "You don't need us. Or any

human help. You've got a hundred Reboots here. When you break the others out of New Dallas, you'll have double that."

"Eighty-three," Riley corrected. "A bunch took off."

"Get the doors unlocked, like you did last time," Tony said to Addie, "and everything will be fine."

"Everything will be fine" seemed optimistic to me. I hadn't considered it before, but Wren and Addie had taken a terrible chance by going into the Austin facility. They could have been trapped inside. HARC didn't just build locks; they built locks with steel doors with pass codes and cameras, in a facility safely behind two different fences.

Getting us inside another one was incredibly risky, even with eighty-three Reboots.

"What about the other facilities?" Addie asked. "Are you going to help us with those?"

A pained expression crossed Tony's face, so Desmond answered for him. "No. We've talked to the humans in the area, and everyone agrees we should focus on rebuilding here. We're going to make this a HARC-free zone, and work on bringing in humans from other cities."

I ran my hands down my face with a heavy sigh. They expected us to invade the facilities and rescue the Reboots. Maybe it wasn't even that crazy of an expectation. They'd always made it clear they wanted us to leave after we deprived HARC of Reboots. Why was I even surprised?

I glanced over at Riley and Addie. We were the only three

Reboots in the house, and it was as if the humans had drawn an invisible circle around us. They all danced around it, keeping their distance like we couldn't be trusted not to lash out and attack them at any moment. Some of them had witnessed me do exactly that, and maybe they would never see anything but a Reboot who murdered a human.

Wren had been right. I'd given the humans too much credit because I'd still seen them through my old human eyes. I'd remembered how they treated me when I was alive, when I was one of them. I'd ignored how they treated me since I Rebooted—they screamed, they attacked, they feared.

Why had I wanted to save them? Why had I been horrified that Wren didn't? Of course she didn't. She'd been dealing with this for five years. She knew they would never trust us.

"Okay," I said, crossing my arms over my chest. "We're going to take all the Reboots willing to help to New Dallas tonight. Only as many that will fit in one shuttle, though, because we'll need the other one for the new Reboots."

Riley frowned. "Do you think we can get two shuttles safely in and out of the city?"

"I have no idea." I turned to Addie. "We need to explain to everyone how dangerous it's going to be. They need to understand there's a possibility we'll be shot down or trapped in HARC or killed. No one has to go if they don't want to."

"Got it," Addie said. "I think plenty will still want to go. Wren helped save the Austin Reboots, after all."

"Reservation Reboots might be less inclined," Riley said. "But I bet there's some."

"Tell them I will be eternally grateful." I turned back to Tony and the other humans. "And we're done."

Tony raised his eyebrows.

"After I get Wren back, we'll empty out the rest of the facilities. Or as many as we can. Then we're leaving. Good luck with HARC. Good luck if Micah comes back. You're on your own."

I paced up and down the grass in front of the big shuttle that afternoon as the sun began to set. I'd already prepared the Reboots, and Riley had raided HARC for more gas. Of the eighty-three Reboots we had left, almost all agreed to go with us. The humans would have to protect Austin by themselves.

Now I just had to wait, and it was killing me.

"Callum." Addie grabbed my arm, making me stop, and held out a plate. "You should eat."

I looked down at the sandwich. I didn't feel hungry, but I suddenly couldn't remember the last time I ate. It must have been at the reservation. If Wren were here, she would tell me I needed my strength.

I took the sandwich off the plate and held out half of it to David, who sat next to Addie on the grass. He hesitated, then gave me a small smile as he took it.

"Thank Gabe," Addie said, tilting her head toward him.

"He's the one who thought to clean out HARC's food before it went bad."

"They cut the power to the facility a few hours ago," Gabe said. "But we've got some people working on getting it back up."

"Thanks," I said in between bites.

Gabe plopped down on the grass next to Riley and Addie. He squinted at David. "You made a bunch of them at Tony's feel bad."

David gave him a confused look as he took a big bite of his sandwich. "What'd I do?"

"Some of them have Reboot kids. Seeing you so relaxed about a Reboot family member made them feel guilty."

"They should feel guilty," I muttered. "But our parents did nothing but scream when they saw me last time, so they're not alone."

"They want to see you now," David said, straightening and giving me a hopeful look. "They mentioned it again this morning."

"Then they can come see me. I'll be at the HARC facility down the street."

David nodded, his face falling a little. I doubted my parents wanted to step foot inside a HARC facility, especially one taken over by Reboots. But I certainly wasn't going to go out of my way to find them again.

"Personally, I'm glad I never knew my family," Riley said. "All this parent stuff seems really stressful."

I almost laughed but it died in my throat, pushed down by the rock of pain sitting in my chest.

"It's going to be fine," Addie said softly. "She's going to be fine."

I nodded as I resumed my pacing. "She is. She probably already burned New Dallas to the ground and doesn't even need us to come get her."

They all laughed and agreed and I tried to force a smile onto my face like I wasn't worried.

"I'm going to feel guilty forever if she's not okay," Riley said quietly, after a long pause. He picked at the grass. "I knew Micah used to drop bad Reboots. I should have warned you guys."

"Guilt isn't going to help anyone," Addie said. She looked pointedly at me. "Is it?"

I didn't know if she was talking about my guilt for making Wren stay at the reservation, or my guilt about killing the human. It had all formed into one giant lump of awful in my chest.

"No," I admitted. "Doesn't mean it's not still there."

"But that's good, right?" David looked up at me. "Before you came back, I thought Reboots didn't feel guilt. It seems like good news that you still do."

"True," I said with a small smile. It was only a few days ago I'd wished away my guilt about killing that man, but David had a point. It would be worse without it.

"I like to harness guilt into kicking people's asses," Addie said.

David turned a worried look from me to Addie and scooted a little farther away from her. I bit back a laugh as Addie arched her eyebrow in amusement.

I glanced back at the shuttles, armed and prepared for take-off. "I think that sounds like an excellent plan."

TWENTY-EIGHT

WREN

MEAT.

My arms wouldn't move. My legs wouldn't move. I was on a hard table and I couldn't move.

I couldn't get to the meat.

I squinted in the bright light at the figures around me, snapped my teeth, and thrashed against the metal holding my wrists.

Mumbled voices floated in the air, and a man came into sight. He was juicy meat, plushy meat, fatty meat.

I growled, lifting my head as far as it would go. Meat moved away.

The voices around me were louder, and the meat was holding

my arms and legs. I flailed until the table began to wobble and the voices grew louder. Panic. I liked the panic. The panic made the meat smell better.

I wrenched one arm free and grabbed at the closest meat.

Everything went black.

I blinked, squinting at the blurry walls of my cell. My head was heavy and cold. My cheek was pressed to the freezing concrete.

I slapped my hands against the floor and started to push myself up, gasping as a wave of dizziness crashed over me. I was going to vomit.

No, I wasn't. There was nothing in my stomach. I couldn't.

The hunger was so intense, suddenly I could barely breathe. I felt sick, and hot, and cold, and confused. I blinked again and the bars of the cell came into focus. How long had I been in here?

I squeezed my eyes shut and collapsed on the ground again, not caring that it was freezing.

The door opened and I mustered the energy to glare at the guard who entered.

He tried to make me shuffle down the hallway in my chains, but I was weak and kept swerving into him. He made disgusted noises every time I touched him, so I fell entirely against him. He yelled and I ended up on the floor. It was not my most well-thought-out plan.

He shoved me along in front of him the rest of the way,

and when we emerged from the elevator, Suzanna and Officer Mayer were waiting in front of the lab. Officer Mayer snorted as soon as he spotted me.

I caught a glimpse of myself in the long lab window. My hair was dirty and messy. I couldn't make out my features very well, but my eyes looked dark and sunken in. I seemed smaller somehow, like I'd shrunk even more. That didn't seem fair. I didn't have any spare inches.

"Feeling better, I see," Suzanna said as the guard hauled me onto the table. "I wasn't sure that antidote would work."

Was this better? When had she seen me last? Ever's face flashed in front of me, that crazed, hungry look she'd had in the days before her death, and I winced as the humans began to shuffle around the room. I now understood her panic, her sobs when I told her what was happening to her. I don't think I fully appreciated the terror she felt until this moment.

Suzanna stuck a needle in my arm and I glanced down to see my blood running into a bag. She poked a hole in my other arm and hooked a bag to that one, too.

"What happens if you drain a Reboot dry?" Officer Mayer asked.

"They pass out. They come back, though." Her lip curled as she looked at me. "They always come back."

"You don't always come back, you know. Sometimes Reboots die for real."

My head fell to the side as the memory edged into my brain,

Riley's voice as clear as the day he'd first said that to me, early in my Reboot training.

"Is this how you want to be in the field? Do you want everyone to see you as a pathetic little mess?" Riley had asked after I'd been shot on an assignment and was curled into a ball in the dirt, gasping for air.

"Up." He pulled me to my feet by my collar. He was tall for a fourteen-year-old. I'd been surprised when he told me his age. The assignment was on the ground behind him, hands and feet bound.

Riley dumped the bullets out of the human's gun and held them toward me. "You always take the bullets out of the gun before you go back to the shuttle. And you hold the gun by the barrel. If a guard sees you approaching holding a gun by the handle, they will shoot you."

I whimpered, crossing my arms more firmly over my blood-stained shirt.

Riley sighed, lowering the gun and bullets. "Do you want to die? Again? For real this time?"

I just stared at him. Maybe I did. Maybe death was better than this.

"Because if you let them kill you, what does that say about you? Is that who you want to be?"

I'd swallowed, his words pulsing through my whole body. That wasn't who I wanted to be.

"You can be the best," he said. "You're One-seventy-eight. Do you want to be the biggest disappointment, or the greatest success?"

I didn't want to be a disappointment. I'd felt like one most of my life.

"I know it's a lot of responsibility," he said, his voice softer than usual. "And I know you're really young. But life isn't fair. Or Rebooting isn't fair. Either way, it was the hand you were dealt. Your choice what to do with it."

I took in a long, slow breath. I'd decided I wanted that responsibility, the pressure of being the best. I'd let it consume me and I'd come out the other side as someone I was vaguely proud of. But now, I think I was only someone HARC could be proud of.

"Your choice what to do with it."

Suzanna and Officer Mayer put their heads together, and I felt a sudden panic zip through my body. I didn't want to die here. I didn't want them to win. I didn't want Callum to think that my choice had been only myself, and that I didn't care what happened to the other Reboots or the humans who had helped us.

I didn't want to be a mindless slave who did what they wanted without question. Who had run away the first chance she got and hadn't wanted to try and help others still stuck in the same situation.

That wasn't the choice I wanted to make. That wasn't someone I could be proud of.

TWENTY-NINE

CALLUM

THE METAL OF THE SHUTTLE CLANGED UNDER MY BOOTS AS
I stepped inside. The seats were already all taken, and Reboots
piled in after me. We had about sixty, which was less than I
had originally thought, but I couldn't expect everyone to jump
on board with saving Wren, even if we were freeing the New
Dallas Reboots in the process.

As I leaned against the shuttle wall, I caught Tony's eye.
He stood outside next to Desmond, watching as the Reboots
boarded. I'd thought Wren was wrong about how self-serving
humans are, and now I felt incredibly dumb. I looked forward
to telling her how right she was.

"Wait! Wait!" a voice called as the shuttle door began to
close. Gabe darted inside, dressed in black clothes and armed.

He nodded at me and I blinked.

"Gabe—" Tony stepped forward.

"You said when I joined you guys I made all my own decisions and accepted the consequences. Going with them is the right thing to do. I accept the consequences."

Tony closed his mouth as defeat crossed his face. For a moment, I thought Gabe's outburst would prompt a show of support from other humans. Desmond looked between the two of us, his brow furrowed in thought, the angry expression he'd been wearing since we arrived gone. But he said nothing as the door slid shut.

I gave Gabe a grateful look as we started to lift off the ground. "Thank you."

He shrugged, bouncing a little from foot to foot. "It could have been me. I almost died of KDH a couple years ago. I don't see staying human as anything more than luck. I don't understand why it's such a big deal."

"I'd say it's bad luck you are human," Addie said, a corner of her mouth turning up.

"Hey, maybe I'll die tonight and I can give you an opinion about it tomorrow."

Addie laughed. "And have you whine about the pain? Stick with me, all right? I'll try to take any bullets for you."

"That might be the nicest offer I've ever had from a girl."

Addie blinked, pink spots appearing on her cheeks as Gabe grinned and started making his way across the shuttle, toward the pilot's door.

"That was weird, right?" She looked at me expectantly.

"Uh, I don't know, Addie."

"I mean, a human flirting with a Reboot is weird." She looked to me for confirmation but I just shook my head in amusement. She nodded, as if convincing herself. "It's weird."

I chuckled, then quickly wiped the smile off my face. I shouldn't be laughing. I needed to focus on Wren. It could already be too late, and I couldn't be laughing while she was dead.

Addie's gaze slid to where Gabe was standing with Riley and Isaac. He was watching her, too. I gestured with my head for her to go and she paused for a second before slowly walking over.

I closed my eyes as I leaned my head back against the shuttle wall. *"Focus,"* Wren would say.

My brain didn't want to focus. It wanted to panic and run through horrible scenarios. Being on this side of things sucked. I didn't like being the one who was fine while Wren was captured. I didn't like being the one the other Reboots looked to for a plan. I could see why she tried to avoid it.

I pushed my hands into my pockets and tried to listen to the hum of the shuttle instead of the shouting in my head. I kept my eyes closed as we flew, ignoring the conversations around me.

"Brace yourselves!" the shuttle pilot called about fifteen minutes later. "We're approaching New Dallas."

Focus.

THIRTY

WREN

MY HEAD HURT WHEN I OPENED MY EYES. I GRIMACED, WONDERING if the headache was a side effect of the drugs, or if they'd done it on purpose. As my vision began to clear, the pain faded slightly, and I realized I was in the lab again. I hated how they could steal my time and I'd wake up with no idea where I was or how long I'd been there. If it weren't for the growing hunger in my stomach (which wasn't that bad yet, indicating it had only been two or three days), I would have had no idea how long I'd been a prisoner.

Officer Mayer drifted into the light and out again, and I heard Suzanna Palm talking from somewhere behind me.

I had a needle in my arm, and I squinted down at my blood

running into a bag. There was a full bag next to it, and I was
woozy.

" . . . eliminate her?" Officer Mayer's voice was a whisper.

I swung my head to either side, stretching my arms slightly.
The metal cuffs around my wrist banged against my skin.

I wondered what Callum was doing. Was he still looking—

I took in a sharp breath. The cuffs. They'd moved around
on my wrist.

I glanced across the room to where Officer Mayer and
Suzanna were still deep in conversation. I barely moved one
arm.

Someone had forgotten to tighten the cuffs.

I began squirming against the cuff farthest away from them.
My hand slipped out in seconds.

I swallowed down a wave of excitement. I slowly twisted
my other wrist around, the one in their line of sight. Officer
Mayer glanced at me and I stopped, blinking blankly at him.
He turned back to Suzanna.

My skin burned as I yanked my hand harder against the
cuff. Suzanna's eyes widened.

"Get her! She's—"

My hand popped free and I shot up to a sitting position,
yanking the needle from my arm. The world tilted violently
and my attempts to hop off the table resulted in me facedown
on the floor.

A hand grabbed my foot and I kicked, gasping as I

desperately clawed at the floor. The world tilted and shook and for a moment I thought it was just the drugs making me dizzy, but Suzanna's face twisted in confusion. Another loud *boom* sounded from somewhere below me.

Officer Mayer grabbed me by the shoulders, hauling me into a sitting position. "I told you we should kill her," he panted.

Yells came from outside. I turned toward the door, hope racing through my body.

"Go," Suzanna said, blowing a curly strand of hair from her eyes. Officer Mayer raced out, and she settled her gaze on me as she pointed a gun to my forehead. "I got this."

My eyes locked on hers. She didn't have the best grip on the gun, and I didn't know why she'd just told Officer Mayer to go. She obviously didn't use a weapon often.

She hesitated, and I forced my vision to focus as I stared at her. She wasn't wavering because she was conflicted about whether it was right to kill me, that was for sure. I knew it was because she was weighing her investment, her loss if she wasn't able to research me further and put me back in the field. Her disappointment in me was just as obvious as Officer Mayer's.

A smile started to form on my face, and Suzanna gave me a confused look. I was proud that I disappointed them. I wasn't emotionless or hardened or the perfect monster they thought I was. I was trained.

I lunged forward so suddenly Suzanna gasped, almost dropping the gun in an attempt to fire it. I snatched it out of her hand and slammed my palm into her chest. Her back hit the ground.

She dove for the gun in my hand again, growling as her fingernails dug into my arm. I fired one shot into her head.

I let out a sigh of relief as my legs gave out and I hit the ground. I didn't usually look at humans after I killed them, but I stared at her blank eyes. I'd killed her in self-defense, and I couldn't say I minded that she was dead, but I wished I hadn't had to do it at all. Maybe that was what Callum meant when he tried to explain the difference between me and Micah. I'd never killed someone if I didn't have to.

I turned away from Suzanna, a strange mix of relief and sadness mingling in my chest as I crawled for the door.

THIRTY-ONE

CALLUM

THE NEW DALLAS HARC FACILITY LOOKED VERY MUCH LIKE ROSA from the roof. It was empty, but the door was propped open, just as Tony had said. The small ground team had already jumped off the other shuttle, and smoke lapped up the side of the building from their bombs.

The shuttle took off as the last Reboot stepped onto the roof, headed for the front entrance to pick up Reboots as they escaped.

"We're in the basement." I put a hand to my ear as Isaac spoke through my com. *"She's not down here. Guard is saying they took her upstairs."*

"Which floor?" I asked, running for the stairwell as I pulled my gun from my pocket.

"*Hold on.*" There was a brief silence before he spoke again. "*He's saying two or three. Not sure. Medical floors somewhere.*"

"Okay." I threw open the stairwell door and rushed down the steps, sixty Reboots flying after me.

"*All Reboots to your rooms immediately.*" The voice on the intercom was loud and firm.

I cursed and ran faster, rounding the tenth-floor landing. We'd hoped to get to the Reboots having dinner in the cafeteria before HARC ordered them to their rooms and locked the doors, but given that announcement, it didn't look good. Hopefully Addie would be able to get to the control room and unlock the doors again, like she did in Austin. I twisted around to see her and Gabe and a few other Reboots opening the door to the eighth floor, where the control room was.

I passed the sixth floor, where the Reboot rooms were located in this facility, and the rest of the Reboots split off. Only Riley and Beth stayed with me.

I flew onto the third floor and ran down the hall, Riley and Beth close behind me. Everything was locked up tight, the white walls blank. I turned around and sprinted back to the stairs, rounding them down to the second floor. I glanced behind me as I threw the door open wide enough for Riley and Beth to get through.

I ran smack into something, and I blinked as I wrapped my fingers tighter around my gun.

Officer Mayer. His eyes widened in recognition and he took several quick steps backward, stumbling slightly. I raised my gun as I strode after him, locking my gaze on his as I aimed the barrel at his head.

He reached for the weapon on his belt and I lunged forward, twisting his hand and extracting the gun as he yelled.

He wrenched away and whirled around like he meant to run, but I kicked the back of his knees, hard, and he hit the ground with a crunch. Around me, the building shook, the echo of gunfire sounding through the hallway.

I grabbed his shirt and yanked him around to face me. Leaning down closer, I pressed the gun to his forehead.

"Wren," I said.

He was breathing heavily, wheezing as fear started to spread across his face. He shook his head. "I don't know."

"Then we should eliminate you," I said slowly. "There's no room here for a human who doesn't perform well."

His mouth opened and closed, panic in his eyes at his own words being thrown back at him. "I . . . I can . . ."

"So you don't think I should eliminate you, then." My grip on his collar was so tight he couldn't breathe anymore, and he clawed desperately at my fingers.

"Callum."

I looked up at the sound of Riley's voice to see a blond head crawling out of a room a few doors down.

Wren.

Relief washed over me with such force that I started running for her right away, forgetting for a moment about Officer Mayer. I turned to see him scurrying down the hallway, throwing terrified glances over his shoulder. Riley and Beth were right behind me, the human forgotten behind us. Riley fired off two shots, but Mayer was already pushing through the door to the stairwell. Beth made a move like she was going to follow, but two officers burst through the door, and she and Riley started shooting at them.

Wren lifted her head, her eyes widening as she spotted me. I scooped her off the ground, the gun she'd been holding falling from her hand as I propped her against the wall. A woman lay dead in the room behind her. The officers at the stairwell slumped to the ground, and Riley glanced over his shoulder at me with a nod.

I pushed Wren's hair out of her face, keeping my other arm around her waist to hold her upright. "Are you rescuing yourself?"

She laughed weakly. She was pale and dirty, old blood covering her clothes. Her eyes didn't focus quite right, and I was fairly certain if I let her go she would drop to the ground.

"I might need some help," she said.

"*The Reboot rooms are all locked.*" I tightened my grip around Wren's waist as I listened to Addie's voice in my ear. "*They've changed the program. We can't get them out. And the guards keep coming up here. We can't hold them off much longer.*"

I cursed under my breath, and Wren tilted her head curiously. "I've got Wren," I said into my com. "Are they ready in front?"

"*Yes,*" Addie said, a hint of a relief in her voice. "*The extraction team is ready there. We have to leave the Reboots for now, though. HARC reinforcements are coming and we don't have enough people to take the whole building.*"

"All right," I said with a sigh, turning to Riley and Beth. "We have to go. They can't get the Reboots out."

"We can break the doors," Beth said, reaching for her gun. "There's enough of us. We'll smash them in."

"Addie said there are HARC reinforcements coming. They're barely holding the guards off as it is."

Beth cast an annoyed look at Riley. "We can't even try?"

Riley peered down the hallway. "We're going to go to the Reboot rooms and look, okay? Get her out of here." He and Beth took off for the stairway at the other end of the hall.

I swept Wren up into my arms. "You did this with two Reboots and a few humans," I muttered.

"Barely," she said with a cough.

I talked rapidly into my com, telling Addie that Riley and Beth were on the way to the sixth floor. Wren wrapped her arms around my neck as I ran for the staircase.

I bolted down to the first floor and Wren only lifted her head as we entered the lobby. The front doors were broken; a few dead HARC officers lay scattered around the front desk. I scanned the space, searching for other Reboots, and found

Isaac waving frantically at the front door.

"Let's go!" he yelled.

The sound of gunfire exploded through my com, followed by Addie's voice. *"It's chaos at the Reboot rooms. There're too many guards."*

"Get out," I said, my heart pounding in my chest. "We'll come back for them."

I couldn't understand her response through the screaming and blasts. Gritting my teeth, I tightened my arms around Wren, pushing through the doors and onto HARC's front lawn as our shuttle began to descend.

Thumps sounded behind me and I turned to see Reboots raining down from fourth- and fifth-story windows. A few more were running through the lobby, and Isaac ushered them all out and took off across the lawn.

A sea of black-clothed HARC officers followed them.

I ducked down, trying to protect Wren's head with mine as bullets whizzed by all around me. Riley appeared at my right side, limping on an obviously broken leg, his gray shirt covered in blood splatters.

"Beth?" I called as we ran.

He shook his head with a grim look.

"Addie?" I said, panic making its way into my voice.

He pointed and I threw a glance over my shoulder to see Addie running behind Gabe, trying to block any bullets before they hit him.

The shuttle landed and I hustled inside, pressing my back into a corner as I slid to the ground with Wren in my arms. Reboots piled in around me, bleeding and talking loudly. There weren't enough, and I craned my neck as I tried to see if more were coming. There were a few stragglers on the lawn, but had we lost everyone else? We'd come in with sixty and we were leaving with what? Thirty? Forty? Plus one more.

I pressed my lips to Wren's cheek and ran my hand into her hair as I let out a shaky sigh.

"You terrified me," I said, breathing heavily.

She smiled, leaning into my neck. "I terrify lots of people."

I wrapped my arms around her tighter, and a scuffle at the shuttle doors made me lean over. We were lifting off the ground, and I saw Addie's face, tight with fear. Her hands were covered in blood, pressed into the chest of someone. I stretched my neck to see.

Gabe.

"What do we do?" Addie asked, looking around frantically. The Reboots exchanged baffled expressions. "Who knows what to do with a gunshot to a human?"

THIRTY-TWO

WREN

I SHIFTED AGAINST SOMETHING WARM AND SOLID AS I WOKE UP. MY vision was tinged with purple, a side effect of something Suzanna and Officer Mayer had given me, and I squinted at the glass wall in front of me. I took in a sharp breath.

I was in a HARC facility.

"It's okay." Callum's voice was in my ear, his arm looping around my stomach before I could jump away. "We're in the Austin facility. HARC's not here anymore."

I slowly pulled away from him, blinking as spots appeared in my vision with the movement. I was weak and hungry and my body didn't feel quite right.

We were in a Reboot room, on one of the beds. The other

one was empty, and the room was bare except for the beds and a dresser. The facility was deserted outside the glass wall, but I could hear the nearby murmur of voices.

Callum had dark circles under his eyes and spots of blood on his white T-shirt, but he smiled widely at me and I crawled into his lap. I wrapped my arms around his neck and he pulled me close.

"I'm sorry," I said, extracting myself and looking down at my dirty clothes. "I'm gross."

"No you're not." He scooped me back into his lap. "I think you look pretty good for what you went through the past three days."

I moaned against his shoulder. "Was it only three days? It felt like a hundred."

His arms tightened around me. "Yeah, it did."

We sat in silence for several minutes, the sounds of people talking drifting into the room. I finally pulled away enough to see his face.

"So you want to explain how we're hanging out in an empty HARC facility?"

"After you went missing, I gathered up the Reboots and we stormed the city. Got HARC to leave. And we figured you'd head here if you could, so we stayed."

I nodded. "Well, I tried."

"I know. Addie told me."

"Which HARC facility was I at?"

"New Dallas. We tried to free all the Reboots there, but . . ." A pained look crossed his face. "We didn't have a lot of Reboots and no human support. We couldn't get the doors unlocked." He pushed my hair back with a small smile. "But the point of the mission was to get you, so I'd say it worked."

"Are all the humans in Austin gone?" I asked in confusion.

He shook his head. "No. HARC ordered them all to New Dallas, but lots stayed here."

"Ah. They just didn't want to be part of a Reboot rescue mission."

"Freeing Reboots is no longer their main priority." He rolled his eyes and scooted off the bed. "Anyway. Are you hungry? I snagged you some food from the stash downstairs."

"I'm starving. I haven't eaten since the reservation." I slid off the bed and quickly realized standing was not the best idea. My legs were shaking and the world started to tilt again. I grasped the edge of the bed and quickly plopped down on the ground.

"You okay?" Callum sat down in front of me with two pieces of bread and a jar of peanut butter. He dipped the knife into the peanut butter and spread it across one of the pieces of bread, holding it out to me when he finished.

"I'm fine." I took a big bite and then another.

"You passed out in the shuttle. I was a little worried. They didn't give you something we need an antidote for, did they?" He cracked a smile. "Although, there are a few left upstairs. We could just start giving you stuff."

I moaned. "No thank you. I'm fine. I think I've had enough weird HARC drugs to last a lifetime."

"All right. But if you try to eat me, I'm going to go grab a few."

I laughed and took the second piece of bread he offered me. "So, the humans. It must be going okay, considering you're all living here together."

Callum's face hardened as he leaned back on his hands. "Not really. The rebels are mad Micah betrayed them and most of the other humans are probably only tolerating us because they have to."

I raised my eyebrows, surprised. "Have you seen Micah since you left?"

"No. I'm thinking that can't be a good sign. Who knows what kind of revenge he's planning?" He leaned forward, reaching for another piece of bread as I finished my second. "I think you were right. Maybe we should go."

"Before we get everyone out of the facilities?"

"I don't see how we can. We lost even more Reboots because of my stupid plan, and the humans don't care what happens to us. You were right."

"Your plan wasn't stupid," I said softly, taking another piece of bread from him. "Worked out well for me."

"Yes," he said. "And thank goodness. I think I would have lost my mind if I'd lost you." His eyes met mine. "But you were right. It isn't worth the risk. I just want to leave with you and let the humans figure this out for themselves. Is it really our problem?"

His voice was heavy, his shoulders slumped, and I sort of missed the overly optimistic Callum, even if he'd driven me crazy at the reservation.

"The humans were never going to come around right away," I said. "And don't pretend like you're totally okay with running off and abandoning everyone. You're not."

"But I insisted we stay and you got hurt and—"

"I'm fine," I said with a frown. "And I made my own choices. I could have taken off by myself if I wanted."

"We both knew you weren't going to do that. You like me too much."

I laughed as he grinned at me. "True."

His mood shifted and he shrugged, eyes downcast. "But I think you were right. They hate us. They're *not* helping us."

"They're scared," I said. "They got rid of HARC and now they want to stay and not worry about anyone else. I can sympathize."

He expression turned incredulous. "Are you seriously arguing for the humans right now?"

"I . . ." I trailed off, considering how much easier it would be to agree with Callum and take off. It's what I wanted, just a few days ago.

And it felt wrong now.

"I was thinking," I said softly. "The night before Addie got strung up at the reservation, she asked me to help her. I just blew her off. I didn't want to stick my neck out and she got hurt. And we both got dropped from a shuttle." I glanced at the bed on the other side of the room. "With Ever, it was sort of the same. I had an opportunity to help her, and I didn't even try to fight for it. I did what I always do, which is to follow orders and keep my head down."

"Ever's death isn't your fault," Callum said.

"I know. It's HARC's fault. But that doesn't mean I don't still feel guilty about it."

He reached for my hand. "I didn't know that."

I ran my fingers over his. "I'm tired of HARC controlling everything and thinking they can treat us like this. The first time it got better was when I finally got up off my ass and fought for you. So let's do it. I'm ready."

He laughed softly, looking at me with happy, hopeful eyes. "Are you sure? The rebels really aren't on our side any-more."

"Let's just go talk to them," I said. "If they won't help, we'll figure something else out."

He nodded, squeezing my hand. "Okay."

"But not right now," I said, glancing down at my dirty clothes. "I could really use a shower first. Does the water still work here?"

"It does. HARC cut the power, but we got it back up." He stood and offered me his hand. "Gabe got some people working on it before we left. He got shot in New Dallas, but Tony thinks he's going to be okay."

I took his hand and let him pull me to my feet. I vaguely remembered a commotion in the shuttle and someone yelling about a human.

"Hop on," he said, leaning down and gesturing to his back. "I'll give you a ride."

I felt steadier on my feet after the food, but the world was still swaying. I gave Callum a grateful look and hoisted myself onto his back, wrapping my arms around his neck.

He walked into the hallway. The rooms we passed were empty until we turned a corner. There was a group of Reboots standing in the hallway ahead, and more gathered in some rooms. I recognized a few and they waved at me.

"This isn't everyone, is it?" I asked, twisting around as Callum reached the stairwell. There were maybe twenty or thirty Reboots here.

"No, most of them stayed in the city. Took over houses and apartments humans vacated. Some of them built tents. Said it creeped them out to be in here."

Maybe it should have creeped me out, but it didn't. Not now that HARC was out. A HARC facility had been my home for five years. It felt familiar. And safe, oddly enough.

"But we lost some in New Dallas," he said softly. "Beth. A few other Austin Reboots."

I squeezed his shoulders gently. I hadn't really known Beth

or any of them, but I knew it must have been hard for him to lose people on a mission he'd been in charge of.

Callum turned into the girls' shower and gently set me down on the ground. It was similar to the Rosa facility, with stalls lined up and curtains down every row. I opened the shelf to my right and found a small stack of towels.

"Oh, I have some of your clothes," Callum said, stepping backward. "You mind waiting a minute? I'll grab them."

I nodded and he disappeared out the door. I slowly walked across the tile floor and sank down in front of one of the shower stalls.

It was eerily quiet, the only sound a leaky tap dripping water somewhere. The showers had always been a source of discomfort for me. I'd hated watching the Reboots run around, flirting and laughing, half-naked.

It seemed silly now to judge them when they were simply trying to make the best of a terrible situation. I ran my fingers over my scars through my shirt. It really seemed ridiculous to worry about my scars so much. I had probably made a bigger deal out of them by being so weird about it.

The door opened and Callum sauntered in, a bag in his hand. He set it down next to me. "It's just some of your stuff from the reservation."

"Thank you." I grasped the edge of the shower stall to help me to my feet.

"I'm going to go shower on the other side," he said, taking

a step back. "You okay by yourself?"

I nodded and he smiled at me before turning away. "Callum." I hooked my fingers into the collar of my shirt before I could change my mind and pulled the material down to expose the center of my chest.

He turned around, surprise coloring his features as he registered the state of my shirt. He glanced up at my face, then back down to the staples that stretched across my skin before disappearing inside my bra. He looked for several seconds, then met my eyes.

"I'm sort of disappointed," he said, his voice amused. "I thought they'd be bigger."

I burst out laughing, dropping my hands from my shirt. He took two big steps forward and ran a hand under my chin as he leaned down to kiss me.

"Thank you for letting me see," he said quietly, more seriously.

"Thanks for wanting to see."

"Heck yeah, I want to see." He leaned forward, eyes on my shirt. "Can I see again right now?"

I grinned, rising up on my toes to kiss him again. He laughed against my lips and I melted into his arms, making the decision to forget about the insanity around us for as long as possible.

THIRTY-THREE

CALLUM

I WALKED ACROSS THE FRONT LAWN OF THE AUSTIN HARC facility that evening, fingers laced through Wren's. After a shower, more food, and several hours' rest, she had finally healed fully and looked like her usual slightly scary self.

Well, almost. She caught me watching her and smiled, an easy, relaxed smile. She hadn't talked about her experiences the last few days much, but it was like they'd unburdened her in some way instead of adding to the weight on her shoulders. She seemed lighter, happier. She'd even whipped off her shirt to let me see her scars again earlier, when I'd jokingly asked.

I'd wanted to lay low in the HARC facility for the night, but she'd really wanted to go see the rebels.

I wasn't sure what to make of it. Part of me was happy she'd come around; the other part wanted to scoop her up and make a run for it before she got hurt again. But she seemed so calm and pleased about her decision that I'd dropped the idea of leaving when she refused a second time. Despite my annoyance with the humans, I had to admit I was relieved she'd changed her mind about staying to help.

I glanced at her again. It wasn't just her that was slightly different, but everything. The air between us seemed lighter and heavier at the same time since she'd shown me her scars. She kept giving me this look that made me want to grab her and crush her against me.

She turned her head toward a pile of rubble that used to be a house as we walked past it. "This is pretty impressive, Callum."

"What? That I destroyed everything?"

"No. That you managed to unite the Reboots and take over Austin. I thought it would be years before we could that, if ever."

"I went with a 'I'm coming, deal with it' approach." But I smiled at the compliment and squeezed her hand.

"I approve of that approach." She paused. "Did you go check on your family?"

"David came and found me," I said. "He wants me to go see our parents. I told him they could come to me if they wanted."

"But he came."

I smiled at her. "Yes."

We turned onto Tony's street and the usual chaos came into view. Humans streamed in and out the front door, and several people sat on the front lawn. I recognized one of them immediately as David, and he hopped to his feet when he saw us coming. A flash of recognition crossed his face as he looked at Wren.

"Hey," he said as we approached.

"Hi." I tilted my head toward Wren. "This is Wren. This is my brother, David."

"Nice to meet you." She held her hand out, and when David shook it I saw him blink in surprise, likely from her cool skin. He cast a quick glance down at her wrist and his eyes widened slightly.

"You too," he said, glancing from her to me.

A yell sounded from inside, and I raised my eyebrows. "What's going on in there?"

"I don't know. They've been yelling at each other since I got here. I decided to stay outside."

Wren slipped her hand from mine and headed up the stairs to the house. I followed her with David close behind, pushing through some humans crowded near the doorway.

Tony and Desmond stood at the edge of the kitchen, matching angry expressions on their faces. There were grumpy humans everywhere, actually. Gabe, pale but still alive, sat on the couch with Addie and Riley. A white bandage poked out from his right shoulder, and he smiled when he spotted me and Wren.

The room grew silent as they noticed Wren, and Desmond ran a hand through his hair with a sigh.

"Hey, One-seventy-eight," he said. "Good to see you."

She gave him an amused look, since his tone said the exact opposite. "You too. What's going on here?"

"There have been attacks on Richards and Bonito," Tony said, crossing his arms over his chest. "Reboot attacks on the cities. And they tried to get the Reboots out of the facilities. Without any regard for human life. Word is, the cities are mostly destroyed and lots of humans are dead."

Wren took a quick glance back at me and I shook my head.

"That's not us," I said to Tony. "Everyone is here. It has to be Micah and the few that stayed with him."

"That's what Addie thought, too." Tony twisted his mouth around. "They were outnumbered and it didn't go well. HARC killed all the Reboots in those facilities. And in New Dallas."

Wren cast a horrified look in my direction before returning her attention to Tony. "All of them?"

"That's what they're saying."

"What about Rosa?"

"The facility is still running, and remaining personnel have been transferred there. New Dallas was open for longer, but we think they must have decided to eliminate all the Reboots because of the attack. But . . ." Tony winced and glanced at Desmond.

"But they'll probably be eliminated in Rosa, too," Desmond

finished. "HARC doesn't want to risk another incident like here. They don't want any more Reboots escaping."

"Word is they're shutting down the program," Tony said. "Suzanna was the biggest supporter of the Reboot experiment, and apparently she's dead."

"Yep, last time I saw her she was definitely dead," Wren said.

"She had some other supporters," Tony continued. "But with everything that's happened, it's not looking good. It won't be long."

I took a step forward. "We need to move quickly then. Come up with a plan of attack." The room was silent. The humans avoided my eyes, and I couldn't say I was surprised.

"You want to let them all die," Wren said quietly.

"Apparently it's the smarter plan," Riley spat out.

"Considering what the Reboots did to Richards and Bonito, it's the only choice we have," Desmond said.

"We didn't have anything to do with that." Wren's voice was still calm, but I could hear the anger beginning to seep through. "We worked against Micah from the beginning. Callum risked his life to get word to you guys about what he was planning!"

"And we appreciate that," Tony said quietly.

"You appreciate it so much you're going to let hundreds of our fellow Reboots die," Addie said.

Silence again, for several seconds, until I spoke. "We can't go in alone. We tried it in New Dallas and it failed. HARC has beefed up their security. We need human support if we're going to have any chance of doing this."

Tony looked at Desmond. "They could help us take down HARC."

Desmond threw up his arms. "We've been through this! I don't—"

Shouting overtook the room again and Wren turned to me, a worried expression on her face.

"Wait." Riley's voice rose over the others. "Stop. Stop!" The humans fell silent as he jumped from the couch, his hand on the com in his ear as he listened to something. "There are shuttles at the fences. Several already on their way into the slums." His eyes flicked to the other Reboots in the room. "They're saying they think they're Reboot piloted."

Micah. I balled my fingers into fists.

"We need to—"

Riley's words were lost as a giant explosion rocked the ground. I flung myself over David as the house crumbled around me.

THIRTY-FOUR

WREN

I COUGHED AS I PUSHED PIECES OF WOOD AND DEBRIS OFF MY legs and struggled to a standing position in what was left of the living room.

It wasn't much. The house was almost entirely gone. About half the kitchen was still standing, and some of the back wall was there, but a hole had been blown completely through the living room and I could see the sky. I spotted a few dead humans, and others were shouting and moaning beneath the rubble.

"Wren? Wren!"

I jumped over a piece of the kitchen table to where I could hear Callum yelling. He had a hand on his brother's arm, pulling him from the wreckage. His expression turned to relief when he spotted me.

David looked fine except for some cuts on his arms. It appeared Callum had taken the brunt of the blast for him. One of his arms was cut so deep I could see bone, and the front of his shirt had been ripped open and his chest was black and red.

"You all right?" Callum asked David, taking a quick survey of him.

He nodded, his eyes wide and horrified as he surveyed Callum's injuries.

I heard a rustle behind me and turned to see Riley, Addie, and Gabe limping out of the house. Riley shouted something into his com.

I grabbed Callum's arm. "You have weapons, don't you? Where are you storing them?"

"In the shuttle that's parked by the schoolhouse." He ran his hands through his hair as he looked around. "Some of them are alive under there. I need to get them out."

"I can help," David said.

I rose up on my toes and planted a kiss on Callum's lips. No matter what he said about us leaving and not working with the humans, his first instinct was to stay and save them, and I liked that about him. I hadn't realized it at first, but I liked that he had a deep sense of right and wrong and stuck to what he believed.

"Be careful," he said quietly.

"You too." I gave his hand a squeeze before turning to take off down the street behind Riley.

There were only two shuttles in my line of sight, and Reboots ran past me on all sides with weapons. One of the shuttles hovered over a clump of houses at the other side of the street, firing until they were nothing but a pile of rubble.

Riley made it to the shuttles in front of the schoolhouse first, and threw a handgun and giant knife in my direction, along with a helmet. "There's not much left!" he yelled as he slipped a gun into his own pocket.

"This is fine," I called over my shoulder as I plopped the helmet on my head and bolted down the street. The roar of motorcycles made me turn, and I spotted Micah, Kyle, and Jules speeding past on their way to the heart of the slums. About ten or fifteen other reservation Reboots dashed in the opposite direction, guns raised.

I broke into a run. Riley and a few other Reboots pounded the dirt behind me as I sprinted after Micah. The shuttle I'd seen earlier began to spin erratically and plummeted to the ground with a loud bang.

The grocery store and the other shops made up the center of the Austin slums, and as I approached the wooden buildings I saw smoke billowing from several of them. I darted in between two shops and came out on the wide, dirt road that ran through the center of town.

Micah stood a few yards away, legs on either side of his

motorcycle as he aimed a rocket launcher at a nearby store. He whooped and glanced behind him, doing a quick double take when he caught sight of me. He quickly masked his surprise with a wide smirk that looked anything but happy.

He kicked the stand on the motorcycle and hopped off. "Wren! Nice to see you again. How'd the bounty hunters treat you?"

I reached for my gun, even though we were both wearing helmets. I had no interest in any more chitchat with him. He grabbed his own gun, and I fired off a quick shot to his hand. The gun flew through the air and landed a few feet away. I aimed again as Micah charged me, and I squeezed off the next one too quickly. The bullet sailed past his ear as he tackled me.

We hit the ground together, the gun falling from my hand in the scuffle. Micah tried to wrap his fingers around my throat and I kicked him off before scurrying through the dirt and hopping to my feet.

His eyes were furious as he stood, his mouth set in a hard line. He rushed at me again and I slammed my foot into his knee. With a gasp he stumbled back, and I punched him across the jaw.

He retaliated so quickly I didn't know he was swinging until the punch hit my stomach, and then my cheek. I wheezed as I ducked his next punch, slamming both my fists into his chest.

He hit the ground with a grunt. "You should be ashamed," he said as he hopped up on one leg.

"About which part? I'm not the one who pushed a couple Reboots out of an airborne shuttle."

"No, you're the one who ensured we're going extinct."

I laughed as I inched my fingers closer to the knife hanging off my belt. "I'd say you're the one killing us. Hundreds of Reboots in the facilities were killed because of you."

His eyes narrowed, his fingers balling into fists. He screamed as he ran for me, limping on his left leg.

I pulled the knife from my pants. Swung it through the air.

Micah's body crumpled to the ground. His head rolled off in the opposite direction.

I winced as I turned away, wiping the bloody blade on my pants. Riley stood over another dead Reboot body a block or so away, and he raised his arms like, *"Victory!"*

It didn't feel like a victory. Callum had said once it was only appropriate to kill someone in self-defense, which this had been, but it still made me feel uncomfortable in a new, unwelcome way.

I slipped the knife back in my pocket and picked up both guns off the ground. With a sigh, I headed in the direction of gunfire.

There wasn't much left of Austin an hour or so later. Homes all around me were destroyed. I was still on the wide road in the middle of town, and the shops and apartment buildings had huge holes in them.

I holstered my gun as I watched Riley and Addie drag Micah's body into the pile we'd made. Burying Micah and his crew was impractical, so we'd decided to get them all together to transfer them to the edge of town for cremation.

Riley sighed, wiping a dirty hand across his forehead. It was late, the sky was black, and my body felt heavy and tired. The bodies had all been cleared and piled up, and when Addie said she was going to Tony's house, we followed.

The roads were filled with humans, all headed in the direction of the schoolhouse. One glanced at me and I braced myself for a yell, or a glare, but one side of his mouth lifted in a smile. I blinked in surprise and turned a confused look at Riley and Addie, but a tall figure at the end of the street caught my eye.

I quickened my step and Callum's face lit up when he saw me. A young boy was on his back, his arms wrapped around Callum's neck.

"Hey," Callum said, reaching for me. He leaned down for a kiss. "Everything okay?"

I nodded, glancing at the trail of humans behind him and the boy on his back. "Who is this?"

"I don't know. I pulled him out of the rubble but he won't talk."

The boy frowned at me and buried his head in Callum's shoulder.

"I'm going to the schoolhouse to see if anyone knows him.

A lot of the humans are gathering there for the night. Come
with me?"

I nodded and wiped a streak of dirt off his forehead. He was
covered in dust, from his neck down to his pants, which had
two huge holes in the knees.

"Is your brother okay?" I asked.

"Yeah. The other side of town wasn't hit as hard, so he went
back home. He was good. Helped me sort through the rubble
of a lot of houses and get people out."

I ran a hand down his arm and we turned to head toward
the schoolhouse. Humans were spilled out onto the front lawn,
and a woman shot across the dirt as soon as she spotted us,
making some sort of weird, strangled noise that made me want
to take a step back.

Callum knelt down, sliding the boy off his back, and the
woman whisked him into her arms, crying as she kissed his
cheeks.

"Thank you, thank you," she said, grabbing Callum. She
hugged him with one arm, blubbering something I couldn't
understand.

"You're welcome," Callum said hesitantly, shooting me a
baffled look as she released him.

Tony was across the lawn next. He grabbed Callum and
wrapped his arms around him. He thanked him, his voice
cracking slightly, and turned to quickly walk away.

"Why is everyone hugging you?" I asked.

"I don't know. I'm likeable?"

I grinned at him, because I knew exactly why everyone was hugging him, and so did he. A human caught his eye and smiled, and he nodded at her. Callum had said that saving people was one of my favorite things, but it was he who needed that, who could muster up that kind of passion for people he barely knew.

"Rumor has it the HARC facility wasn't hit," he said. "I could use a rest before we figure out what to do."

"Me too." I laced my fingers through his and pulled him closer as we headed away from the schoolhouse. We walked in comfortable silence, his thumb occasionally rubbing circles on my hand. I considered telling him I'd killed Micah, but the words died in my throat. I was happy he was gone, but I didn't want to celebrate, or brag, or even talk about it. Callum didn't ask, so maybe someone had already told him.

Although the look he was giving me suggested he wasn't thinking about Micah at all. He should be exhausted, but his eyes were bright as they met mine.

When I stopped at the entrance of the facility and rose up on my toes to give him a kiss, he grabbed me around the waist and pressed his hands into my back, bringing my body closer to his. I traced my fingers across his jaw as his lips met mine. He started to pull me closer, then stepped back, glancing down at his clothes.

"Maybe I should shower before . . ." He let his voice trail off, leaving me to imagine what we'd be doing after.

"Me too." My cheeks were warm, but I held his gaze, his dark eyes burning into mine.

We walked to our room for new clothes and back down to the showers. I cast a smile over my shoulder at Callum as I pushed the door open to the girls' bathroom.

I was the first back to the room, and I sat down on the bed, swallowing down a sudden flurry of nerves. How exactly did this work? Was I supposed to say, "Hey, let's have sex!" or did he already understand? I thought we'd sort of been giving each other signals, but maybe it was in my head.

I looked over at the glass wall. The other Reboots were around the corner, out of sight, but I certainly wasn't getting naked for everyone to see.

The other bed still had sheets on it, so I hopped up and pulled them off. I pushed a dresser closer to the door and stepped on top. I shoved the edges of the sheet into the crack between the glass and the wall and released it. It fell down almost to the ground, covering half the room. I grabbed the other one and put it on the adjacent side, so the whole room was obscured. It was kind of obvious what we were doing in here, but maybe that worked in my favor. I wouldn't have to say anything to Callum. He'd pick up on the hint by himself.

The sheets moved as I pushed the dresser back in its place, and Callum emerged from behind them.

He looked from them to me, a small smile on his face. "Good idea."

"I spent long enough with those stupid glass walls," I said, sitting down on the bed. He walked to me slowly, hands in his pockets, his expression nervous. I was relieved he wasn't totally calm, because my hand was shaking as I reached for his arm. When I ran my fingers over his skin, he slipped his hands from his pockets and leaned closer to me.

I looped my arms around his neck and scooted forward on the bed until my legs touched his. He placed his hands on the bed on either side of me, his lips barely brushing against mine. I grabbed the buttons of his shirt and brought him closer to me, until his soft lips on mine made warmth zip through my body.

I pulled him closer and closer, until we were tangled together and he was running his fingers down my scars and I was laughing when he told me I was like a hot cyborg. Then there was nothing but the sound of his breath and his warm skin against mine and I forgot to keep one ear on the door or watch for threats or scan the closest location of weapons in my head. It was just him, his smile against my lips, his arms around me, and I was gone.

THIRTY-FIVE

CALLUM

I WOKE THE NEXT MORNING TO WREN ASLEEP AGAINST MY CHEST, her arms tucked up underneath her chin. She was wearing my shirt, which I'd wrapped around her when her arms had begun to prick with goose bumps. She'd buttoned it crooked, and I could see the tip of her scars, the first few of the metal staples holding the skin together. I tightened my arms around her and pressed my lips to the top of her head.

I hadn't slept so well or so long in weeks—not since I was a human—and I blinked in the dark room. Was it too much to hope that everyone would leave us alone and I could spend the day right here?

Murmured voices trickled in from the hallway and I sighed

inwardly. Of course it was. HARC was still out there and, thanks to Micah, we could already be too late to save the Reboots in the Rosa facility.

Wren stirred, and a smile crossed her lips before she even opened her eyes. She snuggled closer to me so her face was in my neck.

"Good morning," she mumbled.

"Good morning." I brushed a kiss against her cheek.

"Is it too late to take you up on your offer to leave and forget about everyone else?" she asked, humor in her voice.

I laughed. "Never. Let's go right now."

She grinned at me, because we both knew it was way too late for that.

"Hey, is Callum Twenty-two in here somewhere?" a voice nearby yelled.

I sighed as I swung my legs over the bed. "Yeah?"

"There're people downstairs in the lobby for you. They say they're your parents."

I blinked in surprise. Even though David had said he thought they wanted to see me, I didn't think they'd actually come.

Wren rolled out of bed and reached for her clothes. "Want me to come with you?"

"Yes. Please."

I pulled on my clothes and shoes so slowly that Wren was standing by the hung-up sheets, watching me in amusement as I tied my boots.

"We could sneak out another door," I said, half joking. "Or jump off the roof."

"Breaking our legs just to avoid your parents is a little extreme."

I released an exaggerated sigh as I stood. "Fine."

Wren reached for my hand and tugged me from the room and down the stairs to the ground level. She pushed open the door and light flooded the stairwell. I walked out onto the black floor.

My parents and David sat in the chairs at the far side of the room, like they were waiting for an appointment with HARC officials. I took a tentative step forward and David, spotting me, jumped to his feet, a big smile on his face. My parents stood, too, and started toward me.

We all met in the middle of the lobby. My mom looked like she was going to cry, and I wasn't sure what to make of that. My dad just seemed nervous.

"This is Wren," I said, glad to have something to start the conversation with. She dropped my hand to offer it to my parents, and my dad shook it first, his gaze falling to her bar code.

"It's nice to meet you," she said, noticing his glance. "It's One-seventy-eight."

My mom's eyes widened briefly but she shook Wren's hand and turned a tentative smile to me.

"We heard . . ." My mom cleared her throat. "Well, we heard a lot of things."

"I hope some of them were good," I said.

My dad laughed. "Of course."

I felt awkward with them staring at me like I was a hero. It was better than last time, though, when they saw me as a monster. I tightened my hand around Wren's. "Is everything okay at the house? David said you weren't hit too bad by the attacks."

My mom nodded. "It took a bit of a beating, but it's still in one piece. Nothing that can't be repaired."

"Good." I felt a rush of relief, even though I never planned to live there again.

The front doors banged open and Riley and Addie walked through with several other Reboots. He gestured at Wren and she looked up at me.

"Go ahead," I said, slipping my hand out of hers. "I'll be over in a second."

My parents watched her walk away, and my mom turned to me with a questioning look on her face.

"She was there, that night you came to see us."

"Yes. We were in the Rosa facility together. She helped me escape."

"Oh." My mom smiled. "That's wonderful. I didn't know Reboots escaped."

My dad eyed my bar code. "Rosa? What's it like there?"

"Rosa is . . . a mess. I like it better here."

"Are you staying?" my mom asked. "People were saying this morning that if we saved the Reboots in the last facility, we might drive HARC off for good."

I cocked my head in surprise. I didn't know who she'd been talking to, but it sounded like the humans were having a change of heart.

"I should go check in and see what the plan is," I said, gesturing back at Wren and Riley. "A lot of the humans have been gathering at the schoolhouse. Have you been there?"

My dad shook his head. "Not yet."

"You should probably check in with them. I'll catch up with you guys later."

My mom nodded, stepping forward like she was going to hug me. She stopped, her face twisting in worry.

"Do you still hug?"

I laughed, quickly covering it with my hand. I held my arms out. "Yes. I still hug."

She wrapped her arms around me and gave me a quick squeeze. If I felt different to her she didn't show it. In fact, she was teary-eyed as she pulled away and I quickly took a step back as I felt a lump grow in my throat.

They turned to go and I headed for Wren. She slipped her arm around my waist and gave me a kiss. I put my hand on her cheek and made the kiss last a moment longer.

"Do they approve of me?" she asked when I pulled away. "Am I too blond?"

"Yes. That's what stuck out in their minds about you. You're blond."

Riley turned to us, an amused look on his face. "Are we done making out? Does anyone maybe want to come with me to figure out how the hell we're going to rescue the Rosa Reboots?"

"Fine," I said with an exaggerated sigh, grinning at him.

He charged ahead of us with Addie, and I slipped my hand into Wren's as we followed them out the door. It was sunny but chilly as we walked through HARC's front lawn and back into the heart of the slums. The city looked worse in daylight, many homes and buildings destroyed and not a human in sight. Maybe my parents misunderstood and the humans were uniting to kill all the Rosa Reboots. Take revenge for Micah's attack.

Riley stopped in his tracks as he and Addie turned a corner.

"What the hell?" Addie exclaimed.

I jogged to their side, reeling back at the scene in front of me.

There were humans everywhere. Like the most I'd ever seen in one spot. They covered the schoolhouse lawn and took up an entire block.

And they all turned to stare at us.

I had a sudden urge to run even as Tony and Desmond appeared from the crowd and headed in our direction. Ordinarily that many humans against four Reboots would be terrifying.

"Hey," Tony said with a tired smile as he and Desmond stopped in front of us. "Where are the rest of the Reboots?"

"Still at the facility," Wren said. "What's going on here?"

"Word got out that we'd taken Austin back from HARC. After HARC killed the Reboots in the cities, most of the humans decided to come here instead of New Dallas or Rosa."

"To do what?" I asked.

Desmond shoved his hands in his pockets, his eyes moving between me and Wren. "To join One-seventy-eight in the fight against HARC."

"Sorry, what?" She let out an incredulous laugh.

"The officers in New Dallas didn't keep their mouths shut about you escaping. Everyone knows. And when they heard Micah and his crew hit Austin, too, they figured out who the good guys were."

"Imagine that," I said dryly, looking pointedly at Desmond. He'd given me an utterly baffled look yesterday when I'd pulled him out of the rubble, like he didn't believe I'd stick around to help him.

"We all figured out who the good guys are," Desmond said quietly. I nodded, trying not to give him a smug look.

Tony smiled at Wren's increasingly confused expression. "They're here to partner with the Reboots to take down HARC."

THIRTY-SIX

WREN

"THIS IS DEFINITELY A TRAP," ADDIE SAID.

I looked at her in amusement as we ushered the last of the Reboots out of the facility and instructed them to go to the schoolhouse. "If it's a trap, it's a very elaborate one." I followed her into the hallway and we walked past the glass rooms together.

"It is, but it's brilliant. They lure us to an entirely different city under the guise of helping us, and then drop us straight into HARC's lap!"

"I think that's highly unlikely." I raised my eyebrows at her, unsure if she was kidding.

She grinned at me. "If you get captured again, I'm leaving you. No rescue this time around."

"Noted."

I pushed open the door at the end of the hall and headed down the staircase, our footsteps loud in the empty building.

"I heard you decapitated Micah," she said. "I approve. I wish we could have pushed him out of a shuttle first, though."

I glanced at her as we stepped into the HARC lobby. "I don't know. It felt kind of . . . wrong."

"In what way? You probably saved half the humans in this city by getting rid of him."

I shrugged. "I'm tired of getting rid of people. It's what I've been doing for five years. I want to . . ." I didn't know what I wanted to do.

"Make more people?" Addie asked, trying to keep a straight face. "Have some babies?"

I groaned. "No."

"Are you sure? You can do your part to save the Reboot race. I have a knife right here. I can take out that birth-control chip for you now if you'd like."

"I will stab you with that knife."

She laughed as we walked into the sunshine. "So you and Callum are putting it to use." She shot me a look, a wicked glint in her eye. I shoved her lightly. "Okay, can I ask you a question not about killing people?"

"Why not?"

"Would you ever be with a human?"

"How do you mean?"

"You know, like . . ." She waved her arms around. "Like . . . together. Like you and Callum."

"I don't know. I think it would be weird."

She kicked a rock. "Yeah."

I cocked my head to the side, something Callum had said about Addie protecting Gabe when they rescued me floating through my memory. "Gabe?" I asked.

"Yeah." She looked at me sheepishly. "He kissed me last night."

"Was it weird?"

"No, it was nice. But it made me think about the future. If we win and Reboots start living among the humans, what's gonna happen? Are they going to start dating? Having kids? What is a half Reboot half human going to look like?"

"I don't know; I never thought about it." I shrugged. "Maybe Micah was right."

"That's terrifying."

"Not about everything, but about the evolution stuff. He had a point that Reboots are simply evolved humans. So maybe we're just in the tough part right now. Eventually everyone will sort of meld together into one superhuman Reboot."

"A Rehuman. Or Huboot."

"Maybe not Huboot." I laughed as we turned the corner and the schoolhouse came into view. Callum was talking to a group of humans, a map in his hands.

I forgot to breathe for a moment when our eyes met and his

lips curved up. I didn't know whether to blush or jump into his arms every time he looked at me. Flashbacks of the previous night were on repeat in my head, and it seemed ridiculous that everyone around us was going about business as usual while I was standing in a slightly shifted world.

Addie punched my arm, snapping me out of my trance, and when I turned she grinned at me. She lifted one eyebrow and I blushed, scurrying to where Riley and Isaac were standing with a few Reboots.

"How's the ammo situation look?" I asked.

"Not bad," Riley said. "Micah and his team had a lot on them, so we took that. Combined with what the humans took from the cities, we're in pretty good shape."

Callum joined us, spreading the large map he was holding on the table in front of Riley.

"Do we have a plan?" I asked. Desmond and Tony were standing a few yards away, their heads bent together as they spoke. "One the humans are okay with?"

"Yes." Riley put his finger on the map. "We're here." He moved his finger along the river to the north. "About thirty miles north is Rosa." He traced the route farther up. "Twenty-five miles north of Rosa is New Dallas. Everyone has agreed to go into Rosa together to get the Reboots first since HARC has set up headquarters there. If we can take Rosa, we'll hit New Dallas right after. Apparently there isn't much left of HARC now. Most are in Rosa." He put his hands on his hips. "Tony got in contact with Leb, and they think they can get together enough humans in the city to support us."

"Seriously?" I said doubtfully. "They're not exactly the most Reboot-friendly humans in Rosa."

"I still have the scars from where they captured me and beat me in the middle of the street," Callum said.

Riley rolled his eyes. "You don't get scars."

"Emotional scars, then." A smile tugged at the edges of Callum's lips.

Riley chuckled. "Leb said he and the other rebels have been working on the people in Rosa, especially recently. You have support from a few officers inside of HARC, which is what's really important. Don't go around killing any of them unless they strike first."

"Are humans coming into the facility with us?"

Riley shook his head. "We're going to position some outside, though, to try and prevent more officers from getting in before you guys have a chance to escape. Our hope is we can get all the Reboots out of the building quickly and fight HARC off in the street. It will be easier. Well, relatively." He raised an eyebrow at me. "And Leb said Officer Mayer is back in Rosa. I thought you might appreciate that information."

A blip of excitement ran through me at the prospect of cornering Officer Mayer and eliminating him. I glanced at Callum, who'd had the chance to kill the officer and hadn't taken it, but his expression was neutral.

"Do they know all these humans came here to help us?" I asked.

"No idea," Riley said. "We suspect if they do know where they went, they don't know they want to partner with us."

Addie looked down at the map, then back at Riley. "What's the plan for the humans? Assuming we win? It's not realistic to think they'll all be okay with living among us."

Riley shrugged. "Don't know. The idea of splitting us up in each city was mentioned."

"Like a *rico* side and a slum side?" Callum asked dryly.

"Hey, maybe we could lock all the humans in some sort of building," Addie said.

"Oh! And they could help us out with stuff like policing and capturing criminals," Callum said. "But they may not like that, so we should probably keep them pretty tightly contained."

Riley gave me a "make them stop being ridiculous" look, and I laughed.

"Let's install trackers in them, in case they try and run away," Addie said, her serious face starting to crack.

"And we should probably just get rid of them when they get too old, because you know how adult humans are." Callum made a talking motion with his hand. "Blah blah blah, rebellion, blah blah blah, let's fight back. And they're not as strong when they get older anyway."

"This is productive. Thanks, guys." Riley shook his head as he rolled up the map.

"Oh, come on!" Addie called as he walked away, a smile spreading across her face. "We'll give them really good food!"

Riley turned to give us an amused look. "Callum, fill them in on your plan."

"You have a plan?" I asked, turning to him in surprise.

"A brilliant plan!" Riley called over his shoulder.

"Well, I don't know about 'brilliant,'" Callum said with a shrug. "But I was thinking about how screwed we were in New Dallas with that intercom system. HARC gets on there, says three words, and the Reboots do whatever they say. So I thought we should get a com and let you talk to the Reboots instead."

"That *is* a brilliant plan," I said, smiling at him.

He looped an arm around my waist, pulling me closer. "I plan, you do the punching-people-in-the-face part. I like how this works."

THIRTY-SEVEN

CALLUM

I STOOD BY THE LARGEST OF THE SHUTTLES THAT NIGHT, WATCHING as our human allies climbed on behind the Reboots. Tony and Desmond filed in, and Desmond cast a glance in my direction. He nodded at me as he leaned against the shuttle wall.

We didn't have nearly enough shuttles for everyone going to Rosa, so the pilots were going to have to make two trips. The first wave was mostly Reboots, but there were a few humans with us.

I turned to the other shuttle to see Wren walking in my direction. She held her arms out as she got closer and I took a step forward and scooped her up, lifting her off the ground so she wrapped her legs around my waist. She ran her hands behind my neck and pressed her lips against mine.

"You're not allowed to die," she said quietly with a small smile. "I'm ordering it, as your former trainer."

"Got it," I said, kissing her again. "You either. Or captured. Or anything."

She leaned closer, so our foreheads were almost touching. "If we get separated and it looks like this isn't going to work, if it looks like we're losing, I want you to run. Meet me at that spot halfway between Rosa and Austin where we stopped and ate. Remember?"

I nodded. "Only if things get really bad, though."

She nodded in agreement as her lips touched mine again. I tightened my arms around her and held on until she slowly began to pull away. She hopped down to the ground.

Our shuttle was now fully loaded. Wren grinned at me, the kind of grin that made my insides turn over.

"I probably love you," she said.

I let out a surprised laugh. "Probably?"

She laced our fingers together and tugged me toward the shuttle, glancing over her shoulder. "Probably. It's hard to tell with me, you know?"

I laughed again. "I probably love you, too."

"I figured."

I wanted to grab her and kiss her again, but I settled for a smile as we stepped inside with the others. The door banged shut as I ran my fingers down her cheek, and she returned my smile as the shuttle roared to life.

* * *

The day I arrived at the Rosa HARC facility, my first day as an active Reboot, I'd been brought in by ground transportation. I'd sat in the back of a HARC van, my hands cuffed, a guard on either side of me.

I'd been able to hear my heart beating, and realized I'd never asked if a Reboot still had a heartbeat. I'd understood the general idea of Rebooting—the body shutting down and coming back stronger—but I'd never considered what exactly the body still did (or didn't do) after it happened.

I remembered sitting in the van as the Rosa fence opened. My palms were clammy and I felt sick. It had taken me a minute to remember I was a Reboot, and to realize I still had all the same emotions and feelings I did as a human.

I hadn't known whether to be relieved or terrified. Relieved to be the same person; terrified to have to go through being a HARC Reboot while I still had a conscience and happy human memories.

We approached Rosa on foot this time, the shuttle parked a mile behind us. My fear was the same.

No, not the same. It was still there, but it wasn't fear of HARC or worry for my future. It was fear for Wren, fear of messing up, fear of the plan not working and all the Reboots dying. But I could keep the fear under the surface now. No sweaty palms or pounding heart.

I glanced down at Wren, who was staring straight ahead, her expression blank. I might not have been as good as her at keeping my emotions in check, but I admired the way she could push them back and pretend they weren't there when it suited her. I wouldn't have ever guessed I'd like that about her.

She stopped, and the Reboots and humans behind us paused as well. Riley, Addie, and Isaac were following us, with about twenty Reboots. The human group bringing up the rear was small, only about ten or so.

We were so close to the gate I could see the towers. It was silent, the usual buzz of the fence gone. It had been turned off, just as Riley had said it would be. That seemed like a good sign. Maybe we had enough human support in Rosa after all.

Wren gestured for us all to stay put and walked to the gate. She wrapped her fingers around the wire without hesitation and paused for a moment. I winced, thinking of the charge that could have gone through her body.

She nodded and Riley and Addie ran forward with wire cutters. They snapped them quickly, the wires falling down loose toward the ground. Once there was enough space for us to get through, Wren went first, followed by the Reboots, then the humans.

My eyes darted to the towers as we quickly formed a half circle, humans in the middle, and took off toward the city. We'd been told to go to this location because the guards in either tower would pretend not to see us, but I still braced myself for bullets as I ran.

They didn't come. It was silent as we passed the towers and headed for the HARC building looming ahead.

THIRTY-EIGHT

WREN

THERE WAS NO FENCE AROUND THE ROSA FACILITY, SINCE IT WAS set so far away from the houses of the slums. I'd rarely seen it from this angle, my view usually obscured in the shuttle, although I would occasionally glance back at it from assignments.

The humans split off into the slums as we neared the facility, and I took a quick scan of our surroundings. The area around the facility was deserted, but the idea that they weren't guarding the place was ludicrous, especially now.

I glanced up. They likely had guards on the roof. Probably snipers. There also had to be guards at every door. We'd had no direct guard or officer support in Austin—the HARC rebels who were inside steered clear of us—and it felt odd that the plan was to walk right straight to a HARC officer and ask to be let in.

We rounded the corner and everyone slowed as we came into full view of the facility. Nothing but a few yards of dirt between us and the entrance now.

I took a step forward.

A shot rang out.

I jumped, my eyes immediately going to the roof. But the shot came from the slums and was quickly followed by another one.

"Run?" Callum whispered.

I nodded and we took off, footsteps pounding the dirt. Two guards were standing at the door, faces turned in our direction. Neither had their weapons drawn.

I slowed, holding out my hand as Riley grabbed his gun. "Wait." I came to a stop in front of the guards, their faces serious beneath the bright light above the door.

One of them was familiar, though I'd never known his name. Perhaps the other one had been around as well, but I'd never paid much attention to the HARC officers inside the Rosa facility, other than Leb. They mostly stood against the wall and tried not to make eye contact.

They were both staring at me now, though. The taller one pulled his access card away from his belt and swiped it across the pad next to the door.

"Move fast," he said quietly, holding the door open. "Leb

can only distract them from the cameras for a few minutes."

I darted into the lobby, casting a glance over my shoulder. "Thank you." If we failed they were going down, too. The camera had just recorded them letting a bunch of Reboots into the building.

The lights were still on in the lobby. It was dinnertime, and if we had timed it right, all the Reboots were in the cafeteria right now.

The man behind the desk looked casually in our direction. His eyes widened to saucers as he processed what we were, and he scrambled for the com on his desk.

"Hands up," Riley ordered, drawing his gun as he strode forward.

The man paused, his finger poised over the button on his com.

"I will shoot you," Riley said. "Drop the com on the desk."

"Gently," Callum quickly added, running past Riley.

The human scrambled away as Callum got closer, abandoning the com on the desk as he raised his hands.

"Sit on the floor," Riley said, gesturing. "One sound and you're dead."

An alarm shrieked through the lobby and I winced. "Too late."

Callum grabbed the com and twisted a button on it. He tossed it to me. "I'll stay with the guard," he said to Riley as he raised his gun. "You guys go."

"All Reboots to your rooms immediately." The voice over the

speaker made Addie jump, and she gave me a worried look.

I lifted the com to my mouth as I ran for the stairwell. "Reboots. Stop. Don't go to your rooms." I took the stairs two at a time as I raced for seven, the cafeteria. Reboot rooms were above that, on the eighth floor, but hopefully they weren't there yet.

"This is One-seventy-eight," I continued. "HARC is losing control of the cities. They will kill all of you if you go to your rooms."

I rounded a corner and burst onto the seventh floor to see Reboots crowding out of the cafeteria door. Their eyes were wide as they met mine, growing bigger as Riley and the other Reboots flowed in around me.

The guns in the cafeteria went off.

Screams.

"Run!" I darted away from the door and gestured for them to go down the stairs. I raised the com again. "We have a lot of human allies. Confirm they're hostile before you attack."

That produced a few baffled looks. I gave them a stern expression in return and turned to the cafeteria as more shots rang out. I wrapped my fingers around my gun and pulled it from my pants, swallowing hard as memories of Ever began trickling in.

A hand roughly clapped down on my helmet, forcing me to duck as several bullets flew right over my head.

"Watch your head, newbie!" Riley said with a grin as he released me.

I shot him a grateful look before he turned and began shooting at the guards coming down the hallway.

Hugo ran out the cafeteria door, holding a smaller Reboot close to him. His face broke into a grin when he spotted me. "I knew you weren't dead!"

A guard flew around the corner before I could respond, gun pointed at Hugo's head. I fired off a quick shot and the guard crumpled to the ground.

"Get the gun," I said to Hugo. "Did any Reboots make it to their rooms?"

"Maybe a few," he said as he scooped up the gun.

"I've got it," Riley said, gesturing for a few others to follow him.

"Lock down the building. All personnel to the lower level."

I slipped the com into my pocket as the voice spoke, and ran for the stairs. The sounds of screams and gunfire grew louder as I got closer to the bottom floor, and I tightened my hand around my gun.

Bullets immediately pelted my chest as I passed through the door on the bottom level. Callum sprinted in my direction as soon as I stepped into the lobby, and I grabbed him and pulled him down to the floor with me as bullets raced over our heads.

The lobby was full of HARC officers. Dead bodies littered the ground, too many of them Reboots. There was gunfire everywhere, and bullets zipped all around me as I pushed my way to the building entrance.

HARC officers were lined up on the front lawn. They formed a solid wall around every exit, bullets exploding from their guns.

"Stand back! Reboots, stand back!"

Isaac's voice barely carried over the chaos in the lobby, and the officers were all moving back from the building, arms over their heads.

Callum grabbed me around the waist as the blast shook the building, and we hit the ground together. His body covered mine as the front windows exploded and glass rocketed across the room.

Another blast shook the lobby and the screams around me faded, replaced by a high-pitched ringing in my ears. I squirmed against Callum and he sprang off me, pulling on my hand to help me up.

The lobby windows were completely gone and smoke partially obscured our view of outside. Bodies of HARC officers littered the ground, and Reboots jumped over them as they made a run for it.

Several of the Reboots stopped in their tracks as they encountered a wall of guns. Humans.

Tony was at the front of the crowd, and he lowered his gun slightly as he jerked his head. "Come on! Get out of there!"

I grabbed Callum's hand and rushed for the exit. The other Reboots followed, and Callum turned to grin at me as the cool air hit our faces.

A familiar sound overhead made me turn. A massive HARC shuttle was headed right for us. And on the ground, coming around the corner, at least a hundred heavily armed HARC officers.

They swarmed toward us and I positioned myself in front of the line of humans.

"All Reboots without a helmet back with the humans!" I yelled.

A hand yanked on my arm and I swung around, crushing my fist into an officer's face. He grabbed for me again and I fired a quick shot into his chest.

Riley was fighting off an officer right next to me, and I took a frantic glance around for Callum. He'd disappeared.

"Wren!"

I whirled around at the sound of my name, but saw nothing but a sea of bodies.

Someone behind me grunted, and I turned in time to see a HARC officer grab Addie's helmet and try to rip it off her head. I lifted my foot and kicked him as hard as I could. His hands flew off of Addie and he collapsed in a heap a few feet away.

I pulled Addie to her feet and ducked at the sound of a blast. Flames were coming out of the HARC building, as well as from a bunch of buildings in the slums.

Two big bodies slammed into me and I hit the ground, almost losing my grip on my gun. I held it tightly as one of the HARC officers who'd hit me scrambled across the dirt, pointing his gun in my face.

I kicked both my feet into his face and shot to my knees, grabbing the other HARC officer by the collar.

"No, no, no! It's me, One-seventy-eight!" Leb's eyes were

wide as he stared at me, his hands up in surrender near his face.

I let go of his collar and jumped to my feet, offering him my hand.

"Thank you," he said with a long exhale, straightening the helmet on his head. Like all the other HARC officers, he was in full gear.

His face changed as his eyes found something behind me, and I turned to see Addie with her back to us, gun poised for the next attack.

"Addie!" I grabbed her arm and she whirled around, her panicked expression changing to surprise when she spotted her dad. She raced forward and threw her arms around his neck.

I suppressed a smile as I jumped in front to block them from the HARC assault. "This isn't really the time for hugging!"

"Yes! Right!" Addie pulled away, pointing. "Get back there with the rebels! You're going to get shot up here. Take that HARC shirt off or something!"

He laughed but did as she said, embracing her quickly before running for Tony and Desmond.

I pushed through the crowd, whipping my head around as I searched for Callum. I found Riley instead, who had one HARC officer on his back and was trying to wrestle a gun from the hand of another. Screams echoed around me as I dove for him, wrapping my arms around the waist of the officer on his back and hauling him off. He darted into the crowd as soon as he recognized me, casting a horrified glance over his shoulder.

Riley stood over the other dead officer, breathing heavily. "Thanks."

I started to say "You're welcome" when Riley blinked, putting a hand to his neck. Blood seeped through his fingers, and I whirled to look for the source of the bullet.

A shuttle officer I'd only encountered once stood a few yards away. He'd made me take my shirt off to search for weapons, then was disgusted by my scars.

I dove for him, a bullet clipping my hand. His eyes lit up like he'd succeeded at something.

My heart stopped as I turned around. Riley was already on the ground, a bullet hole in his forehead.

I pressed a hand to my mouth as I choked back a cry. The world was blurry as I started to lift my gun again, but two Reboots were already there, wrestling the shuttle officer to the ground.

I ducked as a barrage of bullets raced over my head and hit my knees next to Riley.

"*Up. Get up now!*" Riley's voice was loud in my head, drowning out the sounds around me.

But I was glued to the ground, my fingers wrapped around his lifeless wrist. I couldn't move, even as his yells grew louder in my head. His bright eyes stared vacantly at the sky.

A Reboot slammed against my back as she shoved a HARC officer to the ground, and I closed my eyes and took in a deep breath. I slid my hand into Riley's and gave it a squeeze, saying a silent thank-you I should have said a hundred times over before now.

I forced myself to stand and wiped a hand across my eyes. I had to find Callum. I had to at least see if he was okay.

Spinning around, I finally spotted him over the sea of faces. He'd been pushed back closer to the HARC building, and he was helping a young Reboot who'd lost a leg over the pile of rubble and bodies. There were no immediate threats nearby and I breathed a sigh of relief.

A door at the other end of the HARC building opened, and I squinted through the smoke at a chubby figure who emerged. Officer Mayer.

He had a large gun in his hand, and I pushed past the Reboots and officers as I ran for him.

He stood at the front of the building, breathing heavily as he observed the scene. He turned to the Reboots making their way out of the building. To Callum.

"Callum!" I screamed, but he made no sign he'd heard me. I fired several bullets in Officer Mayer's direction, but he didn't even flinch. I was too far away.

Officer Mayer raised his gun. He hit the young Reboot right in the head, an easy shot without a helmet.

Callum whirled around, his hand going to his gun.

The officer fired. Callum's head flew back. His body was still for a split second and I held my breath as I waited for him to move. He crumpled to the ground, motionless.

THIRTY-NINE

CALLUM

FORTY

WREN

BLACK TINGED THE EDGES OF MY VISION AND I COULDN'T BREATHE.
I couldn't move.

It had been several seconds and Callum was completely still
on the ground. I couldn't go over there. If I went to look I would
know he was dead. He couldn't be dead.

Desmond appeared, horror on his face as he knelt down
next to Callum. He turned to me. Back to Callum.

Panic began to spread through my limbs and I choked back
a sob as Desmond gave me a shocked look.

I charged for Officer Mayer.

He took off running, pumping his arms as fast as he could.
He turned around and fired a wild shot in my direction, which

missed me by at least a foot.

I raised my gun. I could easily hit his back at this point, but that wasn't how I always imagined killing him. In my head, it had always been more intimate.

Now I wanted him to suffer.

There was no way he could outrun me. He'd trained me too well for that. I leaped forward, yanking on his arm so hard it cracked. He screamed as I launched my foot into his stomach.

He hit the ground, firing off another wild shot that missed me. I tore the gun from his hand and tossed it away. I positioned myself over his chest and knelt down.

I wrapped my fingers around his throat.

His eyes bulged and he swung at me. He grasped my shirt in his fingers and tugged, but I dug into his neck harder. He wheezed and began kicking his legs.

His face turned red.

I held on tighter.

He dropped his fingers from my shirt, putting his hands down and giving me a desperate look. He was surrendering.

I didn't care.

I didn't care.

I didn't care.

I let out a scream of frustration and let go of his neck, backing off slightly. Officer Mayer gasped for air, rolling onto his side as his body shook and trembled.

I wiped a hand across my eyes and found they were wet.

Officer Mayer stared up at me, his expression a mixture of horror and shock.

I considered killing him and was struck again with that awful feeling I'd had a few seconds ago. Did I kill someone just because I could? Was that who I was?

I kicked the gun farther from Officer Mayer's reach and pulled two sets of cuffs from his belt. I slapped them around his ankles and wrists.

No. That wasn't who I was.

My body was heavy as I straightened, and I forced myself to turn around to where Callum lay.

Desmond was still crouching over his body. He had something bloody in his hand. A bullet.

Callum slowly sat up, blood running down his cheek from his left eye.

I yelled, sprinting across the dirt so fast I almost knocked him over when I threw my arms around his shoulders. Callum laughed and wheezed as I squeezed him tightly.

"Sorry," I said, pulling away and putting my hands on his cheeks. His eye was a bloody mess, but starting to heal, and I pulled his hand away when he tried to touch it. "Don't. It will heal faster if you leave it alone."

I turned to Desmond, who tossed aside the bullet.

"Lodged in his eye socket?" I guessed.

He nodded with a wince. "Really disgusting, too."

"Thank you," Callum said with a smile.

A loud yell and the sound of shooting made me turn. The scene in front of the facility had changed, and lots of HARC officers were on their knees on the ground. A tiny group of officers were holding out, firing off shots at the rebels. A few officers took off running in our direction, and I jumped to my feet as bullets sprayed through the air.

Desmond sprang up next to me and I darted in front of him, but it was too late. He doubled over as blood spread across his stomach, then his shoulder. Callum caught him before he hit the dirt.

I raised my gun, but a large band of humans swarmed the officers, and wrestled them to the ground.

Tony was at my side in seconds, and Callum moved away as he knelt down next to Desmond. There was no saving him, though. I quickly turned away, my hand finding Callum's.

The gunfire had stopped in front of the facility, but I could still hear traces of it in the slums. The humans were dirty and bloodied, and the Reboots didn't look much better.

I knew I should go into the slums to help stop the violence there or assist in rounding up the HARC officers for containment, but it all felt like too much to deal with at the moment. I holstered my gun and wrapped my arms around Callum's waist, pressing my face into his chest and letting out a long breath.

FORTY-ONE

CALLUM

THE ROSA HARC FACILITY LOOKED LIKE IT MIGHT CRUMBLE AT ANY moment, so we made sure there were no Reboots locked in their rooms and moved everyone out of the area. Dead bodies were strewn across the lawn, and when the sun began to rise the scene was gruesome.

A few of the rebels gathered together the HARC prisoners, including Officer Mayer, and piled them into HARC transport vans headed for Austin. Isaac and a few other Reboots went to New Dallas to check on the HARC situation there, and reported back that most of the HARC officials fled or abandoned their posts when they arrived. Many blended into the human population, giving up their duties with little protest.

Wren went with Addie and Leb to do a sweep of the city and slums and they returned with a few more humans and HARC officers who'd shot at them. Leb said they were using the human cells in the Austin capitol as a prison until they could figure out what to do with everyone. I thought about asking who was guarding this prison, and who would decide the appropriate punishment, but I wasn't sure I wanted to know. Not today, anyway.

Wren had disappeared, and I found her on the lawn of the facility, sitting next to Riley's body. Her arm was slung across her knees, her head bent down, and she didn't move at all when I knelt down in front of her.

"Do you want to bury him?" I asked quietly.

She shook her head, wiping the back of her hand across her eyes before she looked at me. "No, Riley would think that was stupid. We should cremate him with the others."

I nodded, wrapping my fingers around her arm and giving it a gentle squeeze. I stood, intending to leave her alone, but she got to her feet and slipped her hand into mine. We walked off the HARC lawn to where Leb and Addie were standing with a large group of Reboots.

Leb glanced over at Wren, his expression half surprise, half sympathy. She had dirt and blood smeared on her clothes, and her shoulders were slumped in exhaustion. It was obvious she'd been crying. I suspected that was where Leb's surprise came from, because it seemed that even the people who knew her were shocked to discover she had emotions like them.

"Thank you," Leb said. He looked for a moment like he might hug her but seemed to think better of it.

"For what?" Wren asked.

He gestured to Addie. "I didn't think you'd go to get her out."

Wren was almost amused. "I know you didn't."

"Also for saving my life that one time," Addie piped in with a smile. "And that other time."

Wren laughed softly. "No problem. I'd say we're even now."

Addie pointed to a shuttle a few hundred yards away. "Are you guys going back to Austin? That shuttle is going to take some people soon."

Wren looked at me. "Yes?"

"Yes," I confirmed.

"Are you staying here?" Wren asked Addie and Leb.

"We're thinking we'll pack some stuff up and come to Austin for a while," she said. "Dad thinks that's where they'll start electing leaders and establishing a government. We figured we should stick close."

He was probably right, and I was suddenly glad we were going to be close, too. If they were going to rebuild, we needed to make sure Reboots were part of that. My first thought was Riley, and I swallowed when I remembered he was dead.

"I'm going to stay and help my family get things together," Addie continued. "We'll probably be there in a few days." She bit her lip. "Tell Gabe for me?"

"Sure," Wren said.

"Who's Gabe?" Leb asked, looking between them.

Addie patted her dad's arm, which only increased his alarm. She turned to Wren. "I'll find you when we get there, okay?"

Wren nodded. I dropped her hand as Addie stepped forward and wrapped her arms around her. She returned the hug, and Addie leaned down and whispered something in her ear. I couldn't hear what it was, but when Wren pulled away she had tears in her eyes again. She smiled at Addie through them and slipped her hand into mine.

Wren squeezed my hand and pulled me in the direction of the shuttle. "Let's go home."

FORTY-TWO

WREN

I WAS MET WITH LAUGHTER AS I TURNED THE CORNER TO CALLUM'S old house. A group of human kids sat on a front lawn to my left, but when they spotted me they quieted. One of the girls leaned over and whispered something to a boy, and his eyes widened.

I instinctively reached for the weapon on my belt, just in case, but there was nothing there. I'd given all my weapons to Addie days ago.

A grin spread across the boy's face when I glanced back up at them. "What's up, One-seventy-eight? They described you as taller!"

I laughed, and when I faced front again Callum was standing on his porch, watching us.

"Hey!" he called, his voice amused. "She can't control her height!"

I hopped up the steps and pressed my lips to Callum's, smiling as he pressed a hand into my back.

"They do describe you as taller," he murmured against my lips.

I pulled away, trying to stand straighter. "Better?"

"No." He quickly kissed me again and pushed open the front door, holding his arm out for me to go first.

I took in a deep breath as I stepped inside. I hadn't seen Callum's family since that day they'd come by the facility. He'd visited them a few times, but I hadn't gone with him. When he'd invited me to come to dinner, Addie had clapped her hands like this was exciting. It mostly just made me uncomfortable.

The house didn't have any more furniture than the last time I'd been here, but the smell of meat cooking drifted out from the kitchen. Callum's dad stood next to a table already set with plates, one hand clasped around his opposite arm.

Mrs. Reyes turned around, spoon in hand. She smiled when she spotted me. It even seemed genuine.

"Hi, Wren." She put the spoon down and walked across the kitchen, holding her hand out. "Nice to see you again."

"You too." Her hand was warm and when she smiled she looked like Callum.

David bounded into the kitchen as Mr. Reyes shook my hand. He lifted his nose in the air.

"What is that?" He peered over his mom's shoulder. "Where did we get meat?"

"Callum brought deer meat," Mrs. Reyes said, walking back to the stove.

I turned to him in surprise. "Did you go hunting?"

He snorted. "Yeah, right. Isaac gave it to me since we'd been helping him with construction so much."

I nodded. Callum and I had both been working on rebuilding Austin, since I'd turned down every request to police the streets or leave the cities to assess the situation in the rest of Texas. There were plenty of Reboots—and even a few humans—more than willing to take on that kind of job. I wasn't doing it anymore. Nor was I training anyone. I'd enjoyed that once, but I couldn't stomach the idea of training Reboots for combat any longer. I'd seen enough fighting.

I didn't even like carrying a gun anymore, which was why I gave them all to Addie a few days ago. The world felt different after I'd chosen not to kill Officer Mayer. After I killed someone I would often feel this far-off sense of guilt, like I knew it was an emotion I was supposed to be having but didn't actually feel. But when I didn't kill him, I suddenly felt proud of that decision, like it was totally mine.

And then Callum had looked at me like I was a hero when I told him and I decided I had no more use for a gun.

"Is deer meat good?" David asked, like he doubted it.

"No idea," Callum said, sitting down at the table and

gesturing for me to do the same.

"Yes," I said as I slid into a chair. "I like it."

Callum's mom seemed delighted by this, though I wasn't sure why.

David plopped down into the seat across from me, his eyes darting between me and Callum.

"Did you decide where you're living yet?" he asked Callum.

"We're at the facility for now, until they finish the repairs at Tower Apartments. I rented the small place across from where Wren and Addie will be."

His dad looked between us with concern. "Are you sure? It's not really that nice over there."

"It's nicer than a HARC facility," Callum said with a laugh. "Besides, the slums aren't so bad. Especially now that HARC isn't around anymore."

"You could both stay here, you know," Mr. Reyes said softly to Callum. I knew they'd asked him to move back in and he'd declined. He said it was too weird and almost claustrophobic after spending time out on his own. I could see his point. We had separate apartments for now as we adjusted to life outside of HARC, though we would probably end up spending more time together than apart. Even so, I'd never had a room all to myself, and it was an interesting change.

"I think we're okay." Callum smiled at his dad. "But thank you."

*   *   *

Callum wrapped his arm around my waist and kissed the top of my head as we walked away from his parents' house later that evening. The sky was dark, the roads mostly deserted.

"I think they might have liked me a little," I said, glancing up at him.

He laughed. "Yes, they did. Don't sound all surprised about it." He swooped down and kissed me, swinging our hands as we walked.

"A new batch of reservation Reboots came in today," I said, glancing at Callum.

"Yeah?"

"Yeah. They seemed pretty skeptical about our setup here, but it's better than Micah's was, I guess." I laughed. "You should have seen Tony's face when he saw a Reboot baby. I'm not sure he's recovered yet."

"Maybe some of them will want to help us out at the capitol. Every government meeting is me and maybe one other Reboot with all these humans."

"It's your own fault you get along so well with humans," I said, grinning at him. He pretended to look annoyed, but I knew he liked being a part of forming a government that included humans and Reboots.

There were a few humans and Reboots out walking around as we neared the schoolhouse, but there were less people in Austin than before, since some had decided to go back to their hometowns. And some humans had gone to New Dallas, which was apparently almost entirely human occupied. Tony said they were keeping an eye on it. I wasn't surprised. I never expected all the humans to jump at the opportunity to hang out with a bunch of Reboots.

A bonfire was lit in the empty field in front of the HARC facility, like it had been every night since we'd come back from Rosa. The Reboots had been gathering there most nights, and sometimes a few humans came. Tonight Gabe was sitting next to Addie, an arm slung around her shoulders.

She grinned when she spotted us and jumped to her feet, pulling Gabe with her. "How was the dinner?"

"Good. Deer meat."

"That's really not what I meant."

I smiled, rolling my eyes. "It was good. I acted normal."

Callum made a gesture like "so-so," and I playfully punched his arm as he laughed.

A flash of movement caught my eye, and I turned to see Hugo striding into the facility with another Reboot, both their faces grim.

"I'll be back, okay? I'm going to go check on the new Reboot situation."

Callum nodded, wincing a little as he looked behind me at the facility. A shuttle from New Dallas had dropped a bunch of sick kids at the Austin fence yesterday, and we'd already had three new Reboots.

"Do you want me to come with you?" he asked.

"No, I'm fine." I knew he was just being nice. He'd been with me yesterday when one of the kids Rebooted, and I could tell it upset him to watch.

"I'll meet you in our room later?" he asked, slipping his fingers through mine and pulling me closer.

I nodded and rose up on my toes, pressing my lips to his. He looped an arm around my waist, practically lifting me up off the ground, and I laughed as we broke apart.

I stepped back, resisting the urge to kiss him again when he grinned. I could do more of that later.

I turned and headed for the facility, crossing through the dark, deserted lobby and jogging up to the second floor. As I opened the door, a blast of light and noise hit me, and a few Reboots I recognized from Rosa smiled as they walked past and into the stairwell.

Hugo stood with a few guys in the middle of the hallway, and he jerked his head behind him. "There's two that just died. And one of the girls from New Dallas died while you were gone, but we don't think she's going to Reboot. It's been too long."

"How long is too long?" I asked.

"About three hours."

"We should stay until four hours, at least. You never know." I glanced down the hallway. "Which room?"

"Third door on the left."

I headed down the hallway and pulled the door open. This

floor had once been used for research and experimentation, and the rooms looked similar to where I was tortured in New Dallas, although we'd tried to make it homier. The computer and other equipment had been pushed against the wall, and we'd covered the hard table in the middle of the room with a few blankets. A girl about fifteen or so was motionless on top of them, a young Reboot in the chair next to her.

"You can go," I said, holding the door open. "I've got it."

"It's probably too late," he said, stretching as he got to his feet.

"I know."

He walked past me and the door shut quietly behind him. I sat down in the chair next to her makeshift bed, glancing quickly at her face. She was pale, her dark hair splayed across the pillow. I'd seen her yesterday when they'd brought her in, but she'd been too sick to talk. None of the others had known her name.

I sighed as I rubbed a hand across my forehead. I wondered if her family had let the human leaders in New Dallas take her, or if the city wasn't letting anyone with KDH stay. We clearly had a long way to go with them.

The girl's body jerked suddenly, and I took in a sharp breath and jumped up. I kept my arms at my side, because I didn't think I would have wanted strange people touching me as soon as I Rebooted. But I would have liked someone there. That I knew for sure.

Her body lurched several more times before she opened her bright green eyes. Her fingers clenched the sheets and she gasped, her head snapping around the room. Her gaze finally settled on me, panic on her face.

I braced myself for screaming, but it didn't come. Her chest rose and fell quickly, but she just stared at me silently.

I let out a tiny sigh of relief as I smiled at her. "Wren," I said quietly. The "One" of One-seventy-eight was on the tip of my tongue, but I swallowed it back. We weren't keeping track of the numbers anymore.

She ran one hand down her arm, a worried expression on her face. "How . . . how long was I . . . ?"

"It doesn't matter," I said. "You're awake now."

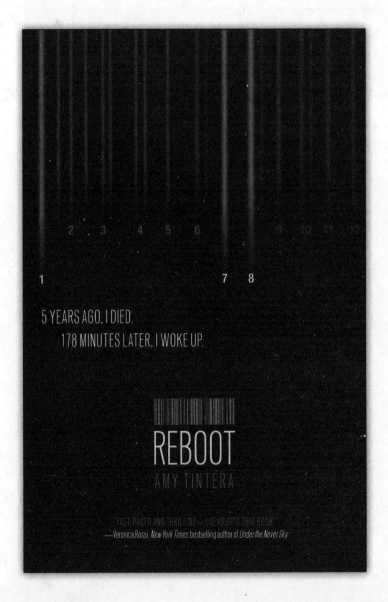

JOIN THE
Epic Reads
COMMUNITY

THE ULTIMATE YA DESTINATION

◄ **DISCOVER** ►
your next favorite read

◄ **FIND** ►
new authors to love

◄ **WIN** ►
free books

◄ **SHARE** ►
infographics, playlists, quizzes, and more

◄ **WATCH** ►
the latest videos

◄ **TUNE IN** ►
to Tea Time with Team Epic Reads